# *Harris* [illegible]

Stanley Middleton w[illegible] Nottinghamshire in 191[illegible] novel, *A Short Answer*, in 19[illegible] 45 novels in a career spa[illegible] years. He was joint winner of the Booker Prize in 1974 with *Holiday*.

Stanley Middleton died in July 2009.

## ALSO BY STANLEY MIDDLETON

A Short Answer
Harris's Requiem
A Serious Woman
The Just Exchange
Two's Company
Him They Compelled
Terms of Reference
The Golden Evening
Wages of Virtue
Apple of the Eye
Brazen Prison
Cold Gradations
A Man Made of Smoke
Holiday
Distractions
Still Waters
Ends and Means
Two Brothers
In a Strange Land
The Other Side
Blind Understanding
Entry into Jerusalem
The Daysman
Valley of Decision
An After-Dinner's Sleep
After a Fashion
Recovery
Vacant Places
Changes and Chances
Beginning to End
A Place to Stand
Married Past Redemption
Catalysts
Toward the Sea
Live and Learn
Brief Hours
Against the Dark
Necessary Ends
Small Change
Love in the Provinces
Brief Garlands
Sterner Stuff
Mother's Boy
Her Three Wise Men
A Cautious Approach

Acclaim for Stanley Middleton

'At first glance, or even at second, Stanley Middleton's world is easily recognisable . . . The excellence of art, for Middleton, is an exact vision of real things as they are. And because he is himself so exact an observer, his world at *third* glance can seem strange and disturbing or newly and brilliantly lit with colour.'

A.S. Byatt

'We need Stanley Middleton to remind us what the novel is about . . . One has to look at nineteenth-century writing for comparable storytelling.'

Ronald Blythe, *Sunday Times*

'Middleton is concerned with what goes on below the surface of lives, what people feel, dream about, hope for, resent, fear – all the things that in real life may be kept hidden . . . Anyone coming to Middleton fresh has a real treat in store.'

Allan Massie, *Scotsman*

'Middleton writes carefully, but his touch is light and astonishingly assured. One rarely reads dialogue as good as Middleton's; it makes his characters instantly alive.'

VS Naipaul

'Middleton is a born writer; unpretentious, discerning, intelligent and virtually incapable of writing a duff sentence. He is the Chekhov of suburbia; I recommend him.'

James Runcie, *Daily Telegraph*

'He is a master of characterisation through dialogue and of a succinct presentation of a complex relationship.'

*Sunday Telegraph*

'Middleton, joint Booker Prize-winner, is a master technician of the form.'

*Financial Times*

'He writes with a delicate, unobtrusive mastery of his craft… and is never for a moment dull.'

*Independent*

'Stanley Middleton, once dubbed "The Chekhov of suburbia", is to the Midlands suburb what Anne Tyler is to the Midwest picket fence. His gentle, careful writing creates an always precise and often unnerving picture of reality.'

*The Times*

'What is so extraordinary about Middleton's talent is that despite implacable domesticity, he is not trivial… Middleton does not want to change anybody's view of the world; he only wants to help the readers understand and better the view of it that they already have, and his quietness and patience do indeed lead him to success in that endeavour.'

Bernard Levin

'He illuminates the important matters beneath the surface that ordinary people feel but rarely talk about.'

Philip Howard

'He is the novelist of privacy, wariness and delicacy of feeling, the literary guardian of civilisation as we have always known it.'

Penny Perrick, *The Times*

'He is a novelist who can do just what Ford Madox Ford presented as the justification of imaginative literature; he can make you think and feel at the same time.'

Allan Massie, *Times Literary Supplement*

'Middleton wrote books you remember decades on... He wrote a calm, whispering prose, full of unspoken suggestion between ordinary acts of living... I think of Middleton, and a few others, who keep still and write and then write more, because they are writers and that's what they have to do, as the real ones, the sort to aspire to.'

Jenny Diski

# *Harris's Requiem*

Stanley Middleton

Published by Windmill Books 2014

2 4 6 8 10 9 7 5 3 1



First published in Great Britain in 1960 by Hutchinson
First published in paperback in Great Britain in 2006 by Trent Editions

Windmill Books
The Random House Group Limited
20 Vauxhall Bridge Road, London SW1V 2SA

Addresses for companies within The Random House Group Limited can be found at:
www.randomhouse.co.uk/offices.htm

The Random House Group Limited Reg. No. 954009

www.randomhouse.co.uk

A CIP catalogue record for this book
is available from the British Library

ISBN 9780099591962

Printed and bound by Clays Ltd, St Ives plc

*For Love that falls on stony ground*

*May feed the singing birds.*

R.M. Hewitt

# 1.

LANDSCAPE with newspaper.

At the end of a summer afternoon the crescent of council houses swept downhill, grained with eddies of dust. In the gutters sheets of newspaper sagged, and here and there sprawled into piles in the privet by a fence bottom.

The two men turned out of the green school-gate and passed the metal green bus-shelter. A crowd of boys were scrabbling there energetically for so warm a day, but pushed themselves into some sort of equilibrium as the masters approached. One boy touched his peak; the majority studied their toe-ends. A six-footer, his cap occupying a small circle over his crown, shouted out from behind a newspaper he was reading,

'He didn't oughter declared. 'E got wor 'e were askin' for.'

The accent was broad midland, of some slum terrace, where a thousand voices shouted from habit.

'Exquisitely expressed,' said one of the men. He was tall, with greasy long hair and a silk, golden sweat-scarf. There was quiet for a minute until they were six paces past and then laughter sniggered up.

'W'et did 'e say?'

'Get you're 'air cut.'

'The poet's tongue, wi' nobs on it.'

The man half hesitated but his companion touched his arm.

'It's Friday night, Winterburn. Your duty to the Committee's done. Apart from your marking and your exam papers and your night school.'

The speaker was small, with dark hair and black eyes sunken deep in the sockets. There was a kind of dapper agility about him with his pale skin and fine, jerky movements of shoulder under a rag-bag of a sports coat. Both wore dark-grey flannels, the school-master's badge, but the smaller man's were burnt and patched on the knee.

'You'll learn,' said Harris, the smaller.

'I could go a foaming pint,' said Winterburn. 'There ought to be a special dispensation for schoolmasters to get the chalk out of their throats. But I suppose you're beyond even so moderate a desire as that, eh?'

Harris rubbed a hand along a dusty privet hedge and then examined his grimy palm.

'You're getting the signs of the profession quick enough,' he said.

'Such as?'

'Everlasting talk. By Friday, I want quiet.'

The other, Winterburn, sniffed gloomily, adjusting his scarf.

'Doing anything tonight?' he asked.

'First,' said Harris, 'I'm going to visit my father. Then I'm going to a quartet rehearsal.'

'Which is worse?' asked Winterburn.

'I'm responsible for one of the quartets; or, at least, the notes on paper. I cannot be held in any way responsible for my dad.'

'Is he keeping all right?'

'Thanks.'

They reached the bottom of the crescent.

'Here's my bus,' said Winterburn. 'Now for country joys. Hope the quartet works out. Sounds and sweet airs that give delight and hurt not.'

He laughed, waved and hopped, his trouser-behind tight, on to the bus. Harris nodded, crossed the road. He pursed his lips as he watched the bus. Winterburn had a ramshackle house seven miles out, two acres of garden and orchard, two youngsters, a strangling mortgage and his feet smelt.

Harris shuffled down a gentler, dirtier hill.

A group of boys on cycles swept past. They raised their caps dramatically, together.

'Good night, sir,' they said. This was precision work.

Harris raised a hand, looked around for more pupils and finding none, ducked under a fence by a railway bridge. He slithered down the grass-bank of a cutting and pulled carelessly at a bunch of wormwood. A ragged litter of leaf came off in his hand and he rubbed it under his nose quietly. He stood. A goods train rattled by; the driver nodded companionably. Harris examined the signals, went over the lines and walked along by the track to the next bridge, where he dodged out again.

He was now in Park Lane, a surprisingly wide road, bounded on one side by a railway siding with piles of sleepers, a derelict hut or two, an unpainted Ford van and vast mounds and stretches of coal slack. All was fenced with a seven foot wire-mesh. The other side of the road had the original village pavement of red house-bricks and grey-blue paving tiles, like mildewed chocolate. It was no more than a yard wide and each inch sagged.

Here and there were cottages, knocked about, slapped one into the other. Then there was a touch of urban order with a terrace of brick houses, 1903, starched lace curtains, scrubbed steps, boys with dangling cherry-bunches, God bless our Happy Home and a gas-lamp. Next lay the wastepiece and, beyond, the 'Standard of Old England,' with a 3? litre Jaguar outside its

Tudor door in concrete. Upstairs were rows of windows in the older station-hotel manner.

Harris lit his pipe.

The first draw filled his mouth and was good. On a hot day he knew that his palate would soon be dry so that there'd be no pleasure. But a bachelor, in his forties, takes what's there. He moved off slowly. There was much to be enjoyed in Park Lane.

Some front doors were open. Through these came the sound of the bustle of tea, of dad back from the pit offering information from the newspaper, of youngsters beginning to tire, of wireless sets and whistling kettles. A group of male old-age pensioners were undulating down the road from some meeting. Their faces were puzzled and they did not speak, as though their deaf-aid sets were switched off.

Harris turned into Burlington Terrace, a row of red-brick six-roomers with lilac trees in the dusty gardens and cricket stumps chalked on every wall. He edged round the back of the houses, through the gardens which were thick with herbaceous plants and roses and at whose end slipped the oil-scummed river, eight feet wide, the Leen.

He opened the back-door. 'Anybody in?' he shouted.

His father grunted. The old man was sitting rocking himself in a chair by a fire. Furniture towered round him; a mahogany chiffonier, a black upright piano, a massive deal table, scrubbed lily-white, high wooden chairs and a quartered tuffet[1] over by the steel fire-guard. The windows were tight closed.

Harris senior scratched his short grey hair noisily.

'Oh,' he said. 'Johannes Brahms, is it?'

This was an old saw with him. When Harris was a boy the rows with his father were frequent, short and nasty. Once he had been playing the Handel Variations when his father shoved in from work.

'What the 'ell are you doin'?' he'd asked the lad.

'Playin'.'

'You don't call that flamin' racket playin', do you?'

'It's Brahms.'

'Who?' The father stuck his hands into his trousers pockets and straddled the hearth. It was such a summer's day as this.

'Johannes Brahms.' The boy pronounced it continental fashion, with rasping, unvoiced S's.

'Johannes Brahms,' his father imitated him. 'Who's he when 'e's at 'om?'

Harris had said nothing. His father knew quite well.

'I as't yer a question, young fellow-me-lad. Who's this 'ere Yo-han-ess Brarmss?'

The boy didn't answer. His father began to unbuckle the belt round his middle. Mrs. Harris had come in, unobserved, from the kitchen.

'Now, then,' she said. 'What are you two up to?'

'I want to know who Yohannes Brarmss iss. An' I'm goin' to get an answer, if I break every bone in 'is body for it.'

'William,' she said.

'I as't 'im a civil question and I expec' a civil answer.'

'Tom,' she said. 'Go out to play.'

'Who's...?' began his father.

Tom made a tentative step towards the door and his father took one towards him.

'William,' said his mother. 'You are a cowardly, boasting brute and a blackguard, but be so good as to listen to me.' Her voice spat.

Tom ran for the yard, frightened to death, but sorry for his father. The weary inevitability of his mother's words shook him. His parents conducted their quarrel like ham-actors in a dud play in front of an empty house.

That night he got a book out of the library, with a picture of Brahms and showed it to his dad. His father picked the book up awkwardly and said,

'Johannes Brahms. That's 'im, is it? Got whiskers like yer grandad Walters.'

He did not hold the incident against the boy, only remembered the name.

'I'm just havin' five minutes,' said his father, now, from the rocking chair.

'How's the world?' said his son, sitting down. 'It's hot in here.'

'My bones gets co'd,' said his father, without fear. 'We'll go into t' front room if you want. It catches t'sun about now.'

'No,' said his son. He knocked out his pipe into the grate.

'Are you stoppin' for a bit o' tea?' asked Harris senior. 'Th' missus'll be back any minute now. She's mother-'ardying it[2] somewhere down t' street. But she'll have the tea laid afore five. Or else.'

'Yes.' His son studied him. The old man hadn't had a shave, but his thin face was red and healthy.

'How's th' schule?' asked the father.

'All right, thanks.'

'Mester Leaman still the 'ead?'

'Yes.' His son smiled. They always had this conversation. 'You don't like 'im, do you?'

'I've met worse, if not much.'

'Tell 'im so,' said the father. 'Straight to 'is face. Listen, bellyache, you say to 'im, I don't like you. I can lump you, like dogs do dumplings, but I don't like you. He'll respec' you then.'

Harris crossed his legs and said nothing.

'You 'evn't got no spirit.'

The father shut his eyes now, as if satisfied. That was what he liked, to put some fool in his place and leave it. He rocked and the chair creaked.

Mrs. Harris came in.

This was not Thomas's mother. The first Mrs. Harris had seen her son to the Royal Academy and then safely in his first job, a public school in Lancashire. She had then died, in Thomas's first term, after a stroke. The old man had lived eight years a grousing widower before marrying a Mrs. Jones.

She had been a boyhood sweetheart; they had courted five years, but she had ideas and had given him up because he refused to get out of the pits and better himself. She had married James Jones, a grocer, a mincing, money-grubbing, bald, hand-rubbing little bit of skin and grief, known as 'Gentleman Jones.' They were childless and when James died during the war, his wife sought out Willy Harris, and, nicely off as she was, married him on his own terms.

She, in her sixties, still had something of the prettiness and softness of her youth. Her hair was white and soft like soap-bubbles and she wore round rimless glasses shaped for smiling.

'Hello, Tom,' she said. 'You might have put the cloth on, William.'

'Pigs might fly.'

'Your dad doesn't get any better,' she said, smiling, fluttering, putting on a show. The men sat in silence.

'I saw Mrs. Davis in the shop,' she said. 'She told me they're playing some of your music at a special concert at St. Saviour's next month.'

'Yes,' said Thomas, 'a quartet.'

'That's nice,' she said. 'Isn't it, William?'

'Get on wi' th' tea,' he said. He looked at his son after his wife had gone into the kitchen. 'A string quartet,' he said, careful with his lips over the words. 'A string quartet.'

'I'll get you a ticket,' said his son.

'Not me, lad. I wouldn't go an' 'ear "Messiah" in that co'd barn.' The father smiled.

'How's the thing you sent to the B.B.C. goin'?' he asked.

'Haven't heard,' said Thomas. 'I expect it back at any time now.'

His father grunted.

'Can't be worse than some of the stuff they put on,' said the old man.

'Right,' said his son.

Mrs. Harris came flying back.

'You're a glum pair,' she said, slapping a trayful on the table.

'We'll look a sight brighter wi' a bit in us bellies,' said her husband. 'Get on wi' it. You're like an o'd 'en scratting for daylight.'

At tea, Mr. Harris did not talk but concentrated on audible mastication. His wife, lower middle to the last, aped the hostess. She talked and handed plates about and smiled.

'Why don't you come back here to live, Tom?' she said. 'It'd be company for your dad. And cheaper than that damp flat. The back-bedroom's very nice. Got a table there and room for your books.'

'I'm all right, thanks,' said Tom.

'Wouldn't cost you so much, not by half.'

Mr. Harris carefully laid a slice of ham and sauce into a sandwich.

'What would he do wi' th' money when he saved it?' he asked. 'I don't know. We can all do with a little bit more, now, can't we?' She nodded at her husband. 'And it'd be very handy for school.'

'Thanks,' said Tom.

'Of course, the neighbourhood's not very class. But we do very nicely, don't we, William?'

No answer.

'Perhaps Tom's right,' she said. 'He's no youngster. Anyway, he must please himself.'

'This 'am's greasy,' said father. 'It's worse nor suckin' pap.' She answered him, and, happy, gave a long account of her shopping. They didn't listen and Tom, unlike his father, tried not to appear rude.

After tea, Tom helped Mrs. Harris to wash up and left. She came with him to the front door.

'It's been nice,' she said. 'And good for your father. He loves you, Tom. He's right proud of you.'

He blew her a kiss.

He got quickly out of Park Lane and took a bus for Forest Road where he lived. The road began on a bus-route among small shops, beer-offs and cafés, but broadened, after an infants' school, was tree-lined before the tall Victorian houses stopped at two churches and a cemetery.

Indoors, he picked up his letters. A bill, an invitation to an organ recital, a circular, a football coupon that had been kicking around on the ground-floor and a long, parchment envelope with large, bold handwriting. 'Thomas Harris, Esquire, B.Mus., F.R.C.O., A.R.A.M., etc., Flat 3, 17 Forest Road, Beechnall.' He put it idly down.

He took off his jacket and tie and sat down in an arm-chair by the window. He could see the cricket-match over the other side of the road, and, beyond, the houses of the Boulevard with the towers and behind them, the straight rows of grey slate roofs leading steadily uphill to the factories on the far side of the valley. Some boys were cycling on the recreation ground, skidding into complicated circles and figures of eight. They were so far away that their voices were thin, like a chatter of sparrows.

He untied his shoe laces, stood up and opened the letter.

*Dear Harris,*

*I've a disappointment for you.*

*Grainger Cooke who is arranging our concert won't have your quartet. He's full of apologies, but firm.*

*Come round at eight Friday just the same. Sorry, old chap.*

*Yours,*

*John Brand.*

Harris threw it to the floor, where it made a little tent (and stayed). He lit his pipe and put his feet up. It was still hot. He puffed his lips out. The same old story. Harris's earth was full of Grainger Cookes, apologising gents, who wouldn't have him at any cost.

He ran his fingers along the arm of his chair; found it got him nowhere; kicked off his shoes and went for a wash in his stockinged feet. In the bathroom he stared at his face in the mirror. He pulled it about, shoved his tongue into his cheek, moved his dental plate. This did him no good for a minute and he returned. He took a kick at the letter. It fluttered a foot and dropped back, tent-like and neat. The boys had gone from the asphalt; a left-hander was running up to bowl; St. Aidan's church threw a spiked shadow across the road.

Seven-fifteen.

Harris sat in the chair, doing nothing, like a man blown after a sprint. His hands dangled over the chair-arms and time passed quickly. He examined his disappointment, and found it unworthy of scrutiny. He looked his socks over.

Now it was time to get up.

He reached for his tie.

Once outside and walking he felt better. Brand lived only ten minutes away. From the outside of the house Harris could hear no sound of the quartet, who were usually hard at it from seven onwards.

Brand let him in.

'We're going out, old chap, you and I,' said Brand. 'So just come in for a minute and wipe the sweat off.' He was tall, handsome, beautifully got up, a factory owner's son and the violist of the ensemble. He had studied professionally, but now worked for money as a director in one of his father's concerns. It was he who drove the quartet, thrashed them into excellence and he who had suggested playing Harris's No. 3 (1956) at the concert.

They went into a large, elegant music room.

'I'm sorry about this, Harris,' said Brand.

'The others aren't,' said Harris.

'They do as they're told,' said Brand, handling whisky. 'Usual orange for you? I suppose you want to know why I'm soft so with Cooke?'

He passed Harris a glass with grace.

'Go on,' said Harris.

'To be truthful,' said Brand, 'I don't know. Why I didn't tell him to stuff his concert is beyond me.'

'It's hard to get engagements,' said Harris, sipping.

'And Cooke can pull all the strings,' said Brand.

'And you've got three animated jellies to take along with you.'

'But we can play,' said Brand. 'Now, you'll admit that.'

'Cooke's hirelings. Leaders of his Philharmonic Orchestra. First desk-men all among Cooke's scrapers.'

'I know,' said Brand, washing his drink round the glass. 'Makes you laugh. I wish to God they had violas in jazz bands.'

'You could start the fashion,' said Harris. 'But Cookey'd corner the racket.'

'Here's to him,' said Brand, lifting his glass. 'Your thing was not quite what he had in mind. We have to play the public a little. Mozart, yes. Haydn, yes. Beethoven certainly.' Brand nodded like a mandarin, imitating Cooke, allowing his slim shape to fall into a crumple of middle-aged fat. 'But, I tell you, John, boy, they wouldn't wear Bartók, you know, and he's as established to you and me as these earlier masters, but not to them. The public for string quartets, my dear laddie, is made up of the solid man, the moral-uplift expert. He wants soothing not salting. Yes, I know. Beethoven's not soft-soap to you and me. He'll have the heart-strings out of you if you're a musician, but he's nice noises to them, ringing in the roof, wandering, floating, as if loth to die. Here, give us your glass, Harris.'

Harris shoved his chin into his tie. Brand raised his newly-filled glass.

'Roll on, Christmas,' he said. 'And let's all have some nuts.'

They finished their drinks in silence.

# 2.

THE evening light was clear so that the outline of houses, trees and railings was sharp. There was dust in the gutter, but the weather was cooler.

The avenue on which Cooke lived was lined with high walls in Bulwell stone and over these branches of trees straggled. It was utterly quiet. About the world of that district was written 'money'. No cars stood at the roadside; nobody was running or talking; the houses were too far back in wide gardens for the sound of plutocratic living to reach the street.

Cooke himself opened the door to them.

He was fat, with a mop of dark, half-curly hair and thick-rimmed glasses. His stoutness made him appear jolly, expansive, a friend and brother.

'Ah, Brand,' he said. 'Brand. And this will be Mr. Harris. Come along in.'

They went into the hall, cavernous as a railway station, lit with delicious wall lamps. The tall windows were of stained glass and one trod silently.

'Sit down, gentlemen,' said Cooke, leading them into a vast room, with plate glass windows overlooking a balustraded terrace. 'And name your poison.'

'Whisky,' said Brand.

'Lime-juice,' said Harris.

Cooke nodded.

There was about him an air of stumbling authority. The son of a rich man, he had during the war tried his hand at concert promotion and made it pay. Now hardly a celebrity appeared in the Midlands except by arrangement with C. Grainger Cooke. He held shares in cinemas, television programmes, a bus company; he grew fat on culture.

The other Cooke, the amateur, was also a force to be met. Hard-hitting ghetto pianists or profiled Italian opera virtuosi made his daily pile; but he arranged Bach and Berg on the side for the cognoscenti of Beechnall. The Philharmonic Orchestra and Choral Society were his; they did not, of course, think so; they democratically elected and rejected. But Cooke pulled the strings. The St. Cecilia Music Society, the University String Orchestra, the Tudor Singers were all Cooke-controlled. He encouraged vicars to rebuild their churches from the proceeds of concerts; he staged musical festivals; hardly a miner in a male-voice choir cleared his throat to sing without Cooke's nod. And even this lot paid. Not handsomely; it would not have kept him in nail-files, but he prevented long-haired musicians from flinging good money after bad. There was much to be said for Cooke.

Now the drinks were out, and they were all sitting, Cooke relaxed. He beamed at Harris, tapping fat fingers on the chair arm.

'You've come round, Mr. Harris, for a fight, I take it?'

Harris said nothing.

'I understand you,' said Cooke, 'very well.'

'More than I'd claim,' growled Harris.

'My dear man,' said Cooke.

'Well,' said Harris. There was a pause. 'What are you waiting for?'

'Mr. Harris,' said Cooke, slowly. 'Before I decided not to put on your quartet, I took professional advice.'

'You saw a solicitor?'

'No, I went to a musician.'

'Who?' asked Harris, interested.

'The professor of music at the university.' Cooke slowly raised his eyes and broad jowl.

'A windbag,' said Harris.

'There are other views, of course. You didn't expect me to get Walton or Britten to read it, did you?'

'I should have thought,' said Harris, 'that with your influence that would have been a piece of cake.'

'I know them,' said Cooke.

'I bet they thank God on their bended knees every night for it.'

Cooke smiled, mandarin-like. He was unaffected by Harris's surliness. Now and then he nodded as if pleased with the way the conversation was shaping. He rubbed a finger over his shaven, powdered face.

'Do you wish to know, Mr. Harris, what Professor Attenborough said?' he asked.

'Not particularly,' said Harris.

'He said...'

' ... that the development of the second subject, though interesting, was not thoroughly worked out, that the potentialities of the instruments were not given full vent, that the general outline of the work, though not without touches...'

'Go on, Mr. Harris,' said Cooke.

'Go on?' said Harris. 'For how long?'

A silence. Cooke stretched his arms, and clasped hands behind his head, laughing up to the ceiling.

'He said,' Cooke spoke distantly, directing words at a chandelier, 'that it was an interesting, even powerful work, and well worth a performance. If I wouldn't put it on, he'd certainly arrange to have it done at the University lunch hour concerts.' Cooke's eyes slapped down to bore at Harris. 'Chap-fallen,[3] eh, Harris? Don't know your friends? Don't know anything, eh?'

Harris laughed.

'Yes,' said Cooke. 'You think Attenborough's all 6/4, 5/3 and the nearest he's got to drama is a 4/2 chord. And you think the closest I ever got to music was the rustle of a five-pound note. So I brought you up here to complete your education.'

'Keep the lesson short,' said Harris.

'Here it is,' said Cooke, 'in words of one syllable. "Cooke is your friend".'

Harris was suspicious. The banality, the appeal of a low-class hoarding, even of the comic turn, left him wondering.

Now he began to smile. He disliked the Cookes of the world because they loomed so large, in their own judgement. But this fellow had deflated, humanised himself. He had reduced himself almost to the sub-human. It was as if he had deliberately wetted his pants to prove himself a man like other men.

'So what?' said Harris.

'I've been watching you,' said Cooke, smiling back. 'This is the appeal to your ego, young man. Just be careful.' He delivered this at quick-fire, like a sports commentator describing some interesting tit-bit on the touchline before he dashed back into histrionics about the football. 'You've got the age, Harris, the drive and the knowledge. I can use you. I know you don't like that. Nobody's going to shove you around. I know all that. But we can do each other mutual good. Another drink, Johnnie,' said Cooke, 'while this character consults his conscience.'

They filled up.

'And,' said Cooke, 'don't consult it too long. I want to go to bed sober. I've got to be up at five.' He walked across to Brand.

'John,' he said, 'tell the gentleman. Am I honest?'

'No,' said Brand, sadly.

'Vindictive?'

'Yes,' said Brand.

'Philanthropic?'

'No.'

'To be trusted?'

'As far as you can be thrown,' said Brand. He seemed out of sorts, had lost the elan of earlier evening.

'You see, Harris,' said Cooke. 'You've had it straight. There's no old buck about me.'

'You've a lovely soul,' said Harris. 'Agreed. Now get on with it.'

'I've come to the conclusion,' said Cooke, 'that it's time a town the size of Beechnall, 300,000 inhabitants, had a performance of the St. Matthew Passion every year.'

'Why?' said Harris.

'I should like to hear one myself,' said Cooke, grandly. 'And now and again,' said Cooke, 'I do somebody a bit of good. The citizens of Beechnall, Mr. Thomas Harris. I could bring a London orchestra down, but I'd lose money. I don't chuck money away. We could do an equally good performance here with local people.'

'All three hundred thousand of 'em,' said Brand.

'Keep your nose out,' said Cooke. 'Mr. Harris, you've a choir called the St. Cecilia Singers. Add them to the Beauvale Colliery Male Voice choir and the Winton Ladies and you've got the finest seventy-eighty voices in the Midlands.'

'Orchestra?' said Harris, interested.

'Beechnall Bach Orchestra, picked and trained by friend Brand here.'

'What's he get out of it?' asked Harris.

'A concert, two concerts in the Albert Hall.'

'And me?'

'Christmas Oratorio for a first fling and The Matthew entire, unabridged, two sessions, at St. Mary's and then at the Cathedral. Think about that man, I'd fix it.'

'Too busy,' said Harris.

'Don't you get across me, my lad,' said Cooke. He was formidable. 'And I've another proposition for you before you start shooting your mouth off.'

There was something about Cooke. He kept his voice down, but you expected him to fling his weight at you across the room any minute.

'The Shakespeare Society's taking the Theatre Royal for a week to do *The Tempest.* You're going to compose the music. Now, hold your horses, man. You want a hearing for your stuff, don't you?'

'What's wrong with Sibelius?' said Harris.

'He's dead,' said Brand.

'And so's this client, from the neck up,' said Cooke, laughing pointing a thumb at Harris. 'Free hand, mark you. It can sound like Anton Webern for all I care. They'll all be listening, mister.'

'Talking it down,' said Brand.

'Step the brass up,' said Cooke.

'It's the other sort of brass I'm interested in,' said Harris. Cooke looked hurt.

'You won't do that for nothing,' he said. 'There's money in the Shakespeare Society.'

'More society than Shakespeare,' said Brand, unpleasantly.

'This is a paying proposition,' said Cooke. 'Brand's orchestra'll be on the B.B.C. before you know where you are. And who's to stop them performing your works? Swallow your pride.' Cooke spread his hand and let his jowl flap over his soft collar, the very image of a man who had gulped pride down by the gallon to the last, bitterest drop. 'You're interested, aren't you Harris?'

'I'm interested to know what your cut is,' said Harris slowly.

'I'm investing in your talent,' said Cooke, softly.

'Sorry,' said Harris, 'but I don't see much in it for you.'

'Much what?' asked Cooke.

'Money, of course.'

'Listen, Harris,' said Cooke. He was sitting up now, galvanized, in action at every joint. 'You can't make any money for me. I make that for myself. I make it in great heaps. I don't ask you to tell me how to get rich. I know.'

'Harris,' said Brand, 'doesn't believe in Santa Claus.'

'But I believe in Harris,' said Cooke. 'I've watched him. He's got it there. You haven't, John, for all your thrust. I haven't. But he has. And, by the left, I'll have it out of him.'

'Print in block capitals,' said Harris. He was not pleased to be spoken of in the third person. No, that was wrong. He was almighty pleased, but he ought to wake up. This sort of thing didn't happen.

'I know what you're thinking,' said Cooke. 'That things like this don't happen. Now, I'll tell you. They do. Every day in my sort of world. You think they don't because you live amongst schoolmasters. What they want is security, moderate remuneration, long holidays, nice, stinking little run-about cars. This world is not made up, thank God, of ushers. Are you interested, Harris?'

'Yes.'

'That's more like it. First, the Matthew. It'll take place, whether you conduct or not. Will you?'

'Yes. If my choir's agreeable.'

'Second. *The Tempest?* You'll do that?'

'I don't see why not,' said Harris.

'Right,' said Cooke. 'That's all settled. I'll send Beauchamp, the producer, round to see you.'

He shoved them out into the dark street.

Harris and Brand walked slowly. They seemed in a smaller, less plangent world. There was time now to do things, to breathe, to look round.

'Well, well,' said Brand. 'And now you know.'

'How much did you know of this lot before?' said Harris. He felt a grudge, an excited displeasure, with Brand.

'Only about the Bach orchestra. Nothing else.'

'Not the Shakespeare?'

'No.'

'It's a snob do, isn't it?' said Harris. 'Orchestra of three titled ladies playing cellos side-saddle and two blond hermaphrodites sucking flutes?'

'If you score it for six Salvation Bands and a football crowd, he'll get 'em,' said Brand. He sounded serious, convinced and serious.

'What I want to know,' said Harris, 'is why he's picked on me?' 'You asked him, didn't you?'

'I'm asking you now. And without the bull.'

Brand stopped and grinned.

'I don't know what's in Cookey's mind,' he said. 'Nobody does. Perhaps he's made enough money and is going in for patronage. The Maecenas of Beechnall. The onlie begetter. Or perhaps he's had a row with old Sturton and the Philharmonic and he's going to wipe the floor with them by staging these marvellous Bach affairs. Or perhaps he's gone off his rocker. I don't know, brother.'

'I couldn't say,' said Harris, 'that I really liked him.'

'Strewth,' said Brand. 'You're not there to like him. You're there to write music. And Cookey's there to get the B.B.C. Symphony Orchestra crawling on its belly and howling to play it. Use your loaf, man.'

'I'm as good as famous,' said Harris, ashamed of himself.

Brand suddenly smacked a lamp-post hard with the flat of his hand. The crack reverberated through the street. Brand swore, looked at his palm; then shoved it in his pocket.

'What's up with you?' said Harris.

'Usual.'

'What's that?'

Brand blew a sigh.

'Didn't you know?' he said. 'Women-trouble.'

Harris muttered some conciliatory sound.

'Cheerio, Beethoven,' Brand said, opening his front gate.

'Brahms,' said Harris, remembering his father.

'No whiskers,' said Brand, fiddling with keys. 'Good night.'

'Unlike my grandad.' But Brand was inside.

# 3.

ANOTHER Friday.

Harris, drenched with the stink of the cod the education committee had provided for sustenance, pushed open the common room door, looking for Winterburn.

The room, large, a squat-L-shape, was brilliant with sunshine after the corridors. It was one of the few rooms in the school which had plastered walls. Furniture was new and bright, domestic, modernistic, Picasso-chintz. Over the bright topped tables and chairs was blown, like ash after an earthquake, a coloured layer of schoolmasterly litter. Piles of exercise books, magazines, open newspapers, chess-boards, ash-trays full of apple-peelings, staggering piles of useful bumf, the odd gown, gym-shoes, cricket-pads, envelopes, dirty cups, mathematical instruments, chalk, pullovers, an overturned jack plane, a half-finished sun-dial face, text-books. Every waste-paper basket was crammed full. Cigarettes were crushed out on the parquet floor. On top lockers were tennis rackets, bats, track-suits, registers, paper-darts, rucksacks, raincoats, confiscated comics. Cupboard-doors were open; a hideous leprosy of paper covered the notice-boards. The room was nearly empty and the morning's smoke practically gone.

A semi-circle of comfortable chairs was placed about the electric fire. Each was empty. At the far-end of the room one table was occupied by five men, the Friday Dining-Club. These were people who had revoked on committee cod. Now they sat at sandwiches. At the end, unofficial chairman, was a Scot, with the thinnest of neat cut meat sandwiches mounted on a thick wrapping from a Sunshine loaf. Next, to his left, a broad man with a poker-face of the raconteur, delicately handled thick whole-meal bread and cheese and a thermos-flask, which he treated like a primed hydrogen bomb. Beyond, an ascetically handsome man, with that aquiline profile that often distinguishes the popular clergyman, was peeling a boiled egg. At the far end, a youngster with a head of thick, sprouting hair was hacking at one of three assorted fruits with his left hand. A quiet man, with sparkling glasses and matching hair off-handedly crossed his legs on the right side.

Harris watched them.

Their heads were fixed over their food, as if they were at some sacrificial feast. It is true that all but the broad man had a magazine, the 'New

Statesman' or 'Sovyetsky Sayuz', though there was little reading. All were talking. But the talk was delivered downwards, at the square of grease-proof paper. Only the Scot showed animation. Now and then he shot out a forefinger; it projected like a rifle and he squinted along its imaginary telescopic sights. Any moment one expected some elephant or wildebeeste out on the playing fields to crash to its knees, an explosive bullet in its vitals. Now and again, something made them laugh, but that was quickly over, and there was a shamed pause, and they were back, eyes down for a full house, again.

Harris moved across. Winterburn sometimes sat here.

'Seen Winterburn?' he asked.

The Scot jumped, half-stood, waved his hands and pointed. In a corner Winterburn was stretched, right down in an armchair.

'Thanks,' said Harris.

'This dispatch rider comes in,' said the broad man, levelly. 'A real scrounger, you know. "Give us a drop of your hair-tonic, bombardier..."' Pause for a tender bite, every tooth in place and mastication.

Harris resisted temptation and wandered over to Winterburn.

'Well, mate,' he said.

Winterburn was slumped low, with his feet on a coffee-table. His unopened packet of sandwiches rested on his lap. He had his eyes closed; his arms dangled limply to the floor like an ape's and his mouth was open.

He grunted in reply to Harris's greeting.

'What's up?' said Harris.

Winterburn shook his head, like a dazed boxer, and put his big feet on the floor.

'I've got a headache,' he said, rubbing his eyes.

'Are you capable of talking?' said Harris. 'I want to pick your brains. Hang on, till I get a couple of cups of tea.'

When he came back, Winterburn looked wider awake, and was pecking uninterestedly at his sandwiches.

'Now,' said Harris. 'Drink up.'

Winterburn did so, clumsily spilling tea on to his flannels.

'I've been asked to write incidental music for *The Tempest,*' Harris said. 'Give us the low-down.'

'Have you read it?'

'Yes.'

'What did you make of it?' Winterburn was alert.

'Fairy-tale. Pretty poem. Nothing very interesting.'

'Now I'll tell you what it's about,' said Winterburn. 'It's Shakespeare getting his own back on the world. He was often fed-up, at his wit's end. Tired of all these for restful death and so on. England then was like England now. If you wanted to get on you kicked and licked.' He laughed to himself.

'What?' said Harris.

'The arse of him below and him above.' Winterburn laughed immoderately, before continuing, 'Just look at *Hamlet.* Pangs of despised love, the law's delay, insolence of office, spurns that patient merit of the unworthy takes. Now I think friend Shakespeare was a vindictive beggar. He stored them up. That's why Shylock's so vivid so early. And look at the King in *Hamlet.* "Offence's gilded hand doth shove by justice. But 'tis not so above." Shakespeare prayed for the day when the proud boyos would catch it in the next world.'

'And?' said Harris.

'*The Tempest* is the next world. In the tragedies, what happens? Somebody commits a minor fault, the tragic flaw appears, a fiddling little thing often enough, and the body cops it hot and strong. Lear misjudges his daughters, Othello listens to a villain, Hamlet's too fine a sensibility for the rotten court of Denmark, Antony wants his oats; result, tragedy, they're goners. Now, look at Prospero.' Winterburn was all alive now, chewing at his sandwiches, spitting droplets of tea about. 'He commits the minor fault. Instead of disciplining his brother and his courtiers, he reads in the library. And he's kicked out, to drown with his baby daughter in a rotten carcass of a butt. But that's where Mister Nasty William gets his own back. Prospero's fiddling in the library's been to some point. His weakness happens to have made him into omnipotent God. Now he's got the power to carve the big bugs up, to put them right back flat on their dirty backs where they belong. That's the point and irony of it. '

'Well, well,' said Harris, rubbing his chin.

Winterburn looked up. He seemed deflated by Harris's casual reception as if he'd expected him to catch fire with the idea. He wiped his mouth with a dirty handkerchief, stuffed it into his pocket, fiddled round, found an apple, caressed it between heavy fingers and finally bit into it hard.

'Of course,' he said, rather shamefacedly, 'you can take that as the Assistant Master's view of the thing. If you asked old Lolly-bags there,' he pointed dramatically at the head's office, 'he'd tell you it was the story of the ideal headmaster, the man of picked and ripe wisdom, given the supreme power that headmasters never get now, with marvellous results. That's what flea-bag'd tell you.'

'Would he?' said Harris.

'And as likely as not you'd believe him,' said Winterburn sourly.

'Certainly Prospero's got enough gas for a headmaster,' said Harris in a conciliatory way.

Winterburn was now back in his chair. The room was filling up. The headmaster himself was there. This was his one descent to democracy, when he came in for a cup of tea and a word with those who caught his ear. He stood half-listening to the senior mathematics master, and glowering, whether purposely or not, at Winterburn, who slowly returned his feet to the coffee-table and lit a cigarette, flicking the spent match high into the air.

'Look at his expression,' said Winterburn. 'Turn the milk sour.'

Harris looked over at the head, who, catching the stare, nodded and smiled affably. His neatly-thick grey head bowed again to senior mathematics.

'Snooping as usual,' said Winterburn. 'Why doesn't he stick on his own dung-heap?'

'He's entitled to a drop,' said Harris. 'What's up with you?'

'Further words,' said Winterburn. 'Tell you after school. No use here. Look at that creeping clown there trying to poke his dirty ear into every sodding word I say.'

He took a bottle from his pocket, tipped out two man-size tablets, shoved them into his mouth with the flat of his hand, belched and closed his eyes.

Harris looked at the handsome, flabby, pale face. Winterburn was hopeless at teaching and it was killing him. Every time he went into a room it was a battle, and lost for a start. He talked too much, and the boys joined him. No child folded his arms without an immediate accusation of insolence. And yet Winterburn tried to keep up the pretence that he enjoyed the life, that he was a jocular clipper of earholes, the quick author of crushing rejoinders.

The headmaster had moved over and stood by Winterburn's chair. The maths man was still earnestly exploring his case, though the head now was obviously taking no notice. Eyes were turned over to the little group.

'... and if you'd look at their syllabus, sir,' said the senior mathematics master, 'I think you'd find that it differed from our own in only a very few ways. It certainly contains some work that I ...'

'Yes,' said the headmaster. 'Aren't you very well, Mr. Winterburn?'

Winterburn opened his eyes. His mouth dropped slightly opened.

'I thought,' said Leaman, 'that you were unwell.'

'I'm all right,' said Winterburn, grudgingly.

'Good,' said the headmaster briskly. 'That table.'

Winterburn looked at it, not moving.

The headmaster made the smallest gesture of disgust, as if he'd be pleased to let the matter drop.

'Yes?' said Winterburn.

'I'd be glad, Mr. Winterburn, if you'd take your feet from that table.' His voice was barely a whisper.

'You would?' said Winterburn.

'I would,' said Leaman coldly. He swished the dregs of his tea round the bottom of his cup, and turned away, making immediately for the door. The mathematics man was left high and dry.

'I say, Winterburn,' he said, 'that was a bit...'

'What you say,' said Winterburn, 'is not my concern. Go and tell him about it. And all the rest of the glorious company of creepers, snoopers, yes-men and responsibility-holders.'

The mathematics master went red.

'There's no need,' he said, rubbing his moustache, 'to take me up like that.'

'Fade out,' said Winterburn. 'Did you hear that, Harris?'

'I don't know,' said Harris, 'who's the bigger b.f:, you or him. You know he's always on about furniture.'

'All he's fit for,' said Winterburn. 'Caretaker in a warehouse for storing cheap sticks of hire-purchase rejects. Clear off.'

He closed his eyes, and took his feet down.

Harris moved across to the Friday Dining Club. The broad man was telling in deliberate and flattened tone how he once made a llama sneeze by giving it a salted sandwich. Harris opened a book of counterpoint exercises by the one boy in the sixth who did examination music. The Club was ostentatiously paying no attention to the reprimand, but storing up and docketing every word.

In the second period of Friday afternoon, Harris had a 'free'. The music-room was unoccupied so that he could knock-about and smoke as he liked in his store-room. He usually spent the time tidying sheet music and gramophone records.

He was barely engaged in this way when a knock disturbed him. It was Leaman, the headmaster. There he stood with long, tidy grey hair, the young face, the silk socks.

'If you're not busy, Harris, I'd like a word.' He courteously motioned Harris into the sole padded chair and sat himself down astride a wooden one which was back-to-front. He grasped the cross-piece with well manicured hands.

'You're a friend of Winterburn's,' he began. 'I want to ask you about him.'

Harris grunted.

'Is he happy here?' said the head.

Harris did not answer, but the head was by no means put out. 'What I say to you, now, Harris, is confidential. I do not wish it to go further, and certainly not to Winterburn himself.'

'One moment, sir,' said Harris. 'My union has a code of professional conduct which...'

'I know,' said the head. 'I'm not asking you to say anything you don't wish to.'

Harris was surprised. The Headmaster, it was said, ruled by means of 'closet government'. Plainly, his ideas were hatched out from casual conversations in corridors, at lunch, in the lavatories. This meant, his enemies said, that only his toadies ever got across; the rest kept their counsel when he was about. Certainly, it was unusual for him to come chasing for advice.

Harris looked over the well-cut suit, at the sun-burnt face; the manner of the best public schools was certainly present, even in the small gestures, the reversed chair, the thoughtful chew at the right thumb-end.

'I'm worried about Winterburn,' said the head. 'And I want your advice.' He smiled, so that deep lines were scored in the smooth face, from nostril to mouth-end. He looked like a photograph in the *The Times* of a successful mountaineer. The head scraped with his excellent teeth along the ball of his thumb for a minute before he started again. 'I'm giving away no secrets,' he said, 'if I say that Winterburn's teaching is not altogether successful. I've had complaints from parents... Oh, yes, I know what you're going to say. I don't swallow every bit of tittle-tattle that comes to my ears. But you've only to walk past his class-room to know all's not well.'

He let his heavy lids droop over his eyes.

'Now, I want to help Winterburn,' he continued. 'He's intelligent, well-qualified, full of ideas, but.' He came to a heavy full-stop.

'Wouldn't it be as well,' said Harris, 'if you spoke to Winterburn himself?'

'My dear chap,' said Leaman. 'I've spoken to him several times. Today: for instance. But he's so infernally touchy. And rude.'

'We none of us like to be told we're no good,' said Harris.

'Exactly. I want to help Winterburn. It's to his advantage and mine. If things go on, Harris, as they are doing, I shall be bound to call in Her Majesty's Inspectors to see him, just to safeguard my own position. But I don't want to do that. I'm sorry for the fellow. But he won't be helpful. My God, I know teaching must be hell if you can't hold your classes down.' The headmaster sighed. 'Can you help me?'

'Take him off the middle-school,' said Harris.

'Well, yes,' said the head. 'That had occurred to me. But there are drawbacks. I don't like interfering with the senior men who allocate the periods. Moorhouse is an excellent man, and if he's put Winterburn down for

4B, I don't like... Besides, it means going over Winterburn's failures with yet another party.'

'Do you mean to say,' said Harris, 'that you've never discussed Winterburn with Moorhouse?'

The head blushed, and, then, smiling ran a flat hand down the side of his face.

'Never in detail,' he said.

Harris blew down a dusty recorder. It tooted and he flushed. The headmaster held out his hand and took the instrument as one takes a toy from a naughty first-former. He stopped the holes with his fingers, twisted the wooden tube, lifted it and blew. It squeaked. He laughed.

'I'd never get a tune out of one of these things,' he said. 'Besides, Harris,' this more seriously, 'it would mean that the other members of the department would have to carry Winterburn, and he's not popular.'

'What of it?'

'Oh, yes. But we have to consider it.'

'You could give him a fair dollop of library supervision. There's only the sixth form in there.'

'The same objection holds,' said the head.

'Or could you think up some new periods, Music and Poetry, with Winterburn and me taking a couple of forms together. I'd guarantee there'd be no larking about.'

'Yes. But we don't know, do we, how Winterburn would take it? He'd probably openly accuse me of calling him inefficient. One has to be careful.'

'You can stand that,' said Harris.

'So I could,' said the head, gracefully putting the recorder out of Harris's reach. 'But in any case, I've practically made up the time-table for next year. It'll be very difficult in all conscience. We're understaffed, you know, since Clarke left. This Music and Poetry idea, I don't know how we'd manage that. You don't get round all the forms in the school for music as things are at present.' He rose and dusted his knees. 'Well, thank you very much. This has been very helpful. I'll see if something can't be done along those lines the year-after-next.'

Harris was angry.

'That won't help Winterburn now, will it?' he said.

'I want to help him,' the head said slowly. 'But I mustn't upset the whole of the rest of the school to do it. However, thank you very much. Very helpful.' He blew chalk off the chair on which he had been sitting. 'Oughtn't this chair to be out there in the music room?' he asked apologetically. His finger rested on the black letters M.R. painted on the cross-piece. He lifted it, swung it lightly, and carried it out to place it with the others.

'Sorry to have interrupted you,' said the head, replacing the chair to his liking. He stepped away, pausing only to close the lid of the piano as he passed and to draw a long line in the chalk-dust on the lid.

Harris sat down fatigued. The flash of anger was gone and he was left numbed and feeble. He tried to work up a rage against all spruce and good-looking men but failed and therefore waited listlessly for the Science Sixth to drift in, apologizing that they'd had experiments to finish. They livened him arguing how you could tell the difference between the music of a good modern composer and mere row, so that when he started down the hill with Winterburn he could at least frame his first words jovially.

'Come on, then,' he said. 'Tell me all.'

Winterburn stared across.

'I don't like your attitude, Harris,' he said. 'This is no bloody joke to me.'

'Come off it,' said Harris.

'It's all right for you.'

'Cor,' said Harris. 'Don't tell me then.'

Winterburn walked on a few steps.

'He sent for me this morning and said he'd had complaints from parents that I wasn't teaching properly.'

'What did you say?' asked Harris.

'What parents?'

'Uh?'

'He said he couldn't tell me because it might be unfair to the boys concerned. So I said that if he couldn't name the accusers I couldn't answer the accusations.'

'Was he pleased?' said Harris, nodding.

'He didn't care what I said,' Winterburn said. 'He just hummed and ha-ed a bit and said we'd pay no attention to these letters then, but that he'd noticed since he'd last had me on the mat that my discipline was no better. He didn't like to mention this because he'd no wish to interfere with anybody's teaching method unless it was absolutely necessary.' Winterburn stopped and Harris noticed that his companion's hands were thrashing about as if quite out of control. When Winterburn began, however, his voice was steady. 'He then said he wanted to help me, that personally he liked me, that I had the makings of a good teacher and the rest of the usual blah.'

'What did you say to that?'

'What the hell could I say?'

'You could have asked him how he was going to do it.'

'Why don't you use your brains, Harris?' said Winterburn nastily. 'You know very well why he adopts this reasonable attitude.'

'Go on.'

'He's made up his mind I'm no good and that I've got to go.'

'You don't know that,' said Harris.

'Oh, don't I? You should have heard him spewing on about the high standard of the school, having the interests of the boys at heart, how unpleasant all this was for him and you'd know what he was angling for. I told him sharp that it was so long since he'd been in a classroom that he didn't know what teaching was like.'

'How did he take that?' said Harris.

'Went red. Said he was sorry to see me take that line and that he was afraid, afraid, mark you, the festering sewer, that if there wasn't some improvement he'd be bound to ask the inspectors to report on me.' Winterburn grinned, unpleasantly. 'I just asked him why he couldn't say straight out that he wanted to get me the sack. And then we got more of his soft soap and personal liking and how sorry he'd be if anything had to happen. I wanted to puke.'

They had reached the bottom of the hill, and almost immediately caught the bus together.

'Do you like teaching?' said Harris gently.

'No.'

'Do you ever think of doing anything else?'

'What the hell can I do? For God's sake, shut up. You're as bad as he is. At least he is paid for it. You're not.'

'All right, all right,' said Harris. 'Sorry.'

Winterburn slumped down, didn't say another word, did not even reply to Harris's 'good afternoon' when he got off at Forest Road. Harris watched the bus move away. Winterburn hadn't moved an inch but sat like a sagging, waterlogged tent.

Harris himself felt utterly fagged out. He walked along without realising that he was moving. Depression was like a lump of lead inside him. He did not fight it; in fact, he barely realised that it existed. It was the tiredness of the term's end; the inability to say anything to Winterburn. He had wanted to say something comfortable to the man, but couldn't. He could not now think of the right sentence. Winterburn and the headmaster were travelling their own way; a whisper behind the hand behind the bridge does not stop the express-train.

He stood in the street and looked about. Here were solid and prosperous houses, built to last. Now they were mostly flats, but steady, reliable people lived in them; people with a bit of something to jingle in their pockets at the month's end.

His shoes were dusty. He dragged them indoors.

The hall was both cool and damp. No letters for him.

A door banged open, letting in light. Mr. Sanderson, the landlord, tall as a bean-pole and in shirt-sleeves came out. 'Mr. Harris,' he said. 'I thought it was you.'

'Afternoon,' said Harris. He did not want to talk.

'I've got something for you,' said Sanderson. 'Hold on.'

Harris sat down on the single, creaking chair in the hall.

'A registered parcel,' said Sanderson, returning. 'A big one.' He handed it over, all smiles, well-done-thou-good-and-faithful-servant in the inclination of his head.

Harris's guts turned over and sank.

'Thanks,' said Harris.

Sanderson stood expressing obligation, fear, delight; he wanted to know what was in it.

'It's a fine big one,' he said again.

'I know what's in it,' said Harris shortly.

'I hope it's nice,' said Sanderson.

'Marvellous,' said Harris. It was his manuscript back from the B.B.C.

'Good, good,' said Sanderson. 'I like getting a parcel. A registered parcel is ...'

Harris went upstairs, the manuscript in his hand. In his room he put it down on the table and took off his shoes. Then with the scissors he cut the string. Now he went out and washed his hands. With clean fingers he turned back the excellent brown paper. They had used the corrugated cardboard he himself had sent. He slowly turned that back.

On top of the thick pile of manuscript lay a formal, printed note of thanks and rejection. He moved it. There was nothing written on the back; no pencilled note to indicate who had seen it; no idea of what the Corporation's musicianly servants thought. He looked at the title. 'Passacaglia, Variations and Fugue for String Orchestra by Thomas Harris.' This in his neatest block print, carefully underlined in red, a double thickness and a single.

Black Friday. His fingers drummed on the notice. He lolled back in his chair; Passacaglia, Fulminations and Tripe by Harris.

The printed notice stung him. This was big stuff. He'd written it over five times. It glowed. It was alive. It did something. He worked through it with Brand, who'd been unlike himself about it. 'This is the real McCoy, Harris, cocker,' he'd shouted. 'This'll set their pretty lug-holes back an inch or two. By the Lord God, this is writing for strings. You've made them do every flaming thing except chuck their fiddles at the audience.' And so on. And here it was politely refused.

Harris wondered who'd read it. Some fiddling, niggling tight-bottomed clerk? Some titled jackass? Some plummy-voiced C.B.E.? He shoved his head down on his arms on the manuscript. It was cool and smooth to his face. He opened an eye. The letters of his title were blurred.

Carefully he rewrapped the pile.

There was a knock on the door. It was Sanderson again. 'There's been a phone call for you, Mr. Harris,' he said.

'When?'

'Now. But it's only a message. It was your dad.'

'Eh?' said Harris. You could hardly get his father near a phone box, let alone into one. Mrs. Harris would have been there with the old man, dialling the numbers, putting in the fourpence, while he'd be swearing and pouring muck-sweat.

'Your father, like,' said Sanderson.

'Like what?' said Harris.

'He was a bit short with me. Didn't want none of my la-di-diddly-di-dah. I ought to wash my muddy ears out. Or get somebody there who had. And look slippy.' Sanderson warmed to it. He bore no malice. 'Proper terror he was.'

'The message?' said Harris wearily.

'Oh, yes. It was a bit hard to make out, really, what he wanted. He was shouting so. I said I'd fetch you. He said what he'd like to fetch me. He's coming up at half-past six.'

'Thanks,' said Harris.

'He wasn't half yelling,' said Sanderson. 'And there was a lady there, remonstrating with him, if I may use the word. And the language.'

'I said, "Thanks",' said Harris.

'He'll be here at half-past six. You've got to be in.'

Harris turned savagely in his chair. Blood suffused his face. If Sanderson said another word, Harris would have knocked him flat. The flesh of his chin was pulled back tight from his teeth; he breathed noisily; his fists were clenched and up. He knew he mustn't move.

Sanderson did the moving. His mouth dropped open; his hands slid down to his knees so that he stopped like some starving ape. Then he jack-knifed upwards and back and was out.

The blood knocked about Harris's temples. He took a great breath of air and blew it slowly, windily out of his jutting lips.

Passacaglia, Variations and Fugue.

Harris got on slowly with a miserable tea. His enervation was back; he no longer felt anger at posh jacks-in-office who wouldn't have him. It would have cheered him to let fly at some such, but he was too idle, or worn, to do this. He washed his cups and plates and settled down to wait for father.

The iron gate outside clinked, the bell rang and a mild hell was let loose.

'I don't want no argy-bargy wi' ruddy flunkeys. An' if you want t' take your high-clarss line with me put your jacket on first. And if you want to make some'at of it keep your jacket off an' I'll poke you into kingdom-come just for the practice. Now, tell Mr. 'Arris we're 'ere, and bein' kep' waitin', and tak' your bloody gormless expression off your face for 'oly, mincin' Moses' sake amen.'

Footsteps waddled on the stairs.

Harris wished he had his father's temperament. Whenever he was nervous, or down in the mouth, or ill at ease, he picked on somebody, bawled them out and was satisfied. It had got him into trouble in his youth, but he was very handy with his mitts. Once he had shouted, or hammered the daylights out of somebody, he was as friendly as a fat dog.

Just outside the door, Harris could hear him saying now to Sanderson, 'Thanks very much, mate. I can see you're a decent sort. Mr. 'Arris thinks highly on you.'

'Your father's here, Mr. Harris,' said Sanderson, opening the door.

Old Harris came in and shouted.

'Come on in Jack. Don't stand out there in the co'd.'

A nervous little man with a pepper-and-salt cap in his hand sidled in and smiled with eyes like sucked aniseed-balls.

'This is my lad, Jack,' said Mr. Harris. 'Tom, Jack Button.'

Button nodded, looking round the room. He had never been in such a place in his life; this was his idea of the ballroom in Buckingham Palace. Harris senior enjoyed this. I've got a son who lives in marble halls.

'Well, 'ere we are, then,' said Mr. Harris. 'Sit thysen down an' mak' thysen less.'

Button took the edge of a chair.

Mr. Harris's bonhomie was going. He was a man of few words except in moments of aggression when glandular activity provided him with a series of well worn insults.

'Well, dad,' said Harris.

'Yes, I'm all right, lad,' said Mr. Harris. 'How's yersen?' He nodded and smiled at this masterpiece of polite behaviour.

There was a long silence. The three of them sat there, breathing. Harris could not be bothered to make conversation.

'Look 'ere, Tom,' began his father. 'Now don't take me wrong. I'm doin' yer a bit o' good. Jack 'ere's got a proposition.'

'Yes?' said Harris.

'Jack's an o'd mate o' mine. He wouldn't do a flea no 'arm.'

'Um?'

'He's the secretary o' the Blidworth Colliery Silver Prize Band.' Further silence.

'Mester Harris,' said Button, 'I've come to ask you if you'll write a march for us band.'

The visitor sat back. It was out now.

'A sort of signature chune,' said Button. 'Your dad said you'd oblige us, like, that you'd be glad to. I know, Mester Harris, that you're a college-trained man, like, but we ain't mugs. Us conductor's L.R.A.M.[4] and...'

There was no stopping him now. The conductor, the soloists, the triumphs, the festivals, the instruments were introduced at length. Harris himself was celebrated; the high glory of his bachelordom of music over a mere set of puffing and blowing colliers. But they were ambitious; they aimed high; they didn't want any old garbage; they didn't go anywhere.

Harris listened. This was his style then. A miners' march to be blasted out at the colliery sports day or the area cup-final. Here was the real level of the Harris of rejected Passacaglias and Fugues.

'You want something like the Dambusters' March?' said Harris, interrupting.

Button stopped, sat upright.

'Mester Harris,' he said, 'we're musicians. Not that I've got owt against the Dambusters and not that we don't play it to please the 'erd, but my lads is more at home with an arrangement of "Crown Imperial" or "The Damnation of Faust" march.'

He spoke proudly, and there was dignity about him.

Harris suddenly felt mildly excited. He was moved. He could have shaken Button by the hand. Here was somebody making his small gesture for humanity and doing it well. Of course, Button spoilt the effect by a long, involved, reckless account of their repertoire, and when and where each masterpiece had been played. Harris listened and his depression lifted a little.

'Mr. Button,' he said, 'how long is this march to last?'

Button was not put out by this interruption.

'Five or six minutes.' He was adequately prepared.

'How do you want it scored?'

Button produced a paper, on which the conductor had written the number of his men. Strong and weak sections were noted; soloists named; weaknesses baldly exposed. This was business.

Harris looked it over.

'I'll knock out a rough piano score,' he said, 'and send for you.'

'Could two or three of us come?'

'Yes,' said Harris.

'Mr. Marby, the conductor, would like to be there. And perhaps the doctor. He's rare for music. And old' Arry 'Arman. He'll be a critic.'

'Right,' said Harris. 'That's it, then.'

'One minute, Tom,' said his father. 'Ain't you offerin' us a drink on it. Jack's come a long way.'

'What would you like?' said Harris, laughing at his father, the social being.

'A glass of sherry.' His father was making an occasion of it.

'And Mr. Button?'

'The same'll do me, thank you, if it's no bother.'

Harris poured out.

'Cheerioh,' he said.

'Us succcss,' said his father gravely.

Button and Harris senior knocked their drink back, and looked in amazement at the empty glasses. Button was swilling his drink round with his tongue like a mouthwash.

'Another?' said Harris.

'No thank you all the same,' said Button. 'Very nice. First time I've ever tasted this 'ere. And very nice. I've got my bus to catch now. I've got an 'ome to go to, you know.'

He laughed and shook hands. Then, oddly, Harris senior came across and shook.

They went out. Mr. Harris was loudly telling Button how he had told him how easy it all would be. Harris could hear the old man's voice half-way up the street.

He sat down again. The room seemed deserted after Button's flat-voiced, enthusiastic chatter. Harris was annoyed with himself. He had taken on a job he did not want. Not that it would cause much trouble to fling together a march that would test Button's crew, but there was the fag of getting it down on paper, once the thing was over and done in his head.

His eye fell on the brown paper parcel.

At least Button's march would get heard. He sat up. Why not send the Passacaglia to Cooke, rather than hawking it round the publishers? It was a cat in hell's chance. Again his spirits rose. He took out notepaper.

*Dear Mr. Cooke,*

*You said something the other night about 'investing in my talent'. I don't know if you meant it, or if it was just a casual phrase to rope me in for your Matthew Passion and Tempest.*

*I send you this work for string orchestra. It's the best thing I've ever done. But the B.B.C. won't have it.*

*Can you do anything with it? Sorry to trouble you.*

*Yours sincerely,*

*Thomas Harris.*

He shoved the note in, repacked the parcel. When it was done, he felt ashamed. He hated those people who pushed their stuff, or used influence. Talent not nepotism every time.

Harris sat down at his piano.

He began to play. 'Nun Komm' der Heiden Heiland'. Bach's flowing prelude pealed out, singing, under his fingers. There was another old buffer who'd had to wait till he was dead. Another second-best client, and no Cooke to pull his chestnuts out of the fire.

Saviour of the heathen?[5]

## 4.

BEAUCHAMP, producer of *The Tempest* was Harris's next visitor. He did not live up to the aristocratic promise of his name. Born in Bradford, he still kept the accent. In appearance, he seemed a lively lad of twenty, but he must have been older in spite of his roll-neck sweater and bandaged glasses.

He burst with energy. He skipped and stuck his teeth out like the pictures of Japanese on the walls of Indian Army Camps. Ek goli, ek Japani.[6]

First he told Harris that Shakespeare wasn't a fool, that the playwright understood the theatre, and that he didn't need any clever fellows mucking about with him. He then proceeded to say how he was going to organise matters. Then he explained how he wanted the songs setting and how quiet the music was going to be in the masques and where and when he wanted the words underlining and how. Harris soon saw himself as a sort of poor equivalent of the stage-electrician. He was given a long sheet of paper, with times of duration, comparative speeds and volumes and ordered to get on with it sharp.

'You know what you want,' said Harris.

'It's likely, isn't it?' said Beauchamp.

'Why don't you write the music yourself?'

'Are you being awkward?' asked Beauchamp. 'Our job's to shove Shakespeare over to these thick-heads, my lad. Harris's mighty symphony'll have to wait for some other time. Sorry, there it is.'

He shoved a tattered school edition of the play into Harris's hand and told him to soak himself in it.

Harris kept his temper and said, 'How do you get on with Cooke, Mr. Beauchamp?'

Beauchamp crossed his first and middle fingers.

'So,' he said. 'Me on top.' He appeared to go through some sort of stage action. Man, with brother who's assistant lecturer in philosophy, thinking deeply. Having completed this he said:

'I shall have Prospero played like Cooke. I've already told him so.'

'What did he say?' said Harris.

'He was pleased.'

'Has he read the play?' asked Harris.

'He's a man of parts who gets things done. He recognises talent. He pushes it.'

'Did he spot you?' asked Harris.

'Harris,' said Beauchamp. 'We can only have one boss in this show.'

'And it's you.'

'Yes, strange to say.' Further performance. Man switching off pneumatic drill before large audience of urchins. 'That's all, brother. Read the words. Learn the words. And then begin. Keep me posted. I want it done before the end of September. And remember it's Shakespeare not Harris they're going to hear.'

'Does anybody love you,' said Harris, 'apart from your mother?'

Beauchamp looked up. Dying tommy sees Angel of Mons. 'Wait until you've had experience of me at work, son, and then you'll forgive the brass-neck. It doesn't go down well at first, but it pays in bright gold.'

He was off. Harris was left holding his play. He opened it. 'Kathleen Connor, Upper Fourth Arts. In case of fire, please throw this book into it,' read the inscription.

Harris had sent his manuscript to Cooke, and had received an acknowledgement. This had not pleased him either. It said that Mr. Cooke thanked him. It also explained that it seemed sensible to Mr. Cooke, if the Passacaglia was all its composer claimed, to wait for Brand to get his orchestra into shape and then let them have first performance. Not only would Mr. Harris have a hand in preparing the performance, it was quite certain that Brand's men would be broadcasting within the next three years. However, Mr. Cooke would have a careful look at the work, and, indeed, would be glad to, though he could, of course, promise nothing. Mr. Cooke was off to Nice for the present, but hoped Mr. Harris's projects were in hand. He was Mr. Harris's cordially, Charles E. Grainger-Cooke.

On the same day that he received this letter, Harris met Brand in the street. He told his friend in a shame-faced way what he had done, but Brand wasn't interested.

He can pull some strings,' he said, 'even if he's not bothered.' Brand seemed nervous. 'Harris,' he said, 'will you do me a favour?'

'It depends.'

Brand smiled in a charming, easy way.

'It's nothing. I didn't go home to lunch today. My wife expected me. Will you come home with me now?'

'What good will that do?'

'It'll put the row back a bit. It might even postpone it altogether if you and my wife hit it off. Anyhow, it'll do her good. I owe her something.'

'And what have you been up to?' said Harris, man to understanding man.

Brand was not annoyed. 'As a matter of fact...'

'All liars start like that.'

'I know,' said Brand. 'Actually, I was called out on some business and left the wet-neck in my office to ring my wife. He, the clever dick, spun some fancy story that I had to stay at the works. Not the first time, either. My wife came round after lunch, and I wasn't there. My secretary knew where I was but I suppose my clever friend kept my wife away from her. Unfortunate, and all that, but I suppose I'm only getting what I've asked for.'

Harris went round with no enthusiasm.

Mrs. Brand was sitting at the tea-table alone. Two empty plates, milk-splashes and crumbs showed where the children had had their meal. Presumably their nurse was putting them to bed.

'Oh, Nance, this is Mr. Harris, who's come in for tea. I want to talk to him about one or two things. Music, you know.'

Brand looked thoroughly guilty. His wife stood up and shook hands with the visitor. She was small, very pretty and birdlike, in that she seemed alive with sharp, minute movements and, if one looked closely, bedraggled or ruffled.

'I'm pleased to have you, Mr. Harris. John's often mentioned you.'

'To my advantage, I hope,' said Harris.

She opened her large eyes wide, studied him wrinkling her nose and said,

'I hadn't thought about that.' She transferred her attention to her husband. Her left hand took up, and began to crumble, a piece of fruit cake left on a child's plate. 'I came looking for you at lunch time, John.'

'I know,' said Brand. 'I was out.'

'I know,' she said very clearly, interrupting him. 'I know.'

'I had to go to Retford. I thought I'd get back, but I couldn't. I had lunch with old Mr. Meyerstein and his son.'

'The young man at the office said you had to stay there.'

'Blast him,' said Brand.

'I was worried, John. I don't know how it was, but I was very upset. I don't know what we should do if anything happened to you.'

Brand took a pencil from his pocket and a slip of paper. He wrote on it and passed it over to his wife.

'There are the phone numbers of Mr. Meyerstein, his son and his secretary. There were three other people there. I've put down their names. They all live at Retford. The exchange will give you their numbers. Ring them up now and ask them where I was. There's hardly likely to be collusion between six of them.'

Brand spoke in an earnest, academic way. To Harris it sounded thoroughly cold-blooded; if Brand had leaned across and hit his wife he would have felt more comfortable.

Mrs. Brand studied the paper. The cake was a mush of fragments now. She was fragile, in danger of shivering away, disappearing into air, the thinnest air. She looked up, all eyes.

'I don't disbelieve you, John.'

'Why did you put the phone down then, when I rang you up this afternoon?'

The pause, the wrinkling of delicate skin, the stare.

'I felt so upset,' she said. 'I couldn't bear to talk. I feel so silly now.'

Carefully, she handed the paper back. Brand took it.

'Please forgive me,' she said.

'It was my fault,' said Brand. 'I'm sorry, darling.'

He went round the table and kissed her. She smiled at the embrace, but it seemed not to alter her. She was like a small, cellophaned, pastel-shaded packet of chocolate; you could not say if it had anything inside or was a shop-window dummy.

Brand and Harris ate, both self-consciously. The conversation was casual and broken. When the meal had ended, Brand said he would go up to the children before they went to sleep.

'You might tell Ethel, John,' said his wife.

Mrs. Brand sat down by the one-bar fire and invited Harris to take a chair on the other side of the hearth. The servant smilingly cleared the table and while she was in the room, Mrs. Brand played at warming her hands.

Finally she sat still, quite straight in her chair, as if deliberately impressing on Harris that his attention was wanted. He, who had been uncomfortably thinking out non-committal openings, was now put further into discomfort.

'Will you talk to me, Mr. Harris?' she asked. It was more like an order. The small voice was authoritative.

'Surely.' He let his voice slide musically over the old word. 'What's the form in politics now?' she said.

The question startled him. Her first sentence had been urgent; now there was the colloquial time-waster. If the first question was the drill-sergeant's rapped order, the second was the second-lieutenant's mouthful between two convivial, expensive whiskies. He thought he'd misjudged her.

'The usual,' he said. 'Talk galore. Nothing doing. Not that I know much about...'

'Will there be another war?' she said.

'I hope not.'

'I said "Will there?"' Her teeth were placed thoughtfully over her lower lip.

'Who's to know?' he said. 'If the governments are sane, there won't...'

'Mr. Harris,' she said, 'I want John to take us to live in Australia. Is that wise?'

'I'd be sorry to see him go.'

'His firm is opening a subsidiary there. If he pressed, his father would let him go.'

'Does he want to go?' said Harris.

'I want to go,' she said. 'If they dropped a hydrogen bomb anywhere on Beechnall, we shouldn't stand much chance here.'

'You wouldn't in an Australian city, either.'

'We shouldn't be in a city. At least not a large one.'

'What about the children's education?' It was a make-weight question on Harris's part, but he felt snobbish and ashamed when he'd asked it.

'What good is education,' she asked, 'if you're blown to bits?'

'True,' said Harris, 'but you can't act on the assumption that that's going to happen. You'd do nothing, or pray or something.'

'That's my assumption.'

Again there was the incisive snap of the skilled N.C.O. Harris looked across. A petite, well-dressed, staring girl, leaning forward, one hand on her ankle. Her eyes, he thought, offered him a glimmer of a smile, of apology.

Brand came in.

'All asleep but one,' he said, a proud father for Harris's benefit.

'Good,' she said, swaying back to relax.

'Now,' said Brand, pulling a chair forward, though it was warm.

'I am enjoying talking to Mr. Harris,' she said.

Brand dropped his chair.

'Oh, well,' he said. 'That lets me out. If you don't mind, darling, I've got one or two letters to write. Are you in a hurry, Harris?'

'No.'

'Fair enough.'

Brand almost ran out of the room. When the door shut, his wife laughed, not loud but quite quietly, and tucked both legs under her in the arm-chair. She did this easily; she was so small.

'I live under that constant fear,' she said. 'I am afraid that my children will be blown to smithereens, or worse, live to produce their children with six thumbs on each hand. It is an obsession with me.'

She said this plainly, but the smile at her husband's scuttle from the room was still on her face.

'That's very silly of me, Mr. Harris,' she said, 'isn't it?' She spoke mockingly. She wriggled her legs down and pulled her frock very tightly round her hips. 'I am a little woman, Mr. Harris,' she said, nodding towards the stretched silk, 'and my children were not born easily. I don't care to lose them thoughtlessly. Do you understand that?'

'Yes, it's understandable,' said Harris.

'I often wonder if an operation on my frontal lobes isn't the only way out. You've heard about pre-frontal leukotomy. Of course, I should lose all sense of responsibility but I shouldn't care any more. I sometimes think I should like that.'

'Well,' said Harris.

'You've got music, Mr. Harris. If things get too much for you, you wallow in that, like a dog in the street. I was nineteen when I married seven years ago, and I liked going to concerts and listening to John and his friends. Now I see music for what it is.' She looked at him, and held a pretty finger out. 'You think I'm going to say it's an escape, but I'm not. It's a nice habit, that's all. Nicer than my rut.'

'Do you ever talk to your husband...?' began Harris.

'Him, and others. I've been to the best psycho-analysts. I know what's wrong with me, but it doesn't cure me. Perhaps I don't want to be cured.'

'You've certainly got it all nicely taped,' said Harris, unpleasantly pleased to get a word in.

'How?'

'Your symptoms, and your comparisons and disclaimers.'

She laughed, she looked like a schoolgirl.

'I've not given you a tenth,' she said. 'You're lucky. And I'll tell you now, since we're being frank, what John thinks it is. I can see you're interested, Mr. Harris.'

Again she paused as if daring him to interrupt.

'He's unfaithful to me. I know that. I don't mind. It's unimportant. But he thinks I've transferred my, er, horror, right word, Mr. Harris? at that to this other business.'

'And that's not true?' said Harris.

'No. It isn't. And I'll tell you why I can explain all this to you nicely. It's because I've explained it to so many other people. It's a relief to me, a sort of indecent exposure.'

'Do you talk it over with your husband?'

'If you fetched him in now,' she said, 'he could give you word for word what I've said to you. He's got it off by heart.'

'Don't you think,' said Harris, in a judicial manner, 'that you've explained it, and discussed it, and put it into words so often that you now believe it's true?'

The large eyes were slowly lifted up.

'You're very ignorant,' she said.

'Do you mean impolite?' Harris said, school-masterly.

A spasm of temper crossed her face.

'I don't enjoy this,' she said. 'I don't talk to you for mere pleasure. That's you musicians all over. Hedonism. Play, fiddle play. What's your Beethoven but a slavering circus clown? Why don't you use your imagination? I am sometimes convinced that my children will die, horribly mangled, and nothing will get that out of my head. Do you think I like it? Do you think that I can't remember the time when I was like everybody else and could hope that horrid thing wouldn't happen? Do you think I haven't told myself to be more sensible? That there are hundreds of other people in the same boat that I'm in who aren't killing themselves with anxiety?'

'One minute,' said Harris.

'What's the use of waiting a minute for you? You can't understand how it is that I can sit here and talk sensibly to you, can you? If I pulled my clothes off and yelped and bit you, you'd be shocked and embarrassed and sorry. Then you'd believe me.'

'The horrible thing is that you can talk sensibly,' said Harris.

'My obsession's not on all the time. When it eases up, I talk, try to bring it out into the open in the hope something'll click.'

'You spoke as if you couldn't help talking about it,' said Harris.

'In a way. It was a habit, a good one at first. I can't resist it now.'

'Your obsession's a habit,' said Harris.

'Now what have you told me?' she asked. 'Do you think that's done any good saying something as obvious as that?'

'I'll tell you something else,' said Harris. 'You haven't got enough to do. If you had to look after your children, and cook and wash, and think twice before you bought three penn'orth of radishes for a treat, as my mother had to, you wouldn't have time for obsessions, except sensible ones.'

'Working-class people go mad.'

'With good reason. You've too much energy and too little to use it on. Go out and char every day and live on what you earn. You'd be so concerned about dirty cracks and wrinkles in your pretty fingers in a fortnight that you wouldn't be worried about hydrogen bombs any more.'

'Isn't it right to worry about them, then?' she said in a childish, sullen way.

'Within reason.'

'But the reasonable fear leads to the unreasonable sometimes,' she said. She was speaking more timidly.

'You make me tired,' said Harris. 'What sort of mother are you? So worried about your babies that you drive yourself mad and leave them without a mother. You're not fit to be a human being. You ought to be stuck in a medical museum. I'd indecent-exposure you.'

'You're enjoying shouting at me,' she said. 'I know that.'

'I'm sorry,' said Harris. 'I've said too much. You're ill.'

'I'm not, Mr. Harris. You said I wasn't.'

'Forget what I said. I'm sorry. I lost my temper.'

'Other people, you know, have said all this to me,' she said. 'More politely, perhaps.'

'Good luck to them,' said Harris.

She sat straight, composed herself, adjusted her position and then spoke.

'I am quite serious.'

Harris felt the blood pound up into his head. His eyes closed slowly, misting his vision and his whole body shook and rocked with anger.

'Then the sooner your husband gets a stick and welts the living daylights out of you the better,' he said.

His ears burned. His head seemed to roll over his neck muscles which were tight as steel-rods. He heard himself blowing out breath again.

'Well, Harris, you dirty, thrashing old schoolmaster,' said Brand. He was standing by the door, at ease, a delighted smile on his face.

'Mr. Harris has been trying to do me good,' Mrs. Brand said.

'It sounded to me,' said Brand, taking a biscuit from an elegant barrel and biting, 'just like a lovers' quarrel.'

'I think,' said Mrs. Brand, 'that I could fall in love with Mr. Harris. Just a little.'

'You naughty girl,' said Brand, kissing her and then sitting on her chair-arm. 'You mustn't say things like that to our Harris. He's pure.'

'Say what the hell you like,' said Harris. 'Don't mind me. I like a smart-society comedy about once a year.' He felt tired and had a headache.

'He is cross,' said Brand. 'What shall we do for him?' 'Dance,' she said.

He bowed very low.

'Would you favour me?' said Brand.

'I am sorry, sir,' she said, 'but my heart is engaged elsewhere.'

Brand jerked up.

'Should us?' he said, sticking his bottom lip out.

'Yus,' she growled. 'O'd me fag, ducks.' She spat off an imaginary strand of tobacco and pushed a couldn't-care-less finger-nail into her hair.

They began a waltz together. Brand, in the Americano-cockney, sang, 'Who's takin' you home tonight?' The initial beat was exaggerated by the dancers so that they slogged forwards on an enormous stagger righted by two small, tip-toe, braking movements. The woman leaned backwards and her husband pressed into her. The raking first strides wheeled them zig-zag about the room. Harris watched the tops of their heads; yard and half forward, sag, jerk. Soon Brand dropped his singing and the steps became utterly complicated. Shining shoes found themselves now close, now there. Once a rug slipped under them, but they eagerly involved the slide in the dance.

Now they were into a kind of quickstep and Brand putting his hands on his wife's shoulders began to bounce with stiff legs, as if he was about to leap-frog over her head. She kept up a kind of back-pedalling shimmy. Harris thought that when Brand went up to go over, she'd retreat so fast that her husband would be flung on to his face. Still the puppet-motion of the man jagged on until finally his left, ramrod leg landed on the table and he was held there, let out, smiling, dependent on his wife. She shifted her hands from his ribs and slapped them on to his chest hard. The outstretched leg slid creaking from the table and he fell backwards.

He had dropped his hands from her shoulder and he fell, professionally cushioning himself like an actor, on his back. As soon as he was down, his wife lifted her skirts and shouting threw her hands on his shoulders and whirled her legs smack upwards in a high hand-stand. Her husband, quick as sight, grabbed her wrists. She held her legs kicking high for perhaps a fraction of a second, but to Harris the time was interminable. He thought for a moment she'd overbalance forwards into the fire grate, but down she flew, her feet cracking like a gun into the floor and one high-heeled shoe twisting clean over, and she stood, astride her husband, holding out her skirt and bowing to Harris. She put out a hand to her husband, who scrambled up.

'Are you all right, Nance?' said Brand.

'Oh, yes, thanks.' Her voice was almost inaudible. She was breathless. When she made her way to her chair, she hobbled badly. After she sat, shut her eyes, let her head loll. Her breathing was fast and noisy.

Brand dusted down his trousers and stood hands on hips in the middle of the room, incapable.

First there was the sharp rasp of the Brands, breathing. This stopped and there was silence. Mrs. Brand was slumped into her chair with her eyes shut while her husband stood, resting, one hand on her chair back. The clock ticked. Harris could hear his heart beating.

Mrs. Brand opened her eyes.

'I've got pins and needles in my feet,' she said.

'Jolly good show, love,' said Brand. 'It's long enough since we've had a dancing session. Harris must've got you worked up.'

'Mr. Harris is shocked,' said Mrs. Brand. 'I can see leg-show's not his line.'

'Mr. Harris will have to be going,' said Harris, comparing his watch with the clock.

'I thought you and John wanted to talk,' said Mrs. Brand.

'It can wait,' said her husband.

Harris stood up.

He walked over to Mrs. Brand with his hand out.

'Thanks for entertaining me,' he said.

Mrs. Brand kicked off her shoes and stood. She did a little, pained dance.

'Oh, my dogs,' she said. 'Thank you, Mr. Harris; come again.'

Brand showed Harris out.

'Thanks old chap,' he said. 'You've worked the oracle this time. Done her good as well as saving me from what I deserve.' He was his smiling, alert self. His eyes and smartness dropped. 'It's worrying, I can tell you. She wrote a poem and showed me. It was about bombed children boiling and dripping off walls like fat off a fowl. Put the wind up me, mate.'

He shook hands with Harris, a thing he had never done before. 'All comes out in the wash-tub, eh?' he said.

As Harris walked back he thrashed the visit over in his head. He could not make out whether Mrs. Brand was bogus or not. That was why he hadn't lost his temper earlier with her. There was a childishness about her, but that was perhaps only his own interpretation of her quick flutters and the slow, impassive stares and her small body. He tended to agree with his own diagnosis that laziness was her trouble; with, maybe, the additional fatigue of a family too early in life before maturity set in, and yet without the ordinary, workaday stresses that would advance such maturity. And then there was Brand, a suave and youthful dirty old man.

He did not remember the talk as forcibly as he remembered the dance. That sad, sexy affair had upset him. Here were a couple of modern, urban, civilized people acting like savages dancing trouble out of existence. It was not right. He couldn't approve of it. But it had gripped him, in throat, heart, genitals and feet and rushed him out of the world of Thomas Harris, a schoolmaster. Perhaps if Winterburn could get jigging he'd set himself straight but the thought of those large, flat, brogue-heavy feet hopping wasn't likely. The tall, stockinged yet naked legs, so much of her had seemed leg, standing like pillars there had rocked him. It wasn't possible so small a person could hide so much leg as that. And the uncovered thighs. We are all dirty old men.

When he got home he fetched his note books out and began the march. A fine, masculine, jagged, upstanding start, ripping weaknesses right out of the band. Masculine. Strong. Brushing the world aside. This was Boss Harris. He worked until midnight and only dropped his pencil down when he was about on his knees.

He began to look through it. As usual he wouldn't wear that. He threw his pencil dart-like at the bust of Mozart and missed by two feet.

'Marche composé aux cuisses de Mme. Brand,' he said.

But he was down to it next day and by the first week of the summer holidays had the full score complete, and nobody consulted.

## 5.

HARRIS wrote to Button and told him to bring the committee down to hear the march.

Button's reply came a week later, written with marvellous care on colliery notepaper, suggesting that Harris should bring the score to Blidworth. He'd be fetched and brought back by car.

Harris had not expected a coal-cart for transport, but neither had he thought a smart Vanguard would be in line. A young fellow, with immaculate flannels and a sky-blue, open-necked silk shirt was shown up by Sanderson.

'Mester Harris? Jack Button telled me to fetch thee ovver.' Harris put on a light raincoat and picked up the folder of manuscript.

'That's it, then?' said the young man and took it from Harris's hand. 'I've nivver seen real composed music afore. 'Ev yer wrote a good part for t'trombones?'

'You'll rip the roof off,' said Harris.

'Offus mouths,' said the young man, pleasantly.

The car made extraordinary pace out of Beechnall northwards, out into the little hills, pelting along lanes, under the great, heavy-leafed churchyard trees and into Blidworth. This was a village, rose and honeysuckle, which sat on the edge of an estate of raw, red-brick miners' houses and the massive, slender buildings of the brand-new colliery.

The young man, who had not said a word, but who, out of deference to Harris, had sung a fierce bass line from Handel's 'Worthy is the Lamb' while they were touching seventy, in the end pointed to a council house and said,

'That there's Jack's.'

The young man made no attempt to move, so Harris got out and before he had taken a step on the unmade pavement the car had rocketed off.

A pretty girl, in a summer frock, opened the door.

'Come in, Mr. Harris,' she said. 'Dad's nearly ready.' She enunciated beautifully.

When Harris entered the living room, he found Button in his shirt sleeves struggling with a collar in front of a mirror propped up on a milk-jug.

'Ah de do, Mester Harris. Just setting mysen to rights, like.' There were contortions with the tie, then Button rose, took his jacket off the chair back, donned it over a fairisle pullover and rubbed his hands.

'Nah, then,' he said. 'Draw yersen a chair up, Mestr' 'Arris.'

The table was heavy with china, gold and blue, a silver tea-pot, a pork pie, ham, brawn, tinned salmon, tomatoes, fruit salad, piled bread.

'I hope you've a good appetite, Mr. Harris,' said the girl.

'That's our Elsie, my daughter,' said Button. 'Twenty-one next month. Works in the Coal Board Offices. Gettin' married at Christmas. Don't know how I s'l manage.'

Harris nodded, and the girl smiled, giving him a serviette. It was enormous and thick and starched. In spite of the heat, there was a broiling fire in the grate.

'We don't say grace 'ere,' said Button. 'We get stuck across it.' Harris, who had already had tea, sat down diffidently.

'You would like just a touch?' said Button.

'I beg your pardon?'

Button went to the sideboard and pulled out a bottle of liqueur whisky. He topped it.

'To wet your whistle, like,' he said.

'No, thank you.'

'Very nice,' said Button. 'Bit of a festivity, like.' He put the bottle on the table.

Harris helped himself to a thin triangle of bread and a tomato, which he began to cut up.

'Salmon?' asked Button. On Harris's refusal, he helped himself, soused it with vinegar and began to eat. 'We're very glad you composed the music,' said Miss Button.

'That's not much of a job for a man of Mestr' Arris's calibre,' said Button. 'My guiney, Elsie, this 'ere bread's as thin as a lace-curtain. It wouldn't do for my snap-handkercher.'

'Is it difficult to compose?' asked Elsie, eating with delicacy.

'Like anything else,' said Harris. 'It's hard work if it's worth doing.'

'I thought the music just flowed into your mind,' she said, 'and all you had to do was write it down.'

'Not mine,' said Harris.

'You interest me,' said Button. 'Get some'at under your waistcoat, Mester Harris. Them tomatoes is my own growin'. No foreign muck about them.'

'Delicious,' said Harris, who was in fact enjoying the fruit.

'Mozart, now,' said the girl. 'It came easily to him, didn't it?'

'In a way, yes. In a way, no. You don't write just like Mozart just because you're talented.'

This started Button, who had a long anecdote about a very talented boy who was at school with his eldest son. He could do anything and everything. The story touched all departments of life; the character of every person named was briefly sketched; the ramifications forked like lightning everywhere. At the end of this magnificent, toppling lecture, Button told in gummy detail how the genius had been killed by a buzz-bomb in London. Even he seemed to see that the story had no point. His daughter listened seriously.

'It were very sad,' said Button apologetically. 'Tragic, really.'

Button talked on. Harris ate much more than he thought possible. Elsie asked pretty questions. As they were about finishing, there was a rattle at the back door and a man came in.

'Anybody at hom', Jack?' he said.

'Eh up, 'Arry, my o'd bird,' said Button. 'Mister Harris, this is Harry Harman, who's come to hear. Elsie, get him a cup.'

Miss Button did so, unwillingly. She did not like Harman, it was clear.

Harman helped himself to a cake, pushed it whole into his mouth and looked round. He was old and as fat and hard as a pig. He picked the whisky bottle from the table. Miss Button pushed him his tea across.

'Thanks, Else,' he said. Her nose went up. He took the cork from the bottle and slopped some into his tea.

'That's gen it a bit o' taste, now,' he said. He returned the bottle.

'Some people would have thought it polite to ask,' said Elsie.

'Little gels,' said Harman, 'should be seen an' not 'eard. Your dad don't begrudge me a sup.'

'He didn't get much chance,' said Elsie.

'Now, then,' said Button. 'Let's not have words.'

'He's no right,' said his daughter, 'to walk in here as if he owned the place, laying his thieving hands on what he fancies. And what call has he got, anyhow, listening to Mister Harris's music? What does he know about it?'

'He had the best tenor voice in the country,' said Button. 'Sir Walter Parratt said to me,' said Harman, 'he said, "Harman, you've got the finest voice I ever heard. If I were a young man, he said, I'd make some'at o' thee." You'll remember Sir Walter, Mr. Harris? A gentleman if ever there was one and he said, "The finest voice..."'

'We've only your word for it,' said Elsie.

'What d'you expect me to do?' said Harman. 'Fetch a medium for him to tell you from the other side?'

'If he heard you, he wouldn't recognise the finest voice,' said Elsie. 'Too much beer's flowed over it since then.'

'You cheeky little vixen,' said Harman amicably.

Button got up. Methodically he began to pack the crockery and carry it into the scullery. When he had finished, he said,

'A drop before we go out?'

'Ah,' said Harman.

'No thanks,' from Harris.

'As you will,' said Button and put the bottle away.

Upstairs from the lavatory Harris could hear Elsie singing in the kitchen. She was giving him her best. 'With verdure clad' from 'Creation'. Her voice was clear as water. When Harris came down, the other two had their top coats on.

'Gets a bit nippy at night,' said Button.

'Do you work on the coal-face, Mr. Button?' asked Harris. 'Not now,' said Button. 'I did.'

'Not 'im,' said Harman. ''E's got a bobby's job, 'e 'as.'

'Nice voice, your daughter,' said Harris.

'Trained,' said Button. 'Dr. Allen.'

'Is he still alive?' said Harris. 'He taught me thirty years ago.'

'No power in it, nor no quality,' said Harman. 'That's right, in't it? Mr. Harris?'

'No,' said Harris.

'She 'as 'er points, I don't deny,' said Harman. 'She lacks passion. Poise and passion.'

They were travelling up the street. It was like a royal procession. People standing at doors, working in the garden, squatting miner's fashion outside the gate, walking arm-in-arm, all greeted Button. He spoke to them all, but his loquacity had gone; his genius, with Harman here, was like Mark Antony's rebuked by Caesar.

'Next stop the 'Orn,' he said.

'The Hound and Horn,' said Harman, battering the aitches. 'To collect Mester Marby, the conductor. Office-worker, he is. Needs his half-pint. Good conductor.'

'Not got the go he should have,' said Harman. 'Too finicky by half.'

The 'Hound and Horn' was a modern place; a kind of brick extension of the colliery. Inside there were green carpets, polished ashtrays, glass-topped tables and a landlord in a blazer.

Marby sat alone, a pint-pot in front of him. He was stout and bald. His face was creased into a smile like that of a baby with wind. When he stood, Harris noticed, he was at least six foot three. He shook hands and asked them what they wanted. A waiter in a short white coat stood by. It was too early for much of a crowd.

Button and Harman demanded beer, Harris orange juice.

The table glistened with light; four pint glasses, a shapely tumbler for the fruit juice, a cut-glass jug of water and a seagreen tray of decorated glass.

'I hear you've brought the full score,' said Marby finishing the first drink.

'Yes,' said Harris. 'I've other things on. I wanted it done.'

'I hope it's playable,' said Marby.

'Mester 'Arris knows how to score,' said Button, quietly.

'He doesn't know my clients,' said Marby. 'Does he, Harman?'

'It's difficult,' said Harris. He pushed the score across.

Marby opened it, shifting drinks. He lit a cigarette. The others watched him, sipping. He turned over a page or two, then went back to the beginning.

'Too 'ard?' asked Harman.

'Who asked you for your spoke?' asked Marby.

'I'm asking you,' said Harman.

Marby slapped his hand delicately on the manuscript.

'This is music, Harman,' he said. 'When the lion's growling, the pussycat licks his bum.'

There was more sipping and Marby took the score on his knee. Nobody said anything. Button called for three more pints and Harris shook his head.

'Cheers,' said Marby, nodding, picking the glass up. 'This'll make 'em sweat.'

'All right, Charlie?' said Button.

Marby didn't reply.

'Like th'Undertakers' Banquet,' said Harman, after a time.

Nobody answered. Marby's eyes worked up and down as well as across. His hand reached for ale. Button ordered again, Harris refused a second time, and studied a long drawing of huntsmen up on the wall. He was content to sit there in mindless content, willing to wait like Button for the expert comment. Finally Button said,

'It's quarter to, Harry. If we're going to get to the doctor's by eight, we'd better look slippy.'

Marby nodded, his head still down to the score. He finished his drink in one gulp. He looked, up at Harman, at Button, at Harris longest of all. He wrapped up the score, replaced it on the table and began to fasten his mackintosh. He stood, scratching his face with a white hand.

'I haven't made it all out, of course,' Button signalled that this was understandable by putting a hand on his sleeve. 'All I say now is, "God knows how you can write like this on orange juice."'

Button dropped his hand. His face crumpled. Harris thought he was going to cry, but he was beginning to laugh.

'Did y' hear that?' he said. 'On orange juice.' His laughter was quiet; the tears were already running down his face. 'Orange juice-t.'

Harman picked up the score.

'Take your hands off it,' said Marby. 'That's a masterpiece, mister.'

They made off together towards the old village. Marby and Harman walked in front, saying nothing. Button was happy now. Harris wondered how these people could give him so much pleasure. This was the second time; Button's claim to musicianship for his band and now Marby's pleasantry.

Harris was suffused with delight. Marby did not look the sort of man who would congratulate out of politeness. Under his soft-handedness he was rough. Harris told himself that it was the praise of such men he wanted. The big noises, he was convinced, were corrupted by the struggle for personal advantage; place-seeking, jealousy and spite were all he expected there. Of course, Marby and company might be impressed by his superior paper qualifications, but they didn't entail the word 'masterpiece.' He watched the high bald head and the baggy mac proceeding ahead.

The doctor's house was enclosed by a fruit-wall. His surgery was a glass and brick place, built outside in the next garden. They went through wrought-iron gates. Harman left the path to walk up the middle of the long lawn.

They went in through french-windows. The doctor's wife, Mrs. Sackville, welcomed them. She was thin, sallow-faced, fast of movement, loud-voiced and could easily be angry. She looked hard at Harris, but greeted the others vaguely and let them quickly in to the doctor, who was sitting reading a book.

The doctor was as quiet as his wife was harsh. He smiled, and his eyes formed massive, delicate crow's feet in the pale skin behind his glasses and he shook hands timidly with Harris. He asked what they would have.

'Some'at to keep the co'd out, doctor,' said Harman. 'Mester Harris is teetotal,' said Button.

'Would you have sherry then, Mr. Harris?' asked Dr. Sackville. 'If you please.'

'Dry or Sweet?'

'Sweet. I've a kid's taste,' said Harris. The doctor looked affronted, and his hands were pressed for a moment on his short, cow-lick hair. His hands were pale and freckled and shook when he brought the drink on a silver, thick tray.

They sat down. Harman took a heavy suck at a big whisky. 'Mester Marby's had a look at it, doctor,' said Button.

The doctor smiled, and fluttered his hands. He did not seem to want to commit himself.

'I'm only an interested amateur, Mr. Harris,' he said.

'Wish there was more like you,' said Button.

The doctor smiled again. Harris decided he liked him. There was silence. Marby was frowning as if he wanted to get on with the important business; Button was pleased but keeping himself in check. Harman was sprawled back in a chair, a disgrace, chanting very quietly at the ceiling.

'At the cross, at the cross

Where the Kaiser lost his 'oss

An' the eagle of his 'elmet rolled away.'

The doctor watched them all, like an old hen marshalling her chicks.

'I think we should hear it now, doctor,' said Marby. 'If Mr. Harris is ready.'

The doctor stood up, opened the piano lid and arranged the stand. A Bechstein grand. Harris finished his sherry and stood fiddling with the glass. Sackville smilingly removed it from his hand.

'Do you want me to say anything about it?' Harris asked.

'Well, if you think...' began the doctor.

'No,' said Marby. 'Play it through first and talk about it afterwards.'

'Yes,' said the doctor. 'That would be wise.'

'Would you turn over, Mr. Marby?' asked Harris.

Marby put his beer down importantly.

'It's in D minor,' said Harris. He didn't know why he told them. Marby already knew; the rest would make nothing of the information.

'Splendid,' said the doctor.

Marby now had the score open at the first page.

Harris wiped his fingers on his handkerchief, felt for the pedals, shifted his stool and began.

The chords, jagged and marching, massed into the room. Here Harris the man of power was showing his brilliant hand for a start. This was music of brass, extrovert, overpowering. After this he had shoved his music into counterpoint, exciting, fighting work, never still, on edge, flashing from one end of the band to the other. The rhythm rocked and junketed, smashed its way into remote keys so that when he restated, in short form, his opening bars it was by way of a palpitating, searing rest before he began, tentatively the broad theme, the Elgar lollipop. But that theme was only half stated, thinly scored, given to a mere ghost of a clarinet with a chasing oboe and bassoon making a husky lopsided trio. At the second appearance it was thickened, given some flesh on the bones but the running counterpoint, mocking at certainty, was prominent yet. Just as the climax was building itself, he'd let it drop again into the slithering keys of the second section, the bravura of everything doing and nothing settled, with a touch of his big tune nodding in B-flat, half starved and finally pushed out in a series of mad arpeggios to fetch the lot back to D major and the Elgarian tune scored for the boys, steady, ponderously marching, grandiloquent, magnificent.

Harris sat with his hands on his knees as he finished. There was silence. Nobody moved. There was the sound of breathing.

Button stood up, put his arm round Harris's shoulders and pressed his face to the musician's, like a continental footballer when a goal's scored. Harris smelt the beer. Harman's eyes were wide open. Marby was stroking the closed score. The doctor sat with his arms between his knees like a man being sick.

Suddenly Harman was singing the big tune and nodding his head to it for joy. Harris knew he'd been a singer, because he carried one note musically through to the next. Mrs. Sackville came in. Button moved back embarrassed.

'Magnificent,' she said. 'Simply magnificent.'

The doctor writhed with pleasure.

'All right, Marby?' said Harris.

'Too good for us,' said Marby. There were tears in his eyes.

Button was like a thirsty dog at a bowl. Harris himself felt like crying.

'This calls for another drink,' said the doctor. 'Splendid, Mr. Harris. My word.'

Harman struggled to his feet.

'Mester Harris,' he said, 'I'll shake you by the 'and if it's the last thing I do.' He did so. 'Receive an old man's congratulations. Mrs. Sackville, you've had your ear'oles opened tonight. There hasn't been...' He staggered back. He sang the tune.

'Yes,' said Mrs. Sackville, moving away from the contamination of Harman's flailing nails.

'More sherry, Mr. Harris,' said the doctor.

'No, thank you.'

'Give 'im an orange juice,' said Button. He and Marby laughed, wrapping arms round each other like comedians trying to climb on to the other's shoulder to escape the snakes hissing from the basket they had dropped.

'Really?' said the doctor. 'Would you really like orange juice, Mr. Harris?'

Everybody was looking at him.

'Yes, please,' said Harris, to please Button, who laughed again and put a hand on the bare shoulder of the doctor's wife.

'Mester Marby in the pub said to Mester Harris,' said Button.

Mrs. Sackville hunched her shoulder and stepped away. Button went on with his story.

Now talk broke out all around. Harris sat by an open window looking out on to the shapes of summer flowers and the lawns slightly brown under the reddening sun. This was success for him. These people had expected something from him and he had done more. He took pleasure in the company, man by man. Harman was drunk, but he could remember the tune. Button was the little impressario, the man who'd made the miracle work. Marby, big and obese, had been knocked over. The quiet doctor, with his hands trembling, was glad he was here; Harris thought of him behaving so, smiling, humming, after some tricky childbirth, pleased among the blood. Only the woman, Mrs. Sackville, had no part because she was not committed.

She came across to Mr. Harris.

'I met a friend of yours,' she said. Her back was towards the rest. They were cut out.

'Who's that?' asked Harris.

'Colonel Leaman,' she said.

Colonel Leaman was the headmaster. Lt. Col R. F. de C. Leaman, M.C. He had a splendid war-record in North Africa and Italy. He was known in this part of the world, too, for his wife had been a Bankes, one of the former colliery-owning family.

'Oh, yes,' said Harris, smiling.

'He spoke highly of you,' she said. 'He wished there were more men of your sort in teaching. I told him you were going to write this music for us.'

'What did he say to that?' asked Harris.

'He said that whatever you did, you did well.'

The compliment gave Harris no pleasure. It was quite unlike the headmaster. In fact, he doubted whether he had said it. And if he had; it should have been said to Harris, not to somebody else, even though there was a chance of it getting back. In any case, it might have been Leaman speaking as headmaster; all my men are good; I don't have 'em otherwise. My staff work's efficient. He'd describe Winterburn as scholarly, and White as sincere.

To Harris the headmaster seemed half-dead. He couldn't convey pleasure as these four men here could. Even when he spoke his regard, it seemed wrung out of him. Perhaps that was the way of colonels and headmasters.

He looked again at his companions. They were singing Purcell's round, 'Under this stone lies Gabriel John, in the year of Our Lord one thousand and one.' They paid no attention to anything but the solemn sound of their voices. Mrs. Sackville was almost snarling. If you invited boozed-up colliers to your house, what could you expect? Her mouth was thin and her eyes mean and narrowed. Harris stood up. He resented her facial criticism of his friends, of these four good men.

Suddenly she saw him standing and her face cracked into a smile.

Mateyness came hard to her, but she moved her head as if she were taking part in the song. Gently Harris pushed past her. His fingers brushed the stiff corset under her summer dress. He wondered why some thin women needed that bracing.

He sat down at the piano and began to improvise over their singing, a fine, dotted, darting tune with trills. The singing swelled until the room was full. Marby fetched them off one by one and the doctor sang last, ''Tis all one' in a light baritone, trembling like his hands and Harris moved down the keyboard to end the sweetness in a Picardy third.

'Beautiful,' said Mrs. Sackville, 'magnificent.'

Harris loathed her. She, like Leaman, did not know pleasure. She held herself in as she held her little belly with a corset and all she could find was a word or two, a superlative perhaps, but as meaningless as a manly tear from a colonel's eye when he had a fly in it.

'Non, nobis, Domine,' sang the Doctor. He began to sing it. William Byrd. They did it in three parts, Marby conducting.

Just before ten, the doctor made a phone call for Harris's transport. The silent man turned up and had him back home in twenty minutes.

While the car was whistling along, Harris had time to savour his delight. He felt slightly drunk. But it was not with the one brown sherry. He had aimed at something and the result had exceeded expectation. This did not often happen, and when it did, you made the most of it. He felt like forgiving Mrs. Sackville, with her thin, lipsticked mouth. Perhaps her function was that of a catalyst. Her sourness sharpened the sweetness. Her stiff upper-lip, and Leaman's, made the world of living people spin. He didn't like the metaphor; he seemed to see Mrs. Sackville with her mouth down at a school globe turning it, with stingy spots of lipstick round the Tropic of Cancer. But it was a good, drunken comparison.

The young man dismissed him as usual. No movement. 'Well, goodnight, mate,' and the jerk of the clutch jumping in. Bash on.

Sanderson was waiting. He wore a ragged cardigan over his rolled shirt-sleeves, and he seemed to have interrupted himself polishing cutlery.

'Evenin', Mister Harris. Lovely, now, isn't it? Cool, though.'

Harris was affable.

'A man came to see you,' said Sanderson. He liked matters spun out.

'Uh?'

'Surly fellow, dressed ridiculous. Patched corduroys.'

Sanderson retreated from the hall and into his own room. He sat down, dipped a rag into a heap of brown powder and set about an aged knife.

'Name of Winterburn,' he said huffily.

Harris said nothing.

'Wants you to go round tomorrow; if you can. Early as you can.'

'Thanks.'

'Seemed to think it was my fault you weren't in,' said Sanderson.

'Did he say why?' Harris's elation forced him into generosity. He'd prolong the conversation.

'No, he didn't. "Tell Harris to come round," he said, "Mister Harris," I said, and I told him no harm come of politeness.' Harris could not believe this. Energy generated by the polishing had thrown up the arrière-pensée.

'And he said?'

'What could he say? If looks could have killed, the house would be full of detective-inspectors now, but they can't. I never liked educated men wearin' working-men's cloth caps. Golfing affairs, all right. Bit of a lark, you know. Wouldn't be seen dead in the things myself, but fair's fair. But when a man of education goes an' buys four and a tanner's worth of greyhound and whippet, there's some'at twisted in him.'

'Well, now,' said Harris.

'I hope he's not a friend of yours,' said Sanderson.

'He is.'

'Then I'll take back what I've said. My tongue'll be my downfall. But honesty compels me to admit I didn't like his manner.' Harris wondered what paper-backed drama he'd lifted that from.

'And now you're counting the spoons?' said Harris, pointing at the cutlery-box.

'It's a good job I know you, Mr. Harris. There's some would take offence at ...'

'Is my rent regular and on time?'

'Yes,' said Sanderson.

'Do I give you any trouble?'

'No.'

'Very good,' said Harris.

He marched upstairs, not even bothering to look at Sanderson's frightened face. Colonel number two.

## 6.

NEXT morning Harris got out his bicycle and pumped the tyres up

He noticed Sanderson watching him through the back-window. He straightened up and beckoned his landlord out into the yard. Sanderson came as far as the door, where he propped himself in an insolent attitude.

'Mr. Sanderson,' said Harris, rather breathless from pumping, 'I was a bit brusque with you last night. I'm sorry.'

'Pardon?' said Sanderson.

'I'm apologising. I was a bit short.'

Sanderson took his hand off the door post. He was now waiting for the catch in it.

'That's all right,' he said. 'I didn't think anything of it.'

'Then there's no need for me to apologise,' said Harris, equally grudging. 'But I have done and there it is. Take it or leave it.'

'Don't spoil it, Mr. Harris,' said Sanderson.

It was Harris's turn for unbelief.

'O.K., chief,' he said and saluted. They both laughed. The old-fashioned phrase worked the trick.

The post came while he was at breakfast, with another letter of congratulation. It was from Kingsley Forde, the singer. He had been a pupil of Harris's between periods of study at the Royal College and in Germany. Now he had made his name, had just returned from an American tour and had given a recital at the Edinburgh Festival.

There it appeared he had sung three songs by his teacher. Harris remembered sending the songs to Forde, after the singer had returned from Germany, where he had done himself well in opera. Forde had acknowledged them; in his big way said he had liked them and that he'd hang on to them and use them. Harris had then heard no more. Forde was already a great man in his own eyes, and Harris's outpourings would doubtless be regarded as a fitting tribute to a growing, international reputation and shoved into a cabinet to fade.

Harris, it seemed, had misjudged Forde, whose big head he had never liked. He had tried the songs in America, and then sung them at the Freemasons'. He enclosed a programme which included a four line biography of Harris, mainly about Forde, and a cutting from the *'Scotsman.'* This read,

'Mr. Forde ended his second group with settings of poems by Landor, Stephen Phillips and Shakespeare done by Thomas Harris, a modern English composer, under whom Mr. Forde once studied. The songs revealed not only a sensitivity to words and mood but had an eloquently shining piano part to which Mr. Gerald Moore did, and enjoyed doing, his usual ample justice.' Forde apologised that he'd not had time to get in touch with Harris before about the songs and enclosed the address of an American publisher who 'could use them'.

Harris could not make up his mind whether he was mad or glad; finally he decided for pleasure.

He got on his bicycle and clattered contentedly out of Beechnall to where Winterburn lived. There was sunlight, and heavy trees and hedgerows for the last three miles with children squeaking about the gardens.

As Harris pushed Winterburn's sagging gate open, he could see his colleague already at work. He was hoeing a border. As last night, he still wore corduroys but he had on a pair of large, polished brogues. He did not seem at ease, but pushed his hoe in a stabbing way as if the weeds had a personal feud with him.

'Hello,' said Harris.

Winterburn looked up, slowly.

'You're here early,' he said.

'That's what you told me,' said Harris, cheerfully. 'How are you?'

'All right. What are you so pleased about?'

Harris told him about the Edinburgh songs.

'Quite the boy genius, aren't we?' said Winterburn.

'Don't take it to heart,' said Harris. 'They haven't offered me a knighthood yet.'

Winterburn leaned on his hoe, saying nothing.

'Wife and youngsters well?' asked Harris. 'You want to get your boys out here weeding by the look of things.'

'You can take your coat off,' said Winterburn, 'if that's how you feel about it.'

'I don't fight anybody before closing time,' said Harris.

'To pull a few nettles.' Winterburn did not smile, but threw his hoe on to the lawn, where it prised a divot out. 'Come on. Let's go inside.'

It was darkish indoors, and on the table were the uncleared breakfast pots. These Winterburn pushed aside, and took out a bottle of beer.

'I don't suppose you'd have one, will you?' he said. He did not wait for an answer, but went to the kitchen, whence he returned with two glasses, one full.

'Ribena,' he said, putting it in front of Harris. He poured a beer.

'Thanks,' said Harris. 'And while you're at it,' he tapped the loaf on the table, 'I should put this bread in the bin. On a warm day like this, you'll have toast. You might like it, but your missus'll be on to you when she gets back.'

Surprisingly Winterburn did as he was told. Then he poured his beer.

'That's what I want to talk about,' he said sourly.

'What, bread, the care and preservation of?' asked Harris.

'Cut the cross-talk,' said Winterburn. 'My wife.'

Harris said nothing.

'She's left me,' said Winterburn.

'And the children?'

'Taken them with her to her parents.'

'I'm sorry,' said Harris.

Winterburn lifted his ale.

'Cheers,' he said.

'Good health.'

They drank in silence.

'I'm sorry, Winterburn,' said Harris. 'Is there anything I can do?'

'What could you do?'

'I could put you up for a few days.'

'No thanks. The holiday's the only time I can do anything to the house. It'll fall down if I don't get about it soon.'

Winterburn sounded no different from his usual self. There was no hint of anger or tragedy, only his rather childish surliness. He might have been complaining that one of his free periods had gone, because a housemaster had been released to earn his responsibility allowance. Harris compared him with Brand, another case. Brand had seemed genuinely moved at his wife's distress, though in a covert way. Winterburn saw it as a further petty disturbance.

'Do you want to tell me about it?' said Harris, uncomfortably.

'Why the hell should I?'

'I thought you wanted me to come over. I don't know. I thought you might want to spill your troubles to me.'

'You think a lot too much, Harris,' said Winterburn. 'I wanted a bit of company.'

'O.K., chief,' said Harris. The phrase had a charm on it.

'What do you think this is?' said Winterburn. 'A 1926 cowboy film?'

'In 1926,' said Harris, 'I was ten years old. I might well...'

'You might well shut up,' said Winterburn. 'At least I've had a bit of quiet since the silly bitch went.'

'You do enjoy yourself,' said Harris.

Winterburn stood up.

'Get out of my bloody house,' he shouted.

'Ah, get stuffed,' said Harris.

'Harris,' said Winterburn, 'I mean it. Get out of my house before I throw you out.'

Harris looked down into the dregs of his Ribena. With a thumb and forefinger he rattled his dental plate. He took out his pipe and pouch and began to rub up his tobacco. When he had finished he pushed the pouch across the table.

'Have a fill,' he said.

'Harris,' Winterburn shouted, 'I've given you an order.'

'I know,' said Harris. 'Have some bacca.'

Winterburn took no notice. He had picked up the bread-saw from the sideboard. His hand was tight round the vivid, blue handle. Harris looked at the jagged edge. He did not feel afraid, and in fact was the bolder for the fact that Winterburn had needed this useless weapon. He remembered seeing a barrack-room fight in which two drunks had been slogging at each other with bottles. The swearing, breathing and whacking had been horrible, but they were not inclined to do much damage. Winterburn's knife was a stage-prop, not a weapon of offence.

Harris said nothing.

'Are you moving,' said Winterburn, advancing, 'bastard?'

'I am not.'

'You'd better.'

Harris was certain what he would do now. If Winterburn hacked at him over the table with the knife, he'd jump back, pick up the light, wicker-bottomed chair and hammer him. The ensuing row, as well as the blow, when the chair rammed down in the table would cool Winterburn's courage. He sat still, ready.

Winterburn changed direction. He was coming round the table, knife up, left hand supporting him on the table-edge. Now he was no more than two yards away and it was too late for the fancy-work with the chair. Harris sucked at his pipe; it had gone out. His matches were still on the table. He was frightened now. He was certain that though Winterburn was bigger, he could get away, but there was the first blow against which he had no defence. He wasn't sure that the bread-saw was so useless. It could carve a nasty scratch and if it got the eye or ear...

He made himself reach for the match-box. His body was clenched together like a fist against the blow. He tried to squint out of the corner of his eye without moving his head. A match was out now in his fingers. He ignited it.

The jump of flame startled him, ran through him, left him stiffer. He forced it nearer his pipe and laid it over the bowl. When he tried to suck, he found he'd lost the power. His lungs were engaged on some business of their own. Finally, he drew in air and the smoke made him cough violently, jerked his head forward. The match was out. His eyes were thick with water. He began the business again. Finger and thumb in the box. The laying on of the middle finger. The stroke down the sand-paper. The half-turn to let the flame grip. He sat watching the flame burn away. He shook the match out, examined its curved, knob-ended charcoal and snapped it off.

He stood up.

The upper part of his body, neck, shoulders, scalp, cheeks, ear were gripped with a pain like indigestion. There somewhere the knife would dig.

He turned. Winterburn no longer held the knife up. He held it delicately by the blade, parallel to the floor.

'Sit down, mate,' said Harris.

Winterburn went round the table, put the knife by his beer, and picked up the glass.

'I frightened you,' he said, draining away.

Harris lit his pipe, and pushed the pouch across.

'Bacca,' he said.

'Thanks,' said Winterburn, picking it up. 'Were you frightened?'

'What are you talking about?' Harris said. The pain still screwed in his shoulder blades.

'You were frightened.'

'You're off your rocker,' said Harris. 'Now explain yourself.'

'She said she'd had enough. She left a letter. Snivelling silly thing it was. And do you know what the last thing she wrote down was?'

Harris murmured.

'Do you know what the stupid whore wrote?' Winterburn was shouting.

'No.'

'"Don't forget to pay the butcher. I forgot last week." That's what she put down. "Don't forget to pay the snot-nosed cat's meat vendor." That's all she could find to say.' Winterburn's face was red with anger. 'And she made a spelling mistake.'

'Here,' said Harris. 'Let's have a walk round the garden.'

'I didn't think she'd go,' said Winterburn. 'Sit down. I'm not getting excited. Do you know why she left me, Harris?'

'No.'

'Guess, then, instead of sitting there so pleased with yourself.'

'Fed up with your complaints,' said Harris, willingly.

'Because she said the boys were not being brought up in an atmosphere that was good for them. If I thought it proper for my children to be neurotic, she didn't.'

'She wrote that?' asked Harris.

'No. You don't think she just skipped, do you? With a long essay for me to mark? She threatened to go times without number.'

'How did you answer that?'

'I told her that I hadn't noticed that the children of successful fathers were any steadier than those of poor kickabouts like me. She didn't listen. There was nothing wrong with the lads. Her trouble was good old L.M.F., lack of moral fibre. When I was a bit down, she hadn't the guts to try to understand. She dragged the kids in. And that's what I don't forgive.'

'Perhaps she felt under the weather,' said Harris.

'Soft-soap Harris. Thomas Do-gooder. Bless your little cotton socks. What if she did? She hadn't Leaman hanging round her neck, had she? And now tell me he's a decent stick, would go out of his way to help you. Go on. I like it.'

'Did you try to understand her?'

'Yes,' said Winterburn, 'I did.'

Harris bit his underlip. Winterburn rummaged for a second bottle and knocked the cap off on the edge of the table.

'Look at that,' said Harris. 'You've marked the table.'

'You don't believe what I've told you,' said Winterburn. 'Every morning I got up at half-past six and cleaned every shoe in the house. I always washed the tea-things up. I did the ironing once.'

'You lovely man,' said Harris. 'Why somebody doesn't land you a good kick...?'

'Go on,' said Winterburn. 'I'm listening.'

'You're so sorry for yourself,' said Harris, lamely.

'It's my fault, is it?'

'Well, I don't know,' said Harris, 'all the ins and outs of it. But you're always belly-aching about something. Nothing's ever right for you. If somebody tries to help, you say he's interfering in your business. Good Lord, I'm as sorry for you as the next man, but you do nothing to help yourself.'

'Go on,' said Winterburn. He was swilling his beer round the glass.

'That's all,' said Harris.

'Do you mean you can't help me?' said Winterburn, heavily sarcastic.

'No.'

'We couldn't drop on our knees and pour our souls out?'

'It wouldn't do you any harm,' said Harris. 'You're too fat.'

'That's all you're fit for, low personalities. I'm too fat. All right. Give us your recipe. Harris's diet sheet to give the world hips like Sir Malcolm Sargent. I can't wait to hear it.'

'Listen, Winterburn,' said Harris. 'Do you want your wife back?'

'Eh?'

'You heard. And you know you're very sorry for yourself. But you do want her back, or don't you?'

'Yes, I do.'

'Why?' Harris spoke sharply.

Winterburn leaned back in his chair.

'I suppose,' he said, 'you're expecting some guff about love now, aren't you?'

'It wouldn't come amiss,' said Harris.

Winterburn didn't answer that one. Harris thought about Mrs. Winterburn. She was another little person, with big cheek-bones and a scrape of blond hair. He always called her, 'the secondary modern type.' Not that he knew much about her. She'd always been as pleasant as time had allowed.

'You talk like a bachelor,' said Winterburn.

'I'm quite willing to go into my deficiencies,' said Harris. 'But, if you don't mind, we'll sort yours out first. Do you want her back because you don't want people saying that she's left you. Is that it? Or is it because you need her? And what about the kids? And, anyway, what have you done, except swear and kick the furniture?'

'I don't know,' said Winterburn. He seemed helpless. 'How can you sort your motives out?'

'That's it, then,' said Harris. 'You want her because you don't want people talking behind your back. And, now, the kids?'

'What about them?'

'Do you want your children? I don't know what a father ought to be. My dad slapped me about, but it meant nothing. It was just his protest because I was moving up a social class and he knew it. But I'll give the old man credit; he wouldn't have a word against me from anybody else. Suppose your kids are dumb clucks and don't win scholarships and have to go to work in overalls and come back with their faces black, are you going to think as much of them?'

'Intelligence is inherited,' said Winterburn. He said it seriously.

'That's what I mean,' said Harris.

'Alan can read already,' said Winterburn, 'and he's barely four.' He rubbed his hands together, then knotted his fingers. 'And Jack's bright.'

'Well?' said Harris.

Winterburn put his hands flat on the table.

'I'm going to be honest with you, Harris,' he said. 'I don't know why. It won't do either of us any good. You're a musician, now, aren't you? You'd make some claim to be a creative artist. You ought to be able to follow what I'm saying.' He blinked his eyes. 'Not that you will follow. I'm very doubtful about your qualifications, really. You can probably knock a decent fugue together, or string quartet or something; I don't pretend to judge. I'm no musician. But when it comes to sensibility, Harris, you're just not there. Don't interrupt. I've often heard you talk about Mozart and decry those people who think he'd a God-given gift of melody and who think he'd have had it whether he lived in Eighteenth Century Vienna or on an iceberg at the North Pole. Now that's correct. Mozart was a great musician because he not only was talented, and well trained and so on, but because he understood life. He knew what people thought and, better, he knew what people felt. That's so, isn't it?'

'Oh, yes,' said Harris.

'Good. I'm pleased you agree.' Winterburn was in his element, the good sixth-form teacher. 'I wanted you to agree, because I'm not sure the theory's right. I'm not sure since I know so little of music. It's certainly true of poets. If they don't feel utterly what it's like to be other people, then for all their skill with words, they'll only be second-raters.'

'I don't want to interrupt,' said Harris, 'but...'

'Don't then. You haven't got that, Harris. You'll never be any more than second-rate at your very best, and probably the ninth rate is the most you can hope for. You've many good qualities. I'm not denying that. You're compact; you're forceful; you've a short temper which you use; you can stand up for yourself; you're generous and likeable. But you are condemned out of your own mouth. You lack the one quality...'

'Wait a minute,' said Harris. 'Have you ever heard me claim to be in the top class with Bach, Mozart, perhaps Beethoven? And who are your ninth raters? Spohr, Delibes, Max Bruch, Max Reger? I'd be jolly pleased to get as high as that, mister, I'll tell you.'

'Your humility does you credit,' said Winterburn. 'Or would if you meant it, which you don't.'

'I suppose,' said Harris, 'your alpha plus insight into other people tells you that.'

'Exactly,' said Winterburn. 'Exactly.'

'Go and chase yourself,' said Harris.

'Harris, I told you I was going to be honest, and no amount of third form slang will alter the truth of what I've said. Let's admit that I lack the talent for words and notes...'

'Otherwise you'd be Shakespeare?'

'You show yourself up,' said Winterburn, 'every time you speak. I am now speaking honestly. I am probably a fool to do so, but I am speaking with my whole mind. You, you measly man, are shocked and embarrassed. You cannot bear to hear the truth. It's not nice. Well, your comfort's to hand. You can tell your silly little soul that this business of my wife has turned my brain. And that's what you're thinking, isn't it?'

'As a matter of fact, no,' said Harris. 'I was just thinking that when you're doing this whole man act of yours, you don't sound half so constipated as you usually do and you don't swear nearly as much.'

'As if that mattered,' said Winterburn. 'A few swear words are all you're fit for. You, you're so magnificent a composer that you have to stick your head half-way down the lavatory-pan to hear the cistern-flushing, and that's the only music you understand.'

'Not quite first-rate, Winterburn,' said Harris, 'but better than the other muck. We've got to clear the sewage, you know.'

'But I'll go on,' said Winterburn, 'whether you follow or not.'

'Why bother?'

'It might do something to you. You might write a few bars that are worth listening to.'

'Well, before you do,' said Harris, 'fetch me another glass of Ribena, will you? This's thirsty work.'

Winterburn went out grudgingly.

'I've told you this with a purpose,' said Winterburn from the door. He put the glass down on the table, absent-mindedly, slopping it over the top. 'You're trying to make out that I squeal before I'm hurt. Limits of pain are different for every man or woman. Look at my wife. I understand her all right. She's not a sensitive person. She lives a minute at a time. She's never worried about what's coming next, or involved her conscience about what's good. She's more like an animal. Or a plant; alive but only just.'

'No wonder she's left you,' said Harris. 'I bet you went out of your way to make that clear to her.'

'No,' said Winterburn, 'I did not. But I couldn't help observing her. She fussed at this, at that, one thing at once. Nothing overwhelmed her. What would have half-killed me never touched her.'

'Did you know she was going to leave you?'

'No. She threatened often enough. I didn't believe it.'

'Then,' said Harris, 'what about your claim to understanding her?'

'I didn't claim omniscience. It was a misjudgement. I admit it. Carelessness on my part.'

They looked at each other.

'And what are you going to do about it?' said Harris finally.
'What's that to you?'
'I'd like to know how the master-mind plans...'
'That'll do, Harris. I can only stand so much.'
'Tripe,' said Harris. 'I could kick you through that wall with my boots off.'
'You should have seen yourself cowering over that table,' said Winterburn. 'I pitied you. I thought for a moment I'd put my knife right into your eardrum and twist it.'
'Thanks,' said Harris.
'But I couldn't. All bent up with fright. Over the table. I couldn't.'
'I feel sorry for you, Winterburn.'
'Don't talk your way out of it. You were livid with fright. You know you were.'
Harris stood up.
'Pick that bread-knife up again,' he said. He manhandled his chair and stalked round the table. 'We'll see who's frightened.'
Winterburn did not move. He folded his arms and leaned right back in his chair.
'This time, Harris,' he said, 'I am sitting down. I am waiting for you, not cringing over the table. You're angry because I've proved you the pissing little miserable coward you are. But go on. Do as you like. I'll sit here.'
'Pick that knife up,' said Harris. He raised the chair above his head.
'No,' said Winterburn.
Harris let fly with the chair. A leg hit Winterburn over the head and the smile, alleged arrogant, on his face was wiped off and replaced by a gasp of amazement. His underlip trembled. His eyes seemed to fasten high on a corner of the room. Very slowly he laid his arms on the table, rested his head on them and began to sob.
Harris still held the chair in his hand.
The problem was what to do. He imagined what would happen if he did right and put an arm round Winterburn's shoulder. Winterburn would lash out like a child in a tantrum and that would be that. He took a step forward. Very quietly he put the chair down.
There was nothing he was capable of doing. He went into the garden where the sun was bright; there were leaves dancing. He kicked a stone in the path. Over the hedge he could hear people laughing in the road. It was a holiday, summer morning, but indoors was Winterburn, a kind of broken heart. Harris was ashamed. Again he had found himself unfit to do some necessary thing.
On the lawn there was Winterburn's hoe lying. It seemed invested with

Winterburn's tragedy. Harris told himself to stop making a song about it. Winterburn had lost control over himself for a minute; soon it would be over, and in a week or two forgotten. An image of a great barracks or drill hall, the tang of disinfectant wafted out into the street, settled into his mind. He had soldiered there. Now it was finished, and as a civilian he could spit on the wall, unmoved. Spit? That was no indication of a satisfactory apathy.

Harris did what he was capable of. He sat on a bench and felt for his smoking tackle.

It took nearly five minutes to fill and light the pipe. His nerves and muscles were paralysed by his sympathy for Winterburn, by shame for his action, by the world for surprising him. People ought to be always what they are in public, when they are pleased. Not when they are knocked down or arrested. Harris remembered two policemen marching a little, blubbery man fast through Beechnall Market Street, and the man was crying out loud while a trickle of blood bubbled at his nostril. That was not human behaviour. Humanity resided in the girls with fresh dresses, and the women putting baskets into cars and men eyeing themselves in plate-glass windows. But the policemen didn't mind. They were talking cheerfully to each other as they rushed the prisoner along. Perhaps the full story made a difference. It might be that the prisoner had cut a child's throat or kicked a puppy to death.

Harris now saw himself as Winterburn's only friend, the one he had run to. And this friend had worked through a routine of kid's stuff with a chair-leg and Winterburn's heart had been broken. Harris had no difficulty in persuading himself not to be a fool. Sentimentalising the business got nobody anywhere. He did not see himself acting in any other way. Winterburn had asked for and got it. You couldn't blame yourself for being not a saint. It might be the very thing that set Winterburn on his feet. Shock therapy. The phrase was comfortable. You could mouth it, and think of nothing.

Harris's brain raced through this rigmarole, but his body denied it. He felt as if he had been beaten up, and every part of him was registering a shocked and painless complaint. A boy rode past on a bicycle, waving a fishing-net. A bread-van, bright-red, purred along to a nearby house. The sky was full of birds.

He knocked his pipe out on his heel and went back to the house.

His bike stood outside where he'd propped it. He forced himself to go in. He knew that nothing was so bad, when action had started. Once he'd picked up a dog that had been run over. His whole body had revolted but once he had done it, all was well; people did as he said; yes, sir, no, sir, to the man on the job.

But then he had been lucky. He'd never undertaken an action that had panned out wrongly. Suppose he embarked on something and found that instead of his mastery being nicely established circumstances beginning to cosh him about. That's what tragedy was. And it had to start sometime.

He went in.

Winterburn was sitting in his chair, legs crossed before him. He was dry-eyed and his lips were pursed as if he was thinking over some tricky problem. His head was nodding as though mentally ticking off certain factors or imponderables which he had, at least, taken into account. He looked up at Harris and with his left hand signed to him to sit down. A little, enjoyable frown puckered itself between the eyes. Man at work; do not disturb. Winterburn rubbed a hand thoughtfully across his chin.

'I'm sorry,' said Harris. 'I was frightened.'

Winterburn smiled.

'Handsome,' he said. 'Really handsome apology for you, Harris.'

He was quite at his ease, released, jovial.

'That leaves us to discuss what I'm to do,' he said cheerfully. 'Indirect question. What d'you suggest?'

'Go and fetch her back by the hair of her head,' said Harris, relieved, catching the mood.

'I think I will go over,' said Winterburn. 'I'll write first and say I'm a fool. Then I'll go over. Her parents, of course, don't like me, and the saga of my cruelties may have become a set-piece. I hope not. She doesn't bear malice usually, even though her mother's no such scruples. But I'll manage the lot of 'em.' He nodded satisfied. 'How about stopping and pigging it here with me for lunch today?'

'No thanks,' said Harris. 'Work this afternoon.'

'What at?'

*'Tempest.'*

'Good stuff?' asked Winterburn. 'Are you moved by it yourself?'

'Too busy,' said Harris.

'I wish I was you.'

Harris stood up. They shook hands at the door. When Harris rode away he congratulated himself on his luck, but in his shoulder was the faint ache for the knife and in his legs the vestiges of the garden torpor.

# 7.

HARRIS was furiously at work for the next few weeks.

His *Tempest* overture, stormy row, was written and the songs, but the bits and pieces of Act I were a trouble. Beauchamp wanted Prospero's long speech to Miranda underlining. Harris argued about this, said he thought Shakespeare's text adequate, but Beauchamp wasn't having any. It was clear now to Harris that, in spite of his disclaimers, Beauchamp wasn't leaving Shakespeare to carry the day. If the producer had had the space, he would have organised a football match to keep his clients amused, while Prospero puffed on. Failing that, Harris was to make significant noises. Significant was Beauchamp's key-word; it meant 'that which I add'. He had flung his arms back like a delta winged jet as he explained how the music, in this noise-filled isle, would 'revivify audience reaction'.

'You think,' he shouted, 'I'm man-handling Shakespeare. You are wrong. I am giving him a chance. That theatre will be filled for six nights with people who don't want to be there, who only want to see Mrs. This-and-that dressed up to the nines and in a less expensive seat than they've got. What's a play to them? I'll play 'em. I'll play with them. This will be a significant experience for them. They'll go home thinking.'

'Thinking how good Beauchamp is,' said Harris.

'It's a start.' Beauchamp ran a finger round the top of his turtle-necked sweater.

Harris, therefore, was undecided whether to fall in or to write to annoy Beauchamp. But once he began, he forgot both.

He had also in his mind a project of his own. His new choir had not yet started practising officially, but little groups of them had begun to study together. This suggested that he might write a choral work, which he could prepare for himself. The idea troubled him; he made sketches; scribbled groups of notes, but it all lacked reality because he hadn't yet decided on a text to set. But he knew it had to be done. It was there inside him, and the sooner he let it out the better. He wished to God it hadn't erupted so quickly, before he was ready for it, but he never missed the opportunity to write an idea down in a large manuscript headed austerely 'Work for Choir and Orchestra'. He liked a long period of gestation, but knew he mustn't be idle. When he got to the text, if he ever did, what with Shakespeare and the Bach and school, he'd got, he told himself horticulturally, to have the manure well buried.

That was the best of creative work, before the hard grind set in. Then you had the pleasure of creating, or appearing to do so, without specific problems of making this or that fit into shape. It was better, even, than the sense of having done well, for by that time you had hacked the ore out and only boredom and ruin was left; you moved smartly, if you had any sense, to the next field. If people congratulated you, you were pleased, but it was the executant's gratification not the creator's.

In the middle of all this, Cooke sent out a royal command.

Harris was to report at eight o'clock at Cooke's house on Friday to talk about the Passacaglia. He translated 8 o'clock into twenty hundred hours because the summons reminded him of his army days. They told you to report at some hundred hours and you never knew whether it was for a rocket or congratulation. Commonsensical behaviour had the rawest strips torn off it; some daft antic was a marvel. He'd never learnt the drill. But there had been a tremor of excitement; no searching of the soul of course; you'd find nothing there.

He felt the tickle as he was announced by a maid.

Cooke was with his wife and Brand in the music room. Mrs. Cooke was beautiful. She was dark, tallish, with light-blue eyes. There is nothing else to be said except that she was beautiful. Beside her Cooke was so much fat flesh, and Brand a thin lath of polished bone. Her hands were white so that Harris glanced away to his own jacket, which was shown up for what it was, a cheap buy off the peg. His shoes had been cleaned, but were dusty. The neat tie, five shillings, was low in his collar. He felt about her as Winterburn did of headmasters, directors of education, inspectors. He wanted to shout out, 'I'm Thomas Harris I am. I'm somebody.'

'Give the gent a large fruit-juice,' said Brand, laughing. It was wrong that he should be himself in such company, but there was no doubt about it.

'All right, Harris?' said Cooke.

'Please.'

'Sit down next to me, Mr. Harris,' said Mrs. Cooke. Her voice was cultured, far-back, quite unlike her husband's which had the Midland pinch about it. Harris sat down, pulled up his wrinkled socks, and knocked the ice on the side of his glass. He looked up to see if Mrs. Cooke was watching him. She wasn't.

'Cheer up, Harris,' said Brand. 'Down the hatch.'

Cooke shifted himself into an armchair, crossing massive legs.

'I've looked over the Passacaglia,' he said, moving his glasses up and down from the bridge of his nose.

'Well?' said Harris.

'I like it,' said Cooke. 'I like it very much.'

'Thanks,' said Harris.

'And if Cooke likes it, it's good,' said Brand. "That's so, isn't it, Anne?'

Mrs. Cooke smiled.

'I've also got rid of it for you,' said Cooke. He paused.

'He doesn't mean he's lost it,' said Brand. 'For the Lord's sake, Cooke, put the poor bloke out of his misery.'

'I will do it in my own way,' said Cooke, but smilingly. 'Your work is to be performed on the B.B.C.'

Harris felt a stab of delight, and better, an immense desire to be modest. He was glad about his dusty boots and his tie.

'They've changed their minds?' he asked.

'They have had their minds changed for them,' said Cooke. He put his glass down and rubbed his small, excellent hands together. 'I don't want you to think, Harris, that I went storming into the Director of Music's office, and ordered him to perform the work at once. Not at all. That is the way Brand describes my transactions. If my approach were no better than that I'd be walking the Thames embankment with my trousers' behind hanging out.' Cooke was determined to make the moment last. And again there was the vulgar touch. Trousers' behinds were not mentionable within a thousand miles of Mrs. Cooke. 'I took your score along to Charles Mountain and asked him to look over it.'

Charles Mountain conducted the most distinguished British string-orchestra.

'And I said to him, "Look here, Charley boy,"' said Brand.

'I pointed out to him,' said Cooke easily, 'that I had reason to believe he'd think highly of the work. I also pointed out that the B.B.C. didn't want it. He liked that. He would be grateful to prove the B.B.C. wrong. He believes in private enterprise. He's an Odessa Jew. He didn't go to a public school; he hasn't got the up-top accent. People with grey hair and the right, glassy eyes frighten him.'

Cooke fingered his glass again.

'Mountain read it. And he wrote me at Nice.' Harris for the first time noticed Cooke's tan. 'He said he would go into rehearsal with it. There's a festival in Durham in November when it'll get its first performance, and in December they are to broadcast from the Festival Hall. Your Passacaglia will be played there.'

'Now, say "thank you" like a good boy,' said Brand.

'I don't know what to say,' said Harris.

'You've said what you've got to say in that music,' said Cooke portentously. 'That is sufficient. I take no credit on myself. These things are a matter of luck. Mountain wanted a modern work. Yours was the right sort of length. And I'm not saying, either, that I don't put a bit of business in Mountain's way. But he doesn't play every bit and bob that his pals lay in front of him. He's playing it, Harris, because it's good, and no amount of Brand's blarney will make it otherwise. You have put down something unique, and Mountain saw it. Otherwise he would have had no qualms about telling me to hang it in the lavatory.'

'Quite a speech,' said Brand.

'Mountain wants you to go and see him,' said Cooke. 'To talk about one or two little things.'

'How does it feel to be famous?' said Mrs. Cooke.

'No different,' said Harris, lying. He could look the world in the eye, now, but did his best to keep his glance modestly down.

'That's an important question that my wife asked,' said Cooke. 'Once you become known, you change. Not that you're famous yet, but you've a new position to live up to, and a swelled head will do you no good.'

'You sound like the parson at my wedding,' said Brand.

'I wonder, John, whether you can be serious for two minutes on end,' said Cooke.

'Apologies and contrition,' said Brand. 'If I can't be serious, I'll be quiet. Guard to the guard-room, dismiss.'

'And secondly,' said Cooke, 'you will have to consider whether or not your present way of life is the right one. I have nothing against schoolmasters. But their environment tells against high art. If they're good teachers, they waste too much energy. If they're bad, they grow a protective skin which prevents them reaching to life.'

'I'm only moderate,' said Harris. 'And anyway, I've got to live.'

'There you go, playing safe,' said Cooke. 'It doesn't do.'

'Set into him, Harris,' said Brand. 'Hammer the genius-in-the-garret muck. Tell him that the sublime Bach was a schoolmaster.'

'I'll have to think it all over,' said Harris. 'I'm not used to good luck.'

'Mr. Harris,' said Mrs. Cooke, 'would you lose your job for your music?'

'I shouldn't think so,' said Harris.

'That's good,' she said. 'John here is capable of losing his for a woman.'

'I think,' said Harris, 'that Brand is steadier than you think.'

'I'm not denying his steadiness,' she said, 'nor am I telling you he will run off with a woman; I am saying he is capable of it. That's different.'

'You're a naughty girl putting ideas into my head,' said Brand.

'These matters,' said Cooke, 'are to be thought over. Is there enough happening in Beechnall, for instance, to keep you supplied with material? Among your circle, I mean. You are limited there.'

'Why's Beechnall more circumscribed than London?' asked Harris.

'London's different from that which you know. You should get round a bit, see how people live, move amongst those with lively ideas, who'll do some of your thinking for you.'

'I thought I was there already,' said Harris.

Mrs. Cooke laughed.

'With how many people do you discuss music?' asked Cooke. 'On equal terms? How many contemporary works have you heard this year? How often do you study new scores?'

'There's something in that,' said Harris.

He remembered when he had been at the Academy. He was a good student since he did as his professors told him. It had been new and exciting and he took pleasure in following instructions successfully. Of course, he had listened to modern music, had dabbled in it himself, but it wasn't until he'd taken his first job at Hirsham, a public school, that he'd met Hargreaves, a colleague, a man of money, who'd rammed Bartok, Stravinsky and Schönberg down his throat, that contemporary men had meant anything to him. Hargreaves used to call him 'our academic friend.' He had a room full of records and scores and for two years he and Harris got down to it every night of the week. At first, he instructed Harris, but Harris was very shortly his master. Professional training told, and Harris's musical memory. Hargreaves had become angry before they had finished that Harris made so much better use of his music than he could himself. But Harris's eyes were open.

'Not,' said Harris to Cooke, 'that I waste my time.'

'Good,' said Cooke. 'If I can help, I will. Any new work you wish to study...'

'Mrs. Cooke,' said Harris, interrupting, 'I'd like to ask you a question. Why are people always going out of their way to help me?'

'You, Mr. Harris,' said Mrs. Cooke, 'are you fishing for compliments.'

'No, Anne,' said Brand. 'You misrepresent our Mr. Harris there.' He laughed. 'Good old Brand,' he said; 'always willing to return good for good.'

'You see, Mr. Harris,' said Mrs. Cooke, 'what my husband has told you is important. You're going to have a new status, an important one, we hope. And your time is going to be taken up by all sorts of people, begging and praying, and paying for you to do this and that. And it might very easily put you out of your stride. You'll perhaps be so intent on being somebody, that you'll have no time to write music. It has happened. I don't know you well enough to make prophecies.'

'My wife's talking sense,' said Cooke. 'Don't dissipate your real self, Harris.'

'Oh, come off it,' said Brand, 'and leave the man alone.'

'I think you're jealous of him, John,' said Mrs. Cooke.

'All right,' said Brand, 'I give up. But if he'd a ha'porth of commonsense he'd tell you what you could do with your advice.'

'But he isn't doing so,' said Mrs. Cooke, displeased.

'The poor chap's so pleased about his Passacaglia, that if he told him to go home and paint his toenails with raspberry vinegar, he'd sit there with that same soft expression on his face.'

Cooke coughed.

'Carry on, John,' he said. 'We like it.'

'You would,' said Brand. 'Godlike Cooke. Cooke the Creator. And behold it was very good. What you've done hasn't added or subtracted one iota of value from Harris or Harris's music and the sooner you realise that the better.'

'Except,' said Mrs. Cooke, 'that it will now get a hearing.'

'Yes,' said Brand, 'because music's in the hands of tinpot Buddhas like your husband.'

'Tinpot what?' said Cooke. 'Such language.' He laughed till he rolled in his chair.

Harris was astonished at Brand's outburst. Perhaps Mrs. Cooke's hint was right, that the man was jealous. He himself felt goodwill to all men.

Cooke controlled his shaking.

'I'm sorry, John,' he said, and began to laugh again. 'But you really are too much.'

'Go on, giggle away, you oversized parasite,' said Brand.

'And what do you make of that remark?' Mrs. Cooke asked Harris. She spoke quite clinically, perfectly composed and utterly beautiful.

'He reminds me of my father,' said Harris. 'He's always saying uncouth things about people. He exaggerates terribly, but...'

Go on, Mr. Harris,' she said.

'There's often an element of truth in what he says.'

Cooke's eyebrows lurched down. He was surprised.

'It's true,' said Mrs. Cooke, 'that my husband is rather large. That's true. But in what way is he a "parasite"?' Her voice was cool.

'I don't know,' said Harris. 'I expect Brand just meant that your husband annoyed him and so he called him a rude name.'

'Then you were speaking foolishly when you said there was some truth in it?'

'I didn't say that,' said Harris, bewildered.

'No, no. But you implied it.'

'You're trying to catch me out,' said Harris. 'I've reason to be grateful to your husband.'

'And yet you were abominably rude.'

She sat quite straight in her chair, her hands on the arms. 'This is the first time I have met you, Mr. Harris,' she said. 'Charles had spoken very highly of you and your talent. But, to be frank, I cannot say I like you.'

There was silence in the room.

'I'm very sorry,' said Harris.

'I don't take offence easily,' she said.

'No,' said Harris, humbly. He was too cowed to be angry.

'You went too far. After all, my husband is your host.'

'I have said I'm sorry.'

'You have said rather too much for my taste,' she said.

'I'd better go,' said Harris.

'There's no need,' she said. 'My husband won't hold it against you and he invited you here.'

'I've said I'm grateful to him.' Harris's voice was soft.

She looked away. Harris shuffled his feet. Nobody spoke. The three men were embarrassed. Mrs. Cooke gently stroked the arm of her chair.

'I should just like to say something in my own defence,' Harris said. He fingered his five-shilling tie.

'There's no need,' she said. 'The matter's closed.'

'I am going to say something,' said Harris.

She turned the light-blue eyes to look straight at him.

'I said my father was often right in what he said. I did not equate Brand with my father. I gave you a bit of personal chitchat, because I didn't really know what to say. You then go out of your way to make a quarrel of it. I don't know why. Perhaps you take pleasure in turning on people. Perhaps you think you've got a hold on me and so you can have a bit of sadistic fun kicking somebody who daren't kick back. I've every reason to be grateful to Mr. Cooke. And I've no wish to row with you. I've said I'm sorry. I realise that I might have implied an insult to your husband. I did not mean to.'

'I beg your pardon?' she said.

'I did not mean to.'

'Then why did you say it? Freudian error, I suppose?'

She laughed lightly. Harris leaned forward.

'You're a fool,' he said.

'Why, may I ask?' she said. She was not angry.

'You must have a rotten poor life if you have to wait for somebody coming in and then pick a quarrel to give you a shot in the arm.'

'Why should I single you out?' she said.

'How do I know?'

'But perhaps I really was angry with you, Mr. Harris. Perhaps it wasn't just trifling.'

'Then you're off your head.'

'That's not a nice thing to say, is it?'

'I know now,' said Brand, 'why Harris is a bachelor. I took him in to see my wife and he gave her the deuce of a ticking off. I think he does it with all women.'

'He's refreshing,' said Mrs. Cooke, 'but not serious.'

'Mrs. Cooke,' said Harris. 'You're a beautiful woman, but you can't expect your beauty to excuse every lapse your silly tongue gets you into.'

'That's enough, Harris,' said Cooke. 'You've had your niggle at her. Leave it.'

'You're not a queer?' said Mrs. Cooke.

'Anne,' said Cooke.

'Let her yap,' said Harris. 'The answer's no.'

'Why don't you get married?' she asked.

'Harris,' said Brand, 'she's only asking the question most women would want to ask and daren't.'

'It's not,' said Harris, 'that I'm put off by females like her.'

Cooke gave a tremendous cough, that rattled the glass doors of cabinets.

'This is quite as good as the pictures,' he said, 'but we'll call it a day before they start throwing the furniture about.'

'Why do you let him lace into your wife like that?' asked Brand.

'She can defend herself,' said Cooke. 'Besides, what else could I do? "Go and never darken my doors again" is not my style.'

'It would be a nasty smack in the eye for Harris, though,' said Brand, sly.

'Agreed,' said Cooke. 'Shall I tell him to go, Anne?'

'Don't you bother,' said Harris, standing up.

'Yes,' said Mrs. Cooke. 'Kick him out.'

'Sit down, Harris,' said Cooke, 'and let's have some sense.'

'I've never heard anything so stupid since I was in the infant school,' said Harris.

'There are more things in heaven and earth,' said Cooke, laughing. 'Besides, you've been annoying Beauchamp.'

'Is he a friend of your wife's?' asked Harris.

'Now, now,' she said. 'No malice. Reason.' She laughed out loud for the first time.

'You've told him,' said Cooke, 'that he can't produce Shakespeare. Now that's not the thing, is it? What would you say if he told you you couldn't write music?'

'I'm expecting to hear it from him any day now,' said Harris.

'The truth is that Beauchamp's good. He's an obnoxious, loud-mouthed, crawling, dirty little creature but he knows his stuff. You wait until you see what he makes of the play.'

'It's all right without him making anything.'

'I know how you feel,' said Cooke. 'I was the same once about the man. You see him as if he were producing the "Beethoven A minor, Op. 132," played by four nude women with blue bows in their hair. The crowds would come in ...'

'I'll say,' said Brand. 'Let me help 'em turn the music over.' '... but just imagine that they gave an utterly inspired performance.'

'Then they can put their frocks on again and play it,' said Harris.

'But suppose they can't. That's the point. They need to strip to play. What then?'

'Lock 'em up,' said Harris. 'Lock the dirty bitches up.'

'That's Beauchamp. For all his alterations and fooling about Shakespeare will stand out like a rocket. Don't you go interfering,' said Cooke.

'And if I do?' said Harris.

'You go. Out. Quick.'

There was a little pause. Cooke leaned forward.

'I'm not the man, Harris, to be fooled with. When I say something, I mean it.'

'Jupiter Cooke,' said Brand.

'I don't hold what you've said tonight against you. It shows you can be mean-mouthed and spiteful, but my wife asked for it. I don't bring you here as a paragon of virtue. But your job is to write music, as, when and how you like. But I don't allow ushers to get in my way. I pass several of them every morning in the toilet. I'm speaking straight out to you now, and you can say back to me anything you please, because I'm not a bit interested in your words. But, Mr. Harris, one action out of place, and down you go.'

'Righto,' said Harris. 'Your wife said we wanted reason, not malice. So I'll ask you in a quiet way what you mean by these "actions" that are going to get me into trouble.'

'And it might do you some good,' said Cooke, easily. 'I'm not your kindly headmaster clucking round his chickens.'

'Chuck it,' said Harris. 'You've got schoolmasters on the brain. I shall suspect that you're getting your own back for the nasty time you had. Were you bottom of the class?

'Good for you,' said Brand. 'Pitch in, Harris. Draw your chair up, Mrs. C. This is the goods.'

'I was a clever boy at school,' said Cooke.

'So were we all,' said Brand.

'Go on, Brand,' said Cooke. 'Give us a stretch of the matchless autobiography.'

'Not at all,' said Brand. 'You two bash on, regardless.'

'You annoy me sometimes, John,' said Cooke pacifically.

'I thought words were all right,' said Harris, 'and only actions got the high kick.'

'Ah,' said Cooke, 'the yelping Harris.'

'We're all waiting,' said Harris.

'Don't interfere with anything I do. That's all,' said Cooke.

'Simple. Easy. You can't go wrong. But if you do...' He waved an annihilating hand.

'Is annoying Beauchamp within the meaning of the act?' said Harris.

'If it holds up production, yes.'

'I like you, Cooke,' said Brand, 'in this Olympian mood. It seems to fill a long-felt want in this godless world.'

'You'd do well,' said Cooke, 'to look after your wife at home.' He did not sound annoyed, even interested. He spoke as if he were delivering some tennis-club committee ruling. 'You might find that while you've been skylarking round dragging the drawers off all and sundry, you've lost the little woman.'

'Something in that,' said Brand. 'Glands, I think.' He was equally cool.

'That'll do,' said Mrs. Cooke. 'You're baiting my husband. I won't have it.'

'Anne,' said Brand, 'you ought to be glad, and he ought to pay me. The trouble with the world today is that all the high-ups are surrounded by yes-men. There's nobody there to tell them not to be such b.f.s. Just note, Harris, the cunning way the blow is softened. None of your assault-and-battery here. Cooke is placed amongst the most high, and he's so pleased he doesn't give a tinker's whistle for what I say next, do you, Cookey?'

'I'm not listening,' said Cooke, laughing.

'I am. And I don't like it,' said Mrs. Cooke. 'When Charles says something, he means it.'

'I didn't mention the yes-women, but there you are,' said Brand.

'Mr. Harris said something very true just now,' she said. 'You can't expect your beauty to get you out of trouble every time. And one of these days, John, by God, you'll catch it.'

'You've impressed the lady, Harris,' said Brand.

'I mean it,' she said.

'You're beautiful too,' said Brand.

Cooke pressed more drinks on them, quietly. He lumbered round, apparently detached from what had been going on. Harris could suppose that he had been annoyed by the content of his answers, and not by their manner. The ragging of his wife did not touch him at all. Harris wondered what sort of life they led, how long they had been married, if they were happy.

Cooke affably gave an account of what Charles Mountain had said about the Passacaglia, and even told one or two good stories of the conductor's oddities. Soon after Brand got up to go. Cooke, apparently launched for conversation, made no attempt to stop him. Harris went with him.

On the way out, Cooke said, 'They tell me that's a splendid march of yours, Harris.'

'How do you know about that?'

'It's to be put on at Blidworth Festival Hall next month, isn't it? I own the place. Another of my little sidelines.'

He poked at Harris thoughtfully with his middle finger.

'You see what I mean, don't you? I don't want you blotting your copy-book, boy. You've got possibilities. I don't care what you say; it's what you do that matters.' His voice trailed away as if he'd lost interest, and then Brand and Harris were outside.

'Gor blimey, O'Reilly,' said Harris.

In reality, Harris was not displeased. He never liked things to go too swimmingly. Since he had been brought up as he was, he always feared the worst. Nothing was ever handed to you on a plate. Therefore if the evening had been one of unbroken congratulations and drinks all round, he would have been looking for the snag. Even now he wouldn't have been surprised if Mountain had sent a message saying that circumstances forced him to withdraw his offer. In Harris's sort of life there were always circumstances. The quarrel with Mrs. Cooke, if it could be called that, was therefore something of a good omen. This was all very superstitious, but that was common in Harris's environment; the black cat or the cracked mirror were important in a situation over which you had no control at all. In other circles, the pater pulled strings and you could smash every bit of reflecting glass in the house and it did not matter; papa knew how to work the oracle.

'A rum set-up,' said Harris, now walking.

'You think so,' said Brand. 'The rummest thing about it is, that what

Cooke says is true. He's a power in the land.'

'You seem to enjoy yourself there.'

'The licensed clown,' said Brand. 'Cookey knows he can't do me any harm. My money's safely in hosiery, not music, and so I can say as I like. And that's a change for Master Cooke. He rather goes for it.'

'And Mrs. Cooke?' said Harris.

'Ah there, you have me,' said Brand. 'What do you think of little Annie?'

'Very beautiful,' said Harris. 'It oughtn't to be allowed.'

'My, my,' said Brand. 'Bold words for a bachelor. But she's a cold 'un, sonny.'

'You've tried?' asked Harris.

'And succeeded,' said Brand. 'Not enjoyable.'

'Does Cooke know?'

'No,' said Brand. 'Shouldn't think so.'

'Would he mind?'

'There again,' said Brand. 'Cooke, the loving husband, is a bit beyond me.'

'He didn't seem to mind me getting after her overmuch.'

'No,' said Brand, 'any more than he'd mind a fly settling on her hand. One movement of her fingers and it's gone. It wouldn't be any use his breaking out into spots, would it?' He laughed in a tired way. 'Sorry, Harris, that sounds insulting. But I just want to make out to you what Cooke thinks of himself. He's the nearest thing to God you'll ever meet in this egalitarian time.'

'Do you know,' said Harris, 'I wondered whether you'd, er, well, cuckolded him.'

'You should put aside impure thoughts,' said Brand. 'Why?'

'The only time he seemed to be annoyed was when he turned on you and said if you weren't careful, you'd be losing your wife.'

'No, no, no,' said Brand. 'That was a subtle compliment to you, old chap. Nance was there the other night praising you up to the skies, and Cookey thought she might have a soft spot for you. Not that he's interested. Beetles don't bite gods. Look at the way he talked about naked women. He didn't care. He knows Beauchamp will draw 'em in with some choice wench for Ariel with nice legs and a little bit of delicate bottom showing, but he won't catch cold unbuttoning his flies. It's power he's after.'

'Power to do what?' asked Harris.

'To do as he likes.'

'But you tell me he doesn't like doing anything,' said Harris.

'Naughty mind,' said Brand. 'He doesn't want the things we'd have; he wants to push people around.'

'A dictator?'

'Of sorts,' said Brand. 'In his limited sphere. He doesn't want political advantage, if that's what you mean. Not our Cooke.' They walked the rest of the way to Brand's house in a fatigued silence. They stood there for a moment under a street lamp.

'You get your music out as fast as you can,' said Brand. 'Cooke'll do you proud. But once let the critics set about you, not that they will with his nibs to hand, you'll be dropped, brother, like a fag-end at the C.O.'s inspection. You take the limelight while it's going.'

A light flooded the hall of Brand's house and the door opened. Mrs. Brand came out. She had a huge white shawl about her shoulders.

'Hello, Mr. Harris,' she said. 'I'm glad you're here. I thought you might be. I've a question to ask you.'

'Come on inside, then,' said Brand. 'and answer it.'

'It's late,' said Harris.

'I'd be glad if you'd come in,' said Mrs. Brand. Her face was tilted upwards at Harris, and her eyes were excited in the lamplight. She was like a still from a film about the nineties; all ghosts and handsome, mad husbands with cruel walking sticks.

They went in.

She let them into the dining room.

'If you don't mind,' said Brand, 'I'll just stay for the question and not the answer. These shoes are killing me.'

'Right,' said Harris, embarrassed.

'Sit down, please,' said Mrs. Brand. Harris sat.

'I only wondered,' said Mrs. Brand, 'if you were one of those men who disliked women, Mr. Harris.'

Brand laughed out loud.

'Twice in one night,' he said. 'It's a great life. Excuse me while I go and pamper my poor old dogs.'

He went out, still laughing.

'Don't mind John,' she said, twitching the Cashmere shawl.

'Ought I to ask you that question? Is it too rude? But I'm very interested. I really am.'

'You've had too long on the psychiatrist's couch,' said Harris.

'I don't mind how much you shout at me, Mr. Harris, but I would like to know.'

Harris was reminded again of a bird. At a glance, all seemed streamlined, groomed for flight; the most casual second look revealed the tattered feather-ends, the frightened jerks, the stupid staring eye.

'Why do you want to know?' asked Harris. He was gentle.

'I wonder why you compose. John says you're very good. A lot of homosexuals do well as artists, don't they, because they don't fit into society? They have to make up for it. I'm not saying you're not normal; well, that's wrong, I suppose you aren't...'

'Just a minute,' said Harris. 'You're getting very excited. One thing at a time. First of all, I'm not homosexual. I've quite normal tastes. '

'I don't know whether I'm glad or not,' she said.

She looked at him.

'Are you quite insatiable with women?' she asked.

'By no means,' he said. 'A steady average. I've never got round to marrying, that's all. Too much of an inverted snob at one time, too busy at another; here today and gone tomorrow with the sailor's farewell. You know.' He was bluff.

'But if you were only ordinary in that way, you'd only be an ordinary musician.'

'That's all I am,' he said, smiling.

'John doesn't think so,' she said.

'That's kind of him,' Harris said. 'But I'm sure your theory's quite wrong. It's more complicated than you make out. To be a big composer is the result of billions of factors.'

She nodded as if quite satisfied, then stood up and came across.

'Stand up, Mr. Harris,' she said. He did so.

She pushed her body close to his, wriggling into place. She put her hands into his hair pulling his face down so it lay on hers. She was breathing heavily and her hands were running over, massaging his scalp.

'Do you like this, Mr. Harris?' she said, very softly.

'Splendid,' said Harris.

'You're making fun of me.' She nestled closer.

'Of course I am. Now, you go and sit down, Nance.'

'That's the first time you've called me that, darling,' she said.

She did not move.

'And the last,' said Harris, gruffly.

He took her by the shoulders and pushed her back into her chair. His movement was violent, but he felt, oddly enough, schoolmasterly. This was the time for pi-jaw[7] not copulation.

'You don't like me,' she said.

'I like you very much,' said Harris, reseating himself and hoisting his trouser-legs.

'I don't mean like that.'

'What about these children of yours?' asked Harris, cruelly. 'Yes,' she said, sadly, as if she'd just remembered.

'I'm a middle-aged schoolmaster,' said Harris. 'I'm also very busy. I don't intend to make you my mistress, whatever its therapeutic value.' He hadn't meant to be so blunt. 'Moreover, you don't love me.'

'No, I love John,' she said, 'and the children.' She might have been repeating words learnt under hypnosis.

'Good,' said Harris. 'So that's that.'

She was pulling a tiny handkerchief savagely about. 'Careful,' said Harris, 'or you'll tear it.'

She nodded and put the handkerchief on her lap.

'Anything else now,' said Harris, 'while we're at it?'

'Have you ever had a mistress?'

'Yes.'

'I wish it had been me,' she said.

'Well, it wasn't.'

'I'm sorry, Mr. Harris, that I've been so silly,' she said. 'You won't say anything to John, will you?'

'No.'

'You're very deep, aren't you? You're not normal. I know you're not.'

'You act,' said Harris, 'as if you're about sixteen.'

'That's the age I feel with you. Nothing's happened to me yet. I've no experience. That's what I'm like. Be sorry for me, Mr. Harris, please.'

'Are you sorry for yourself?' he asked.

'No,' she said. 'Excited.'

They said no more until they heard Brand coming downstairs. 'Don't say anything, will you?' she asked.

'Hello, hello,' said Brand, in carpet slippers. 'How did the quiz go, Harris?'

'Ask the question-master,' said Harris.

'He did very well,' she said. 'I'd like to cry on his shoulder, John, but he won't let me. I'll have to use yours.'

'Wait till I get the blotting-paper out,' said her husband. He smiled, and she took his hand, snuggling close leaning across to stroke his lapel. Harris felt slightly jealous. She was rubbing her hair along her husband's chin.

'Well,' said Harris, 'time I was off. Or you'll never get to bed.'

'Tut, tut,' said Brand.

When he went, they stood silhouetted together in the door, arms round the other's waist.

## 8.

WITH September Harris started back at school.

The choir was already in full rehearsal. Cooke was right; it was a magnificent instrument. Socially the set up was Fred Karno;[8] the ladies were posh, the gentlemen colliers. But if you asked a drifting pianissimo, a blinding fortissimo, or, hardest of all, a steady mezzo-forte they were marvellous. Harris went for them on notes, and was gratified to see the visiting chorus-masters underlining with a view to next week.

On the third rehearsal, they had another visitor. This was Professor Hedley Attenborough, Drake Professor of Music at the University. Harris guessed he was there as Cooke's spy and was prepared to fight, but the choir treated Attenborough to such distinguished singing that Harris couldn't help being pleased. He and Attenborough had a talk, and the professor invited Harris to his house. He was a pompous ass, and spoke with a silvery grandiloquence that matched his hair. But once under this, and it took some creeping under, Harris saw what a fine Bach scholar he was. He would make comment, rounded and distant, and Harris's hackles would rise and he'd want to reply with one of those short profanities that had made the speechifying of field-officers bearable. Then he'd notice that Attenborough was not only talking sense, but was thoroughly enlightening. Moreover, he was a brilliant harpsichordist. Harris asked him to play the continuo.

'Mr. Cooke thought it an excellent idea,' said Attenborough, 'but I made it clear to him that the suggestion could only come from you. You are holding the helm, my boy.'

He also suggested one of his lecturers, Dr. Morley, as organist, and detailed this young man to attend the rehearsals when he was not present.

That, then, was going well.

The chill in the morning and the smell of bonfire smoke stirred Harris. It reminded him of the time when he was a schoolboy; he'd been bored with the long holidays but he didn't exactly want to start back. It was the only vivid emotion remaining from his schooldays.

In the common room there was the usual bonhomie and talk of how she went over the Alps like a bird. Leaman did his stuff in his stuffy fashion.

Winterburn was back, brown, and in a new hacking-jacket and cavalry-twill trousers. He seemed pleased to see Harris.

'Thought I should be hearing from you,' said Harris.

'Too busy by half.'

'Things all right at home?'

'You mean "Has she come back?",' said Winterburn.

'Yes.'

'Well, why didn't you say so?'

An older member of the staff came up, just back from Venice, to shake hands with Harris. He only nodded to Winterburn and walked off.

'The answer is "She hasn't."'

'Did you go to see her?' said Harris.

'What's that to you?' asked Winterburn. He began to sort some books. 'Yes, I did. Couldn't get any sense out of her. The old bag had been on the warpath.'

'You're living on your own, then?' said Harris.

'I'm doing all right.'

Winterburn dropped his truculent air and said, 'there's nothing to be said really. I wrote and apologized and promised to improve. No answer. I wrote again. Nothing doing. Then I wrote to say I was coming, and when. Not a word. I went. They'd parked the boys out of the way. The old dear handed me a piece of her mind from the word go. I kept my temper, so that the old man was sorry for me, and backed me up when I said I'd like to speak to Mary on her own. We adjourned to the front-room and had an hour.' Winterburn laughed a little as though he were trying to give a comic tinge to the story. 'She didn't seem interested. She'd quite made up her mind that she wasn't coming back. She couldn't give any reasons, and didn't bother to try. Talk of divorce didn't draw her, nor when I said I'd want the boys back. She said that I couldn't look after them, and that her mother would make them all a good home. Pure obstinate stupidity. She couldn't say anything; she didn't feel anything; she looked like a middle-aged slut.'

'You told her so?' said Harris.

'I didn't. I kept my temper. I said that I'd been a poor husband, but that we ought to patch it up on the kids' account and that I'd try to do better.'

'What did she say to that?'

'She gave me that same top-heavy look, and said I was all right in the holidays, but most of the year I was at work and rotten. When I asked her to list her complaints, she couldn't. "You know how it is," she said. She was like a back-terrace woman listening to somebody trying to sell her brushes she didn't want. Pleased to have a minute's break from work, but uninterested, and without the gumption to say a plain "no". When I asked to see the youngsters she said they'd gone out to a party, and there she sat as if she'd got bellyache.'

'I'm sorry,' said Harris.

'I don't know why I'm telling you this,' said Winterburn. 'You've no need to bother your head about it. I'm all right.'

He walked away.

Lessons started; there was the smell of chalk-dust and the slight soreness of the throat. It did not take long to settle to routine.

A day or two later, Harris walked past the classroom where Winterburn was teaching. Through the glass top of the door he saw that at least four boys were standing, grinning. He moved out of sight. There was a lot of noise coming from the class, Modern Four.

'Davis, sit down, will you?' shouted Winterburn.

'But you just said, sir, I could fill my pen from Bertie's, er, Brett's bottle. I can't do that, sir, if I'm sitting down.'

'I'm telling you to get back and sit down,' Winterburn's voice was angry.

'Make your mind up,' said the boy. There was laughter. 'What did you say, Davis?'

'I told Smudger to pull the blind up.'

'You little liar.' There were shouts of 'Oo, sir' and 'Language'. Winterburn called for quiet and didn't get it. 'Any more of your insolence, Davis, and I'll knock your head off.' More shouts of 'Look who's talking', 'Where's your army?' 'Muscle-man.'

A boy stood up and walked out to the front.

'If you'll excuse me saying so, sir, you are not allowed to use corporal punishment.'

'Sit down, Blay,' said Winterburn.

'I was only telling you, sir, in case you had forgotten. The headmaster is allowed to administer such punishment, but even he has to record it in a special book.'

'You're a mine of information today,' said Winterburn. 'It's a pity, Blay, your attention is not directed to those matters you're supposed to learn.'

'I am sorry, sir. But as your language was so violent with poor Davis, I thought in the heat of the moment you might exceed your powers.'

'Your consideration astonishes me,' said Winterburn. 'I am touched.'

The room fairly rocked. Desk lids were banged. People dropped their heads on to their arms to laugh. One joker fell into the aisle, howling. Several put on acts as lunatics, a paper dart skimmed to the front and Davis shouted over the row,

'Even if he is touched, he's no call to say I'm a liar.'

Winterburn thumped the desk.

'Stop this din, you insolent little devils,' he shouted.

The row rattled like stage-thunder; the boys were drumming now on the desks.

Harris went in.

The noise subsided a little, but not much. The class knew that Harris was a strict disciplinarian and would have become perfectly quiet, had it been his lesson. But it was not, it was Winterburn's and Winterburn's alleged control allowed them to continue misbehaving. Blay was standing on his chair, giving an imitation of an ape scratching under its arms. At least half the class were out of their places and even those with books ready were grinning and talking.

Winterburn flushed angrily.

'If you'll excuse me, Mr. Winterburn,' said Harris, 'I'd like to ask a question.'

'Quiet,' shouted Winterburn. 'And listen to Mr. Harris.' There was a lull.

'Who was supposed to put the song-books away last period?'

No answer.

'Was it you, Blay?'

'I'm afraid it was, sir.' Blay had now stepped from his seat, dropped the simian antics, and was polite, in a supercilious adult way. He would never have dared to adopt that tone in a music lesson, but, again, he felt himself under Winterburn's protection.

'You left them lying about.'

'That is correct, sir.'

There was perfect quiet, but several of the class were smiling at the thought of Harris answered back.

'May I inquire why?' said Harris mildly.

'You may, sir. I'm afraid I forgot.'

Harris looked straight at the boy, who stared innocently back and brushed a leisurely hand over his brilliantined hair.

'Blay,' said Harris, 'just come here.'

There was a momentary hesitation, in complete silence, and then the boy walked out, smiling slightly as if in pleasurable anticipation. He stood in a gangway before Harris and then placed his feet apart and his hands behind his back in exact imitation of Harris's own position.

'Why did you not put them away?' asked Harris.

'I'm sorry to say, sir, that I completely forgot.' He tilted his face upwards.

Harris hit him. It was a fast smack with bony fingers across the face. It took the lad completely by surprise and knocked him off his balance. The blow stung and ached so that the boy knelt on the floor, holding on to a desk with his fingers. Harris heard the intake of breath from the rest.

'Go back to your place, Blay,' said Harris quietly.

The boy scrambled up and did so.

'When I tell you to do something, or any other member of this staff tells you, you do it,' said Harris. 'Is that understood?'

There was no answer.

'Is that understood, Blay?' He barely whispered.

'Yes, sir.'

The boy stood leaning on his desk, his eyes full of tears, his left cheek red. His teeth bit at his lips.

'That goes for the rest of you,' said Harris, sharply.

The others looked down at their books.

'I beg your pardon, Mr. Winterburn,' said Harris. 'I'm sorry that I have interrupted your lesson.'

Winterburn glared at him, and mumbled some acknowledgement.

Harris walked out and down the corridor. There was no noise from the classroom. At the end of the corridor, Harris stood by a window that overlooked the playing field. Glancing back, he saw Leaman, a sheet of paper in his hand, marching down. Leaman stood outside Winterburn's room for a minute, then looked in before continuing his walk. Harris went down the stairs.

He was annoyed with himself for the action he had taken, because he'd never had the need to do such a thing in his own lessons. It was Winterburn's fault. The thought of Blay, at his desk, the fight knocked out of him, half-crying and ashamed made Harris angry again.

But there was Winterburn. It was all very well considering these boys as innocent and mischievous but they had driven Winterburn's wife away and taken a father's authority from his children. Blay and company didn't mean any harm; they were like the lad who, bird's nesting, had put out half a county's electricity supply. He didn't mean anything wrong; but hospitals went lightless and the streets were dark. Again, it was Winterburn's fault. If he had any sense of proportion, he could have come to terms with his teaching.

Not that Harris had thought twice before hitting Blay. The lad had deliberately provoked him and had stopped a schoolmaster's smack, heavy, fast and leaving no permanent mark. That was that. Harris was mildly sorry; he hadn't his father's gift of forgetting the immediate past.

He taught his last two periods absent-mindedly.

Winterburn was putting books into his case when Harris came into the common room.

'Coming home?' Harris said.

Winterburn grunted.

'Get a move on then,' said Harris.

'I'll come when I like,' said Winterburn. He sounded huffy.

Harris waited. They put their coats on together.

It was rather late. There were only a few stragglers at the bus-stop. When they were five or six paces down the hill, Winterburn said,

'And I suppose you're bloody well pleased with yourself.'

Harris looked away at an out-or-season game of marbles in the gutter to avoid answering.

'What good did that exhibition do you?' said Winterburn.

'Relieved my feelings.'

'Well, I'll thank you to do it out of my room another time.'

'All right,' said Harris. 'It got quiet, anyway.'

'I'd sooner have it noisy than that,' said Winterburn.

'Leaman wouldn't. And he was snooping around soon after I came out.'

'And I suppose,' said Winterburn, 'you went and told him that, please, sir, you'd been quietening my class for me.'

Harris smiled, lips tight.

'Well, did you?'

'You're not serious, Winterburn, are you?'

'I am serious. I shouldn't be asking, should I, if I didn't want an answer?'

'No, I didn't,' said Harris. 'Look here, Winterburn old chap, you must take a grip on yourself.'

'That's it then, is it? You didn't beat that boy because he hadn't put your blasted books away, but because he was misbehaving in my lesson. That's so, isn't it?'

'A bit of both,' said Harris.

'Who made you my keeper?' said Winterburn.

'Nobody,' said Harris.

'What right have you to come flinging your weight about where you're not wanted? I'll teach my lessons as I like.'

'You weren't doing much teaching when I came in,' said Harris.

'And I didn't do so sodding much when you'd gone. I'll tell you that for nothing.'

'I'll tell you something, then, Winterburn. If you go on as you are doing you'll be up the wall in six months.'

'What's that to you?'

'I like you,' said Harris slowly. 'I don't want you chucking yourself away.'

'The little Leaman,' said Winterburn. 'The poor man's soft-soap king.'

'Shout as you like,' said Harris. 'That's your trouble. You talk too much. I've tried to tell you before. For God's sake, man, give 'em three months on their silent readers and grammar exercises.'

'I'll ask for your advice when...'

'You'll get it now,' said Harris. 'I'm not going to see you mucked about by a gang of kids, whether you like the idea or not.'

'I can expect you in with your strong arm stuff every lesson, then? I'll have everything ready. Now, boys, sit up straight while Mr. Harris comes in and breaks somebody's jaw. My God, Harris, you've got an inflated opinion of yourself.'

'I've got a good opinion of you,' said Harris, 'in spite of all you say.'

'And I suppose I break down now and cry in your arms, you silly-born bastard?' said Winterburn.

'It wouldn't be the first time,' said Harris.

He thought for a moment that Winterburn was going to hit him with his attache case. Winterburn's eyes were wide and he was breathing heavily.

'You lousy...'

'I'm sorry,' said Harris. He put a hand on Winterburn's sleeve. Winterburn stood there at the bottom of the hill, panting. He looked as though he wanted to run away, but as if he had once started his limbs would have darted off in four different directions. For a moment Harris had the idea that only Winterburn's shabby raincoat was holding the writhing body together.

When Winterburn spoke again, his voice was hoarse.

'I will not be persecuted in this way,' he said. 'You'll hear from my solicitor.'

He stood, waiting for an answer.

'I'm sweating blood,' said Harris.

Winterburn rushed into the road. As he ran, whirling his case, he looked like a schoolboy let out early for an unexpected half-day.

## 9.

AT the beginning of October Blidworth Band gave the first performance of the march.

Harris was still madly busy. He had been to see Mountain, who made a few suggestions and then let Harris hear a rehearsal of the Passacaglia. His leader, Felix Manuel, had afterwards asked Harris if he had any 'spare chamber works' and now had two quartets and a violin sonata which he'd decided to perform. Attenborough had arranged for Brand to do the Quartet No. 3 at a lunch-time concert. Kingsley Forde had visited Harris in all his glory and had taken off six more songs; the Edinburgh efforts were now due for publication in England and America. The details of the Christmas Bach concert were at last fixed; in the first half Brand was to conduct the B minor Suite and the 5th Brandenburg, Attenborough on the harpsichord, and Harris was to do the first three sections of the Christmas Oratorio in part two. Cooke had chosen 'outstanding youngsters' from London for the solos, and had already had them once in Beechnall for Harris's inspection and instruction. Finally, *The Tempest* music was scored, utterly condemned by Beauchamp, approved by Cooke and already puzzling the orchestra.

The expected high-polished limousine, different from last time but with a similar laconic chauffeur, fetched Harris over to Blidworth. He'd shaken hands with his cronies, heard the last rehearsal, and had been taken over to a cool tea with Dr. and Mrs. Sackville, some high-up from the coal-board and a homely old soldier who chewed his moustache and was Lord Somebody-or-other. The weather was bright; every ticket was sold; Marby's palms were sweating and a good many visitors from other prize-bands had come back from the Saturday football match and were eating ham and chips and meat-pies in the market cafés. These were reported by Button to be doubtful of the value of the march as music and of the ability of 'Marby's lot' to play it anyway.

There were four rows of cars on the waste ground at the back of the Festival Hall. People milled round in their Sunday best; light greys and electric blues, fairisle pullovers, with cloth caps over the white colliers' faces. Inside there was bedlam. The hall itself resembled its London namesake in that it was not unlike a hump-backed garden shed from outside; inside the main architectural features were the bare rows of girders up in the roof and the savage whitewash on the wall. The audience was enjoying itself. The appearance was of the four-ale bar not the concert-room. People shouted to each other; it was interesting to watch arrivals. Dad would come in, cap still on, followed by our mam, and Brenda, grown-up at fourteen years old. Father's expression was that seen at weddings and funerals, hang-dog, and his hands would be deep in his pockets. Some unutterable young man would frantically indicate the direction of the seats, and then the party would see somebody they knew, and smile, and speak; then a second lot, and smile, and shout. By the time they had reached their seats, they recognised half the people they knew and were laughing and jostling and handing Brenda a right telling-off for nothing.

Harris's party made no such jovial entry. They were whisked from a muddy lane, on to a kind of concrete platform, up some steps, through a zig-zag corridor, all the time past bandsmen, who took their fags out and nodded to Harris. Mrs. Sackville clip-clopped ahead with his lordship straight into the 'Artiste's Room' (on cardboard, specially printed) to find Marby, resplendent in uniform with gold-braid cap and tassels, pulling on a pair of silk socks over his gigantic feet.

Mrs. Sackville did not like that.

She would have preferred banks of flowers, divans, wall-length mirrors, not a plain room stale with tobacco smoke and the chapel-hard chairs festooned with men's jackets.

Marby finished his toilet and officials came in with programmes and snippets of advice. When Marby said he'd like the band on stage, one of the officials opened the door, shoved his head out and shouted, 'Righto, yo' lot. Gerr aboard.' There was some little attempt at formality as the notables were shown to their seats in the front row, but this was somewhat spoilt by the heat and racket and movement of the place and by the fact that the second row was filled with exactly the same riff-raff as the back. The woman behind Mrs. Sackville had a boy on her knee who kept clambering up the seat in front. An eloquent woman behind Harris was spinning a yarn which involved the support of her husband. 'That wa' so, wa'nt it, 'Arry?' she said, and Harry replied 'Ah', a deep note like a bass-player tuning his A string. His lordship, next to Harris, took it in good part.

'Feel sorry,' he said in his staccato way, 'for these folks behind. No leg room. At least we can have a stretch, if we feel like it.'

The curtain went up and Marby walked in. The band all wore their military caps; we've paid for 'em, you shall see 'em. The front row applauded, the rest took to it noisily and with whistles and calls. Marby gave the signal and the audience crashed to its feet for the Queen and back with shifting of kit and rustle of comestible bags.

They were in no hurry to let the concert start. Talking broke out afresh as Marby was seen, apparently, in worried argument with one of his men. 'That wa' so, wa'nt it, 'Arry?' 'Ah.' Marby, himself again, looked the clients over and tapped his stand. Up came the shining instruments and there was quiet, immediate quiet. There was none of that demanding concert-hall cough, no last minute titter. The music was starting and there was a money's worth to be got.

It was a popular programme, as the festivities demanded. 'Tancredi,' 'Finlandia,' two Victorian duets, arr. Marby, for tenor and soprano accompanied, the first movement of 'Beethoven's fifth symphony' and finally a mighty tone poem, specially composed with solos galore for a North-of-all-England Brass Band Competition which Blidworth, against the run of form, had won. This was called oddly, enough, 'Julian the Apostate.' It purported to describe not only the ceremonies, rites, orgies, hecatombs etc. favoured by the emperor, his intense mental anguish, and subsequent damnation but also the steadfast nature and suffering, andante tranquillo, of the faithful Christians.

This certainly was no musical masterpiece, but whoever had lifted it out of Mendelssohn and Wagner, with one eye on Moeran and Vaughan Williams, had unblinkingly set out every trap a band could pitch itself into. 'Marby's lot', however, were not napping. Harris caught himself out thinking that people dressed like soldiers didn't play as well as gentlemen in evening dress. His ears did nothing to support this thesis. At the conclusion, pppp to fff in three bars, the audience went mad.

At the interval there was a rush for the doors and the three pubs opposite. Harris, detached from the elite, found himself in the muddy lane outside. Two stalls, one selling ice-cream and the other hot chestnuts and unshelled peanuts were making their owners' fortunes.

'Comin' in for a quick 'un, Tom?' It was Harris's father.

'No thanks, dad. Got to get back to the nobs.'

'Ah, I seen you sittin' next to Lord Saxondale. I'm two rows behind, on y'r left. Look out for us and gi'e us a wave. I'll be wi' you, lad, shouting like 'ell when your march comes on.'

'Mother not here?'

'Inside. Cherries on 'er 'at. Lord Who, she keeps on asking, our Tom's next to. Saxondale, I says. Owned t' pits. Ah wouldn't sit next to 'im in a public convenience. Ne' mind, son. Keep y'r 'ead 'igh. Goo an' 'ev a word wi' 'er, if yuh can git one in. Ah can't.'

He was off.

Harris found his way back in to where Mrs. Harris was sitting. The main body of the hall was empty, except for a few case-hardened gasbags. 'That wa' so, wa'nt it, Arry?' was still there, talking over Harry, to a nodding woman in a felt hat and raincoat on the other side. Seats had been pushed out of line, and all the gangways were crowded. In spite of 'No Smoking' notices, the men were having a draw; the aisles were as good as outside, especially where the doors were wide and a half gale whirled through. Mrs. Harris was knitting and carrying on a conversation with two women immediately behind her. Although the seats round about were not in use, none had thought of moving. Mrs. Harris only rarely turned her head, but directed her talk, and she was talking most, at her knitting.

'Hello, Tom, boy,' she said. 'Have you seen your dad?'

'Yes. He told me you were here.'

'Very chuff, he is. Pleased as a dog with two tails.'

She turned right round, now, and introduced her step-son to the women who solemnly shook hands.

'I hope you're enjoying the concert,' said Harris.

'Oh, yes.'

'But the second half'll be better,' said Mrs. Harris. 'Won't it, boy?' And give us a nice bow when you have to go up. An' pay no attention to your dad.'

Harris went backstage.

The atmosphere was easier there. The room was thick with smoke. Mrs. Sackville's nostrils were curled, but her husband was smoking a cigarette in an amber holder. Saxondale had a cigar and was with a newcomer, a stiff, white-haired man with glasses.

'Ah, Mr. Harris,' said Marby, 'let me introduce you. Thomas Harris, Albert Morton, the brass man.'

They shook hands.

'Wonderful piece of work, Mr. Harris, wonderful,' said Morton. He spoke with a strong north country accent. 'I was down here last month and had an hour with the band on it. Great work. We'll hear more of it.'

'They never told me,' said Harris.

'No,' said Marby, 'that's our surprise. We're giving your march twice and Mr. Morton's going to conduct it the second time. How's that?'

'Fine,' said Harris.

'Known him for years,' said Marby with pride. 'First clarinet in his band at Rutley twenty-five years ago. Many's the rowsting he's given me.'

'And deserved, young feller-me-lad,' said Morton. 'But it's great writing, Mr. Harris. You know what to ask of 'em. Don't you think so, my lord?'

'Not heard it yet,' said Saxondale. 'Reserve m'judgement, eh?' He winked at Harris.

'Are they back yet, Jack?' said Marby. 'Quarter-hour interval's nearly up.'

'Not them,' said Button, coming in, a rose in his lapel. 'It'll be all of 'a'f-an-hour afore th'King Billy's cleared.'

Mrs. Sackville sniffed. Button heard it.

'Some o'th'band's in, an' all,' he said, by way of excuse. 'It's 'ot in the 'all.'

After thirty-five minutes the band and the majority of the audience were back and Marby advanced to the front of the stage. He tipped his cap back on his head, so that he looked like a disgruntled stationmaster on a hot bank-holiday.

'Ladies and Gentlemen,' he said. He took his cap off and let it swing in his hand. 'You can discard your programmes now, because we aren't playing what's on them.'

'What's up, Marby?' a voice shouted. 'Too hard for you?' Doubtless some rival bandsman. Marby disregarded him.

'First of all,' he said, 'we shall play Elgar's "Pomp and Circumstance No. 4." We're doing that with the intention of letting the men get into it, and also to show you how well our second item, the Blidworth March by Thomas Harris stands up to a real, long-standing classic. Then there'll be a short presentation of the North of England Challenge Bowl and a short item in which you participate.'

A well-known bandmaster began to push his way out, probably to the urinal.

'Don't go, Joseph,' said Marby. 'It's a musical item, not a collection.' There was a large round of good humoured applause. 'Then finally I shall introduce to you, if he needs it, which he doesn't, the man who knows more about brass-bands than anybody else in the world, Mr. Albert Morton.' Howls of delight. Morton was as famous here as any first-division international or television star. 'In fact,' said Marby holding up his hand, 'Albert Morton knows more about the job than even some of those here think they do, and that's saying something.' Stormy home cheering, and the interrupter was slapped nearly through his seat by husky colliers behind him. 'And now,' said Marby, 'I see Joe Sidebottom's back, and that's all the speechifying you'll get out of me.' He rammed his hat on, wheeled, lifted his stick and was into Elgar No. 4 before the audience could get properly into their applause.

The Pomp and Circumstance was well played and acknowledged. Marby then took off his cap and laid it aside.

His stick mounted and dropped, and Harris's great blaze of silver swept the hall. The band was marvellous; every point was made and when they swung at last into the power of the marching tune it seemed as if the whole hall was lifted clean off the floor by the sound. Marby's baton moved lightly, with arrogance, in arabesques over his head and the tears shone unashamed on his face. The magnificence was only matched by the shout of the audience at the finish; it was as though a forest-fire of sound had crashed through the hall. Harris, his head bursting, thought there wouldn't be a stick of furniture left in a piece. Shout on shout, great cannon bursts, exploded from the audience. The ovation lasted all of five minutes.

Harris was dragged on stage, deafened and frightened, to have his hand shaken. The audience seemed quite out of control. It was not several hundred human-beings shouting but a boiling fury of sound, utterly uninhibited and terrifying. Harris stood out there, a little man in a dark suit, the one who had lighted the touch-paper to these shock waves of delirious noise. He had never known such enthusiasm; it crushed; it overwhelmed. It was like a football crowd, a workers' playtime and seemed indecent in the concert hall.

When comparative silence returned, and it was much interrupted by excited chattering, Saxondale and the coal board king handed over the trophy to Marby who laid it on a specially-prepared table at the front of the stage. His lordship made a short soldierly speech but its gruff utterance did not get further than the third row.

The people cheered, but they seemed exhausted after their outburst. Sweat was bright on their faces. Marby came forward again.

'When I knew we were doing the march twice, I wondered what to do for a bit of rest between. So I asked Jack Button. You all know him. And I got what I expected, a sensible answer. He said "Give 'em a sing." and that's what we'll do. "What, Jack?" I said. "The old favourite, 'Deep Harmony'," he said. We'll play two lines over, and then you can let the painter.[9] "Sweet is the work." Four verses.'

Once people began to sing, Harris saw that the exhaustion was only apparent. Tenors and basses strained; motherly contraltos, young Brendas, Harry 'Ah and his wife and guest. They all seemed to know the words. Saxondale and Sackville hummed; Mrs. Sackville looked straight ahead.

Harris turned round. His step-mother was still knitting, her eyes were down, but she was singing. His father had his head right back; his tenor voice, reedy but true, could be heard, Harris thought, all over the hall. The old chap was smiling, shaking his head with enjoyment. It was a pound to a pinch he'd no idea what he was singing about, but he punched Dr. Watts' words as he'd hammered his mates in the ring, for pure joy.

'My heart shall triumph in the Lord,
And bless His works, and bless His word;
Thy works of grace, how bright they shine!

How deep Thy counsels, how divine:'

The old man tugged at his collar between verses. 'It was my lad you was shouting your ruddy 'eads off for just now, and I'll show you there's a bit o' music in his dad. Sing up.'

Then Morton was introduced. He praised Marby; he encouraged the band and made one or two technical criticisms. He then said he'd let them into a secret. They'd hear the Blidworth March, with Mr. Harris's permission, next year played by the massed bands at the All-England Championship. 'It won't be any good, after that, will it now, anybody asking "Where's Blidworth?". They'll all know.'

He then did the march again. Again the violence of the reception. Harris went up-front again, bowed and thanked them. People wrung his hand. 'Good lad', they said. They fought and jostled to touch him, to say they knew his father. One old man, half suffocated by pushing bodies, began the queerest formal speech of thanks. Its heavenly length was soon stopped. 'That'll be enough, Amos,' somebody said. 'You ain't prayin' in t' chapel nah.'

Outside Mrs. Sackville took his hand, smiling, and held it. 'It was an inspiration, Mr. Harris,' she said. 'I'm sorry they spoilt it with that vulgar hymn. But I shall never forget.'

Harris refused all invitations, shook hands with everybody and asked where his father was.

'In th'Bull, I s'ould have thowt,' said Button.

'How will he get home?' said Harris.

'He'll be took,' said Button. 'Thomas 'Arris's feyther'll be looked after, don't you wittle yersen[10].'

But the old man was there, with them, listening.

Crouching, with his parents, in the back seat of the big car racing him home, Harris felt acutely ill. His head rocked with pain. Success had drawbacks. He wished the old people would be quiet, but you don't ask for the moon.

## 10.

HARRIS dropped asleep as soon as he had his head on the pillow.

Next morning, he woke at half-past six, his head clear after last night's excitement. As he lay in bed, he realised that the Adagio of the string-trio, which he'd been niggling at all the previous fortnight without much success, was as good as there. So, nothing *for* it but get up, shave, swill in cold water, put the kettle on, and get the paper out.

By seven-fifteen he was sitting at the table by the window, wrapped in a dressing gown, writing. Ideas flowed, melted, improved themselves; what had been hopeless suggestions a week ago clicked now and were bettered in the act of writing. Good job it was Sunday when he'd plenty of time.

It was pleasant up there. Below he could hear Sanderson knocking about. The landlord provided meals, if you wished, on Sundays; breakfast at nine; lunch at one, so there was nothing to stop the work. It was fine to be able to write like this, and scribble out, and know that the new insertion pleased you more than the old. It was excellent to look out of the window and wonder where that well dressed young man was off to so early in the morning, and to see the twos and threes come talking back from early communion, and know that as soon as your eyes left them, they'd be forgotten in the job in hand.

He went down to breakfast and was told by the only other man in, a culture-addict who was reading the *Observer,* that he had a mention there. He took the paper. Under a picture of Durham Cathedral was a short feature on the Festival, and Mr. Charles Mountain was reported as saying that his orchestra was playing an important new work by the British composer Thomas Harris, whose Quartet No. 3 (1956) was also to be played in the same week by the Manuel Quartet. Nice going.

Until twelve he worked steadily. The publicity did not distract him; the local newspapers had been bandying his name about for weeks. The reporters were a bind; decent fellows but after colour. One of the franker had said, 'Look here, Mr. Harris, what you're telling us would probably get you a good job in a musical academy, but it won't manure my beans.' Harris had liked him, and told him to put down what he liked. And so the locals had been offered the story of Harris aged eight settling like a master to play evensong on a great organ he'd never touched before with a brilliance that spellbound the congregation. This had happened in fact on a chapel harmonium in a mission hall at morning service and he was ten and he'd been told by some saint afterwards that the Lord's work could do without them twiddley-bits o' yourn, thank you.

By twelve fifteen he was well on to the coda, which seemed to grow stronger bar by bar, when Sanderson came up. His face was dirty and he was wearing a woman's apron. Obviously he was cooking.

'Wanted on the phone, Mr. Harris. Can't wait. All be spoilt. Man called Cooke.'

He ran downstairs. This was the only time in the week you could guarantee that Sanderson wouldn't hinder you. Harris would have liked five minutes' chat, no more, when things were going so well. It was one of the delights of composition to put the present, fluent ease back a bit, to make the music wait.

The phone call would do as well.

'Harris here.'

'Hello, Harris. This is Grainger Cooke. Are you busy?'

'Very.'

'All day?'

'No. I'm on at a string trio. Probably I'll have written myself out by tea-time. I've got about a fortnight's work to get down.'

'Can you come and see me about eight?' asked Cooke.

'I should think so.'

'I've a nice little commission in hand for you, boy. Oh, very nice. This'll make your mouth water. No string trio about this.'

'What is it?' said Harris.

'Oh, no. Nothing's fixed yet, so it's too early to start talking. I'm taking you round to see a gentleman. Let's put it like that and leave it like that, shall we? Be here at eight. On time. No earlier or later. I'm busy today, boy. Six days shalt thou labour and on the seventh do the odd jobs. Right you are, boy. Eight o'clock. Here. Glad all went well last night. Albert Morton gave me a ring. Must be off, then. 'Bye.'

After lunch Harris took a walk in the thin sunshine. He wondered what Cooke had lined up for him now. Certainly that man moved. He also considered Master Winterburn. He dragged his feet a bit at that in the sand in the coarse grass on the recreation ground. Winterburn had not spoken to him since the Blay episode, had tried to make it obvious to everybody else that he was cutting Harris. Once the fool had knocked down the book he was reading and Harris, picking it up, had handed it back. Winterburn did not take it. Harris returned it to the arm of the chair from where it had fallen. Winterburn did not re-open it, but picked up another book and began to read. The silly devil. Harris felt sorry for him.

Harris worked on until after four. He was then exhausted and had a cat-nap. When he woke, he felt slow and dizzy but sensed he'd had a good day. He tried to look over the Adagio, but found it too much trouble. He'd started on the last movement, and idly wondered if he could go any further. He made tea and toast, then bathed and dressed himself up for the visit to Cooke.

Reading a book, he relaxed at last.

There were footsteps on his stairs. Below he heard the six o'clock pips on some body's wireless. Sanderson knocked on the door.

'Wanted on the blower again, Mr. Harris,' he said.

'I'm popular today. Who is it?'

'Mrs. Freer or some such name.'

'Never heard of her,' said Harris. They went down one behind the other.

'I'm tired,' said Sanderson. 'I'm always glad when Sunday's over. On the go morning to night.'

'Nip into the "Vernon",' said Harris, 'and see all your pals.'

'No, Mr. Harris, I don't feel up to it. All I want is to get my boots off and my legs up.'

They were downstairs now.

'Hello. Harris speaking.'

'Is that you Mester Harris?' said a woman's voice.

'Yes.'

'Can you, will you, like, come round to your dad's?'

'Why? Is anything wrong?'

'Well, yes, there is ... like.'

'What is it?' said Harris.

'I beg your pardon,' she said.

'What's wrong? Who's speaking?'

'Oh,' she said, 'I'm all flustered, Mr. Harris. It's your dad.' Her voice trailed breathlessly off.

'Is he ill?' asked Harris.

'Yes, he is. He's died, like. This afternoon. Your mother, well, Mrs. Harris, you know, asked me to phone you and tell you to come round.'

Harris stood like an idiot with the phone in his hand. From behind a door he could hear the polite voice reading the six o'clock news. There was a weakness, like a pain, in his legs as if his muscles were knotted. He felt deathly cold.

'I beg your pardon,' said the woman's voice.

'I didn't say anything,' said Harris. 'Tell her I'll be round right away.'

He replaced the phone and took two steps along the hall. His feet were heavy. Inertia held him stock still. He had to go upstairs and take his coat and go for the bus. He rubbed a hand across his face, slowly.

'Hello,' said Sanderson, emerging with a big white bread bin in his hand, 'the lady friend's given you something to think about.'

'Uh,' Harris said.

'Don't you take notice of 'em, Mr. Harris,' said Sanderson.

He seemed much more cheerful than he had been a few moments back, though, perhaps that was only Harris's observation.

Harris forced himself to notice things. It was something he could do. The big urn-shaped knob at the end of the banisters, the cane-legged table with a pair of gents gloves, the fly-blown glass or perhaps it was the silvering worn off, the sandy trilby hat that always hung on the pegs.

'I'm glad I'm past it,' said Sanderson.

'Eh?'

'My courtin' days is over, like.'

'I've just heard,' said Harris, and his throat muscles were bound. Why should he tell Sanderson, anyway?

'Yes, Mr. Harris?' said Sanderson, smiling. He seemed to have noticed nothing unusual either in voice or mien. 'Something, I hope, to your advantage, as they say?'

'My father has died.'

Harris mumbled but the words got across to Sanderson. The grin came off his face, and his mouth dropped open like a spaniel's, begging.

'I'm sorry, Mr. Harris,' he said. His voice was changed. It whispered. 'Is there anything I ...'

'No,' said Harris, 'thank you. I'm going round now.'

He moved forward, past Sanderson who stood there with the bin hanging from one hand, and up the stairs.

When he came down, Sanderson was waiting, but he had lost the bread bin and had put his coat on.

'Don't forget, Mr. Harris, if there's anything...'

'Thanks, Mr. Sanderson.'

'Eh, Mr. Harris, if I could tell you how sorry...'

'I may not be back tonight. I don't know. I'll ring if there's anything.'

Sanderson opened the door.

'At the service in Canterbury Cathedral today, the Archbishop of ...' from the wireless.

People were walking leisurely toward church or the pubs. They all wore their Sunday best. Everything was as it should be.

Harris was numbed as he waited for the bus, which seemed an age coming and his anger revealed itself as shudders of cold, in his back. There was a smiling conductor who wanted to talk. When the bus jerked forward after a stop Harris felt sick. They were held up twice at traffic lights.

He began to run up the hill to Park Lane, but soon stopped that. His whole body was now drained dry, and breathing seemed an impossibility. It was a miracle that he could walk, but he kept on going, past the new grey stone and red tiles of the Baptist chapel, past the tall, thin, falling house with six slate-coloured steps. His misery was precisely situated now as a dull ache at the bottom of his stomach. The road seemed unending. There were few people about; he ran round an old lady pushing a pram with a large baby sucking a dummy. Everything was as it should be. The neon sign was on outside the 'Standard'. His dad wouldn't see that again. Now he was getting closer to the house, it appeared that the passers-by looked at him, curiously and sympathetically. The news was getting about. He rushed round the back of the house.

With his hand on the cold iron of the latch, he suddenly felt embarrassed. He'd got there and he didn't know what to do.

'Can I come in?' he called.

'Is it you, Tom?' said Mrs. Harris.

There was a bit of a scuffle and a woman came out into the kitchen where she switched the light on. She motioned him in. A kettle was boiling on the black-leaded gas stove. He entered the living-room.

'Ooh, Tom,' said Mrs. Harris, 'I'm glad you've come.'

He sat on the arm of her chair. She didn't get up but pushed her arms round him as he sat. He put an arm across her shoulder and they stayed together, not speaking, for a few minutes.

'Ooh, Tom,' she said, at last.

He could see that she had been crying but she seemed quite composed now. Her pretty, curly lamb's wool hair stood on end. She rested her head on Harris's coat and closed her eyes. He tightened his grip.

'It's the shock,' said the other woman. 'That sudden.' She had reseated herself opposite and spoke in the softest whisper. Suddenly she raised her voice. 'Drink you tea, mah ducky,' she said. 'It'll do yer good. Got a drop in it.'

Mrs. Harris opened her eyes and sat up. She tried to smile at the woman.

'That's Mrs. Freer,' she said. 'Next door. She's been ever so good.'

'You have a drink,' said Harris.

'Yes, Tom.' She took a cup, trembling.

Mrs. Harris took a sip or two of the tea, put it down.

'Ooh, Tom,' she said and began to cry. Harris made consoling noises. His own misery didn't seem to matter. He was an automaton, a thing, sticks and stones.

'It's the shock,' said Mrs. Freer. 'Come that sudden.'

Mrs. Harris cried a little longer, dried her eyes and took hold of Harris's hand.

'It were at tea-time,' she said. They had tea early on Sunday.

'Now, don't you go upsetting yourself, mother,' said Harris. His voice sounded very matter-of-fact to himself.

'Have another cup o' tea, mah duck,' said Mrs. Freer.

Mrs. Harris took the cup again, and drank.

'We'd just finished,' she said. 'It was half-past four. I was washin' up in the kitchen and yuh dad was sittin' across there in that chair Mrs. Freer's in, smokin' his pipe.' She looked wildly round, but her voice was steadier. 'I thought I heard a noise an' I walked to that door there wi' a plate in my hand, dryin' it. Your dad was hangin' on to the fire-guard, all doubled up. He must 'a got up to get himself a spill out o' the jar. "Willy, whatever's th'matter," I said, and he sort o' turned his head. I run across to him and got 'im in th' chair. "I do feel bad," he says, and he sort o' put his 'and on his heart.'

'You sup now, mah pigeon,' said Mrs. Freer.

Mrs. Harris did as she was told. The tears were running down her cheeks, but she made no noise. She might have been peeling onions.

'Ooh Tom,' she said, and pressed Harris's hand.

There was a noise upstairs. Harris looked up.

'They just laying him out,' said Mrs. Freer. 'The undertaker's up there an' Mrs. Smith. She allus does it.' She spoke in the same whisper as if to conceal what she was saying from Mrs. Harris. 'We was lucky to catch 'em in. Bless yo', my beauty,' she said to Mrs. Harris.

'I got the brandy and tried to give him some, but he couldn't swallow. "Shall I fetch the doctor?" I says, and he just looked at me, like, his face was proper grey and gave a little moan and he was gone.' She began to sob.

'There, there,' said Mrs. Freer. ''E didn't suffer much. That's one blessin'.'

Once more they settled to silence, then to heavy breathing.

Mrs. Freer poked the fire. The undertaker came down. He was solemnly cheerful.

'Bad job,' he said. 'But it's best to go sudden. Lingering, it's awful. Could tell you some things, if I'd a mind. Cheer up, mah duck. Try to look on the bright side. He's 'ad a good life. You get t' bed early and 'ave an asp'rin and some sleep. I know it's 'ard.' All this came off in a kind of comforting murmur. 'This your boy, Mrs. 'Arris? Like a word with 'im. If you don't mind, sir.'

He took Harris into the front room.

'It's burial,' he said. 'Your mother's told me. At the Wesleyans. Cremation's very nice, you know, but there's them that don't hold with it. You don't want mother worried, do we?' He rapidly sketched his wares, told Harris what had to be done, promised to do it, and left. 'Look after her, sir,' he said. 'She's a good-plucked 'un, but she needs your sympathy now.'

He nodded with a frown, put on his hat and said, 'Good night, sir. And don't you worry. I'll see as all's well.'

When he'd gone, Harris remembered he used to sit next to him in the infant school.

As Harris came back in to the living room, he heard a third voice. It must be Mrs. Smith. 'Lovely, he looks, that there peaceful, might be asleep. Hardly a line on 'is face. You can tell 'e's gone to glory. Proper 'appy.'

These professionals, Harris decided, all had their line of patter.

Mrs. Smith took them upstairs, like a guide. She rattled on that there would be no need for an inquest as he'd been under the doctor and what a blessing that was.

'Look at 'im, now,' she said. 'Lovely. Like a baby. There's nowt on his conscience; that you can tell.'

In fact the old man looked wooden. There was none of the movement that made him alive. He had become anonymous, any old, dead man.

Mrs. Harris clung to Harris, then darted forward, stared, bent and kissed the forehead and buried her face in the bed clothes.

'Nah, mah love,' said Mrs. Freer.

'Don't take on so, mah beauty,' said Mrs. Smith. She'd laid out her thousands. 'That's not 'im. That's only 'is body. The spirit's gone above.'

They lifted Mrs. Harris and took her downstairs. Mrs. Smith chattered on, a curious, half-parsonical stream of advice and reminiscence. She joined them in a cup of tea, hung around for half an hour before she packed her traps and left.

Mrs. Freer stood up.

'Ah'm takin' 'er in, Mester 'Arris, until after the fun'ral. Ah'll just go an' make 'er a bed up and get 'er in the sheets. They'll all be coming round, word o' sympathy and prayer, you know, but she's better beout[11] it this night.'

When she was gone, Harris sat by his step-mother, holding her hand. They said nothing, stared into the fire. There was one of the old chap's pipes still up on the shelf. Harris took a poor view of all tear-jerking, but he dared not look at it. There was a permanent lump in his throat, a listlessness, and a desire to shrink.

'He was a good husband, Tom,' Mrs. Harris said at last.

'Yes.'

'An' a good father.'

'He was.'

'None better.'

They returned to staring into the fire.

'I can hardly realise he's gone, Tom,' she said.

'No.'

'His heart's been bad a long time now. Didn't like you sayin' any thin', though.'

'I know.'

'It was quick. I'm glad it was quick. But I shan't never get him his tea again.'

The conversation lurched on. Harris was relieved when Mrs. Freer came back.

All three went next door.

'Nah, Mr. Harris,' said Mrs. Freer, 'just you lock up and see as the fire's safe then get yourself off 'ome to bed.'

Harris did as he was told.

As he legged it down Park Lane, he was ashamed to notice that his main feeling was again relief. The air was cool, slightly damp. He gulped it down, with pleasure after the heat of the room. Underneath this surface of pleasure there was the knowledge that something was wrong. He probed, and immediately the vague discomfort crystallised into the memory of the corpse in the cold bedroom. His throat swelled. He dragged air into his lungs, hiding precise misery with the veneer of physical pleasure.

He forced his mind to do something. This seemed essential; once he allowed his body to take over, he'd be wretched. The swelling in the throat, the shivers, the cringing of arm muscles, the prickling heaviness of eyelids would rob him of humanity, given half a chance. His mind was directed forwards.

Now, where was the great music appearing from this? Here we had tragedy; the nearest and dearest knocked off without so much as a by-your-leave. But there was no superb funeral march, salting the wounds to heal. No fear. That was preposterous: was Winterburn right then that Harris lacked the sensibility, so that when the crudest sorrow hit him it was barely noticed? Harris rejected that. The test came later. The old problem of aesthetics presented itself for another run-through. 'Ought the artist to welcome disaster as the means to creation?' What tripe. At this moment, the old chap alive, supping a pint in the Standard, would be worth any symphony ever written.

Right. Next question then? Here was the hour of trial. How did the trio Adagio measure up now? That was good this afternoon. He began to run through it, but gave up. It meant nothing or, worse, it meant that the body was to be relaxed to hear it, and once the body got its way, there was Thomas Harris, human being, bang in the gutter.

A little phrase of Bach recitative nagged over in his mind. 'But woe unto that man by whom the Son of Man is betrayed.' It had no significance. It came and went, was a temptation to let the body get in. The drooping minor thirds at the beginning of the phrase reminded him of 'His body sinks to rest.' Put a sock in it.

He stopped on the bridge over the little river. It was lattice, like some rustic work in a pleasure garden, but made of iron. Well done, the industrial revolution. He watched the water, the little, changing flecks of light, the dangling bushes. There'd be newspaper caught in their roots he reminded himself. He picked a stone and listened to it plop into the river. He put his hands on to the cold bridge, braced his shoulders. 'That's the chap that married Anna,' he said.[12] It was always his father's way of encouraging him when he was a lad. The straightening up gave him a sense of well-being, but that disappeared immediately. Body was winning. He stared listlessly into the water.

He looked at his watch for something to do. Eight-thirty. He hadn't realised it was so late. The minutes with his step-mother had seemed endless, but he'd thought that was subjective. There was nothing he could do. Tomorrow he'd have to be running about; that wouldn't be so bad, he promised himself, but now he'd better get home and to bed. His father was on a bed, a wood image under a white sheet. Harris remembered the book he'd been enjoying; that shaped no better than the Adagio.

Eight-thirty. Good Lord, he was supposed to be at Cooke's at eight. Oh well, better ring him up. Can't go round there. He sorted fourpence out of his pocket and went into the phone box at the corner. Nobody in at Cooke's. No answer. He looked at his face in the mirror. He had to lean forward to do it. There was his face; it was as ever. There he stood in the box, in the hexahedron of bright light, a man without a father. The phone in his left hand was still ringing the bell in Cooke's house. Nobody came. That was that. He dropped the phone quietly into its cradle.

Outside the box, he stood still, unable to make up his mind. He had to cross the road and board a bus, a thing he'd done before. But now the world seemed different, as if he'd been engaged within another dimension, or like a blind man seeing for the first time in his life. People walked past; the trolley buses swished along the road; there were lights in the cinema opposite and the metal gates were locked back. But none of this made sense. It was quite fresh, a horrifying world, to him.

'Can you give us three pennies for a thre'-penny, mister? Got a call to make.'

He felt in his pocket, held out the coppers, had the three-penny piece put into his flat hand. He did not speak. To himself it seemed as if he did not understand the language. It was as if the person had asked him in Chinese and he, quite by chance, had guessed and made the appropriate action. Ridiculous. He could still hear in his head the exact pitch and intonation of the voice. He could understand.

His body heaved a great sigh out of him, and he crossed the road.

On the bus he seemed to be two men. One was the cowed, cold man, frightened of death; the other half listened with pleasure to the conversation of a party off for Sunday's celebration.

'Ah don't like eggs,' one old man said. 'Never did. In India we used to call 'em "unders" and in France they was called "oofs". But I didn't stomach 'em nowhere.'

## 11.

THE funeral rushed Harris. There were visits here and there, getting used to shaking hands with long-faced strangers and then taking them into the front room, drenched with eucalyptus, to show them the body in its shift in the coffin on black trestles. The letters and telegrams were, in the end, sent; the funeral tea eaten; Harris's sisters seen off, step-mother with one of them.

Attenborough took the Bach practice on Wednesday, although Harris had started back to school. A postcard of apology had been sent to Cooke. A postcard from Beauchamp demanded his presence at 6.30 on Saturday night at the Vale Road School for an important rehearsal of both music and drama.

At school, reactions varied. Those who knew were solemn and sorry, but obviously glad when Harris switched to talk shop. Others clearly did not know, and approached him with demands for this and that, dubious stories, questions about whether he was feeling better now. Winterburn was in a cleft stick. He felt he ought to show sympathy, but did not like to make the initial move.

On Wednesday evening, Harris saw him coming out of the cloak room.

'Going my way?' Harris said.

'I thought I'd made it plain I wanted nothing to do with you.'

'Righto. Sorry,' said Harris.

'You didn't think just because your father had died that it would make any difference between us, did you?' Winterburn sounded uncertain. 'I'm very sorry. I know you thought highly of him. But that's the only reason I'm speaking. I'm glad you've given me the opportunity to say that, and there we'll leave it, if you don't mind. I don't want to have anything more to do with you.'

'Oh, be reasonable, for heaven's sake,' said Harris.

Winterburn turned away. Harris fell in step with him.

'You can't stop me walking alongside you, can you now?' Harris said.

Winterburn didn't answer.

'Will you have a fag?' he asked a little further on.

Winterburn affected not to hear. When Harris stopped to light up, he went on. Harris hurried to catch up, leaving the cigarette unlighted.

'This is all very silly,' he said. No answer. 'You're acting like a mardy kid.' They took step for step together to the bottom of the hill.

'Carry your bag, sir?' said Harris, desperate. He took hold of the handle of the attaché case. Winterburn rapidly swung it into his other hand.

'Temper,' said Harris. 'You're a big boy now. Your shoelace is undone.'

Winterburn hesitated and looked down. Both laces were tied.

He walked on, sniffing.

'Got you,' said Harris. 'You can hear.'

He said no more until they reached the bottom of the hill.

'Goodnight, Winterburn,' said Harris, stopping. 'Come off it, mate.'

Winterburn was half-way across the road before he'd finished speaking.

When Harris, on Saturday, set off for the Vale Road School rehearsal, it was the first evening he had been out. On arrival it did not take him long to find out what had happened. The previous Monday, an attempt had been made to fit words and incidental music together. With the orchestra in its present state of rehearsal the result was catastrophic. Harris put this scheme down to Beauchamp since he was known to dislike the score, and to be determined to get rid of it.

The actors had refused to continue, and the bemused orchestra had supported them. Brand had resigned. This evening's business though ostensibly a rehearsal was in fact a general meeting and it was known that Cooke, who had been in London all week, was specially coming back. J. N. P. Greenhalgh, Esq., the Society's president and Professor Attenborough were also to attend.

When Harris arrived the rehearsal had broken up and people were talking furiously at each other, going through the extra-ordinary range of gestures that afflicts amateur mummers when they meet and drawing chairs together in the hall, presumably for the meeting.

Ten minutes later Cooke arrived, brief case and Homburg, the fluff of a first-class carriage still on his trouser-legs, to take over. He was introduced by the President who laid it on thick that Cooke had thought so highly of this society that he had etc. etc.

From that moment it was all Cooke. He was exquisite. Harris admired every minute.

For a start he invited criticism of the music. People were slow to speak, but encouraged by Cooke they soon had every sort of complaint that was to be heard. There were those who said the music was hopeless, cat-through-mangle. Then those who said it was fine music but too modern in idiom. Next those who claimed it was unsuitable for Shakespeare. Others thought the orchestra couldn't play the notes so that nobody had any idea whether the music was right or wrong. Odd stragglers rose and were rude about the Establishment, Cooke, Greenhalgh, Beauchamp and, surprisingly, Harris.

Cooke listened to all this, jollied the speakers along, summed up their speeches. He wanted to make it eminently clear, he said, what the complaints were. He treated every speaker with respect, be he insolent, tongue-tied or a mere anecdote-monger. Everyone was encouraged to speak his piece; this was then beautifully summarised by Cooke and all the points that the timid or disgruntled said would never be raised were brought out quite patently by Cooke himself.

Then he opened the defence.

In the same mild way, he said he accepted the criticisms and thanked the splendidly frank Society for them. He himself, he thought, was to blame. He would tell them why. They had in Harris a remarkable talent. Songs performed at the Edinburgh Festival, a great Passacaglia, Variations and Fugue to be broadcast from the Festival Hall, string works accepted by the Manuel Quartet, acknowledged by them all as the finest chamber-ensemble in England. He thought such a man as Harris would shed lustre on the Shakespeareans. Very quietly, he said he still thought so. At the shouts of disapproval he said he'd tell them why, but for the moment he'd consulted an internationally acclaimed scholar, Professor Hedley Attenborough, and he'd say what he thought of the score.

Attenborough rose, held out his notes, told them the time he had spent on the music and then pronounced it 'substantial, carefully-worked out, strong, abounding in ideas, eloquent and moving.' Dramatically it showed remarkable insight and succeeded magnificently as far as another medium could in throwing light on the text in question. He threatened them with detailed appreciation, but Cooke cut him smilingly short and moved him from the stage.

This was not received without retort. Beauchamp had drilled his cronies well, Harris thought. Cooke was unmoved. He mentioned that the first musical critic of *The Times* to whom he'd been talking only yesterday had shown great interest in the proposal to commission Harris. He suggested that people who mattered were now watching the Society. If tonight they turned Harris's music down, it might be taken up by the lurid national press. 'Society Sacks Composer.' The young men in the weeklies, always on the look-out for a cultural smack at the provinces, wouldn't hold their hands. And it was the wrong sort of publicity. This was not what they wanted.

By this time a good part of the audience was with him; he had, in any case, a strong following and if a vote had been taken he would have collared a majority. But he wasn't ready. He suggested that perhaps they'd been unfair. It was to their credit. While actors were preparing, their nerves were on edge. But once let the orchestra master the score, they'd see; no, better, they'd hear.

His final stroke was a masterpiece. He said he, fortunately, wasn't in charge of the production. That was in the loving hands of one he and they trusted, his and their very good friend, Jack Beauchamp. Jack would have the last word. That was right. Cooke led the applause as the producer came up.

Beauchamp looked them over. Wellington reviews his troops. He said he was no musician. This reduced the audience to howling laughter. He yanked his sweater down and said he'd now girt his lions. Listeners in hysterics. Broadly smiling he began to move the palm of his hand over his face. As it progressed downwards it wiped the smile from the features it had passed. At one moment you could see the basilisk eyes and the brash smiling of the lips. It was wonderfully managed. He snapped a finger out and in his broadest Yorkshire said, 'You don't want a speech from me. I suggest,' lunga pausa, 'we get on rehearsing.' He toppled backwards and crab-walked with ludicrous, slow skill to the edge of the dias. Roof-lowering applause.

The revolution was over.

Within ten minutes the rehearsal was on. Beauchamp lorded it; if his underlings felt disappointment in him, they were not allowed to show it. Harris marvelled at the volte-face; but Beauchamp was quite himself. Harris pulled back a chair to listen. Someone interrupted.

'Mr. Thomas Harris?'

'Yes.' Harris looked towards the man. He was young and smart.

'Mr. Cooke would like to see you, in the infants' staff-room.'

'Now?'

'Yes, sir. I'm very glad the decision went as it did. This way, please.'

The fellow led Harris up a flight of stairs. Outside the staff. room was a chair, deliberately placed.

'If you'll sit down, Mr. Harris, please, I'll tell Mr. Cooke you're here.'

There was the sound of laughing inside. The messenger came out. It was all arranged like a big business interview. The school with its smell of disinfectant, stone steps, iron-railings, the Van Gogh and John Piper reproductions, the vases of flowers, all familiar to Harris, had been moulded by Cooke into a high-powered executive's hide-out.

'Mr. Cooke won't be long.'

Five minutes' sitting. There was more laughter. The handle rattled; out of the half-open door a smudge of smoke and heat swirled.

Greenhalgh and Attenborough emerged, shook hands; the president walked away. The professor played over Harris with his eyes, let his smile fall off and said, 'I was sorry to hear the news of your father.'

Harris grunted.

'A sad blow.' He nodded, pressed Harris's hand and stood reeking with sympathy. 'Does Mr. Cooke know you're here?' Harris said nothing.

'Come in, Harris,' Cooke shouted. His mouth sounded full.

Inside the room it was oppressively hot with the gas-fire on full. Cooke was sitting at a long table, with a tray on which were sandwiches, a pot of tea, a large cup and saucer and a silver spirits-flask. His hat and coat were off, his jacket unbuttoned and he was going hard at the food. Attenborough placed a chair.

Harris sat down and looked round. There were green curtains at the window; the piles of books were few and tidy; dangling on coathangers were a couple of maternity smocks such as infant schoolmistresses wear. At Harris's end of the table was a large sheet of brown paper. On it were drawings and letters; A is for Apple, but it was unfinished. He pushed it along towards Cooke.

'Satisfactory tonight?' said Cooke, hardly pausing from mastication.

Harris half-nodded.

'You've good reason to be pleased with yourself. Went our way nicely, didn't it?'

No reply. Cooke looked up, interested.

'Don't think it was easy. I had to be quite awkward with Master Beauchamp before he saw sense. Still, they're playing your music, Harris, and that's that.'

'I'm very grateful,' Harris mumbled.

'Are you?' said Cooke. 'Are you? I hope so, my lad, because I've a bone to pick with you.'

Harris rubbed a finger on the table.

'You didn't turn up on Sunday evening,' said Cooke.

'No.'

'No? Is that all you've got to say? Well, I'll tell you, Mr. No, you missed the chance of a lifetime. I'd got one or two notables gathered and mellowed, all ready to commission a work from you, a big work.'

'And?'

'The drink's worn off. A big choral work to celebrate the four hundred years of Beechnall as a city. And now…' He snapped his fingers.

'Oh,' said Harris.

'Oh,' said Cooke, leaning back and shoving a thumb into his waistcoat as if to test the capacity of the stomach beneath. 'I'd just like to ask you a question, Harris. What exactly do I get out of you?'

'I often ask myself that one.'

'Then I'll answer it for you,' said Cooke. 'Nothing. Exactly nothing. There's not a farthing in my bank account due to you, mister.' He paused, spoke softer. 'I do for you, Harris, what I can, because I think you've got talent. You're worth pushing for your own sake. I tell you that bluntly. But I'll also tell you that there are limits to my patience. I thought twice about coming down tonight, and that's straight. And if there'd been no Cooke here, there'd have been no Harris either, and the sooner you cotton on to that one the better.'

'I've said...' Harris began.

'You've said precisely nothing. You take it all as your right. Again I'm warning you. Quietly, but...'

'I explained,' said Harris, 'why I didn't come.'

'Yeh?'

'I sent a note on Monday.'

'To my private address? I've been away. Not seen it. But that's what I'm trying to get into your thick skull, that a note on Monday's no good to me. Lord, man, can't you see which side your bread's buttered?'

'You don't know, then,' said Harris, 'why I didn't turn up.'

'No. Nor am I very interested.'

Harris sat right forward and stuck both his legs straight out.

He put his hands deep into his trousers pocket and jingled his loose change.

'I didn't come,' he said coldly enough, 'because on Sunday afternoon my father died suddenly.'

Cooke's expression did not change; he fingered together a few crumbs on his plate and stuffed them into his mouth.

'I'm sorry,' he said. 'Very sorry.' He looked up. 'But I'm afraid it makes no difference.'

'No difference to what?' said Harris.

'Your chance of this big choral work.' He shook his jowls. 'This is a competitive world, laddie. The opportunity was there. I'm not saying you'd have got the commission, but if you'd have behaved yourself, who knows? The plain fact is, however, that you didn't come. I'm not blaming you, now I know. But don't you get blaming me.'

'Who? ...' Harris began.

'Sir Archbold Staleybridge. He's going to put the money up. Old Greenbaum. The Duke. The shekels were there.'

'And you're not prepared to do anything for me now?'

'No, Harris, I'm not. I was annoyed last Sunday. I didn't like it. I'm not saying you weren't right to act as you did, but you take the consequences. You've got to realise that if you're going to get anywhere, you've got to put in a bit of spade-work of your own, at whatever the cost.'

'My father died.'

'There's something in the Bible about that,' said Cooke. He scratched his hand. 'Look here, Attenborough, how many composers in the country are there who'd come cap in hand for this commission?'

'No telling,' said Attenborough. 'Good men, you mean. Twenty, perhaps, thirty.'

'Yes,' said Cooke. 'At least. And what of our young friend here?'

'I'm very sorry, Harris,' said Attenborough slowly, 'that you haven't got the commission. Very sorry indeed. But these things need very careful handling, stage-managing. You just don't understand. People won't throw their money about these days. Mr. Cooke has been working for weeks, in the dark, pulling a string here, dropping a hint there. But once the psychological moment's past, the business is dead.'

'He only rang me on Sunday,' said Harris. 'Suppose I'd have been out for the day.'

'Nothing doing for you,' said Cooke. 'That's easy.'

'Mr. Harris,' said Attenborough, 'you just do not know how delicate negotiations are in these...'

'Delicate for everybody but me,' said Harris.

'Listen, Harris,' said Cooke. 'These amateur affairs are my hobby. True I've professional connections, and influence, but I can't fling my weight about as I do when I'm at work. I arrange, set things in motion, but that's all.'

'What a confession,' said Harris.

'You listen to young Brand too often,' said Cooke, 'with his Lord-of-Hosts talk. It just doesn't square with the facts. I was annoyed with you last Sunday, and said some things that didn't do you any good. I'm sorry. But I could no more get you that commission now than I could bring back yesterday.'

'All right, then,' said Harris.

Cooke dusted the crumbs from his waistcoat.

'Talking of Brand,' he said, 'I've a favour to ask of you.'

'You know what...' Harris began.

'Brand,' said Cooke, undeterred, 'has resigned from the conductorship of this orchestra. I want him back. We must all press him. Will you go round and help him change his mind?'

'Why should I?'

'It's to your advantage. You want the job done properly. He's the man to do it. After all, my son, I did come from London to rescue you. Tit for tat, eh?'

'Sometimes, Cooke,' said Harris, 'I almost like you. In spite of myself.'

'Well, well,' said Cooke. 'And I like that. You've learnt lesson number one.

Help yourself. It shifts one of the imponderables. So round you go like a good chap. The sooner the better.'

'Right,' said Harris.

'That's it, then, boy. And no promises, mark you, but I shouldn't altogether despair of that choral work yet. You could make a start. Wouldn't do anybody any harm, would it?'

'Hello,' said Harris. 'The Lord of Hosts is resurrected.'

'There's the door,' said Cooke. 'I'm busy.' He was pleased with himself.

Harris left.

The corridor was chilly after the room. Harris stood, with a hand on the jamb, listening but there was no sound from inside. Nobody was about. He took two steps towards the far end, stood again and listened. There was nothing doing. Why he had stopped he didn't know. He was standing by a cupboard which had a painted, neat notice 'Plimsolls'. Again he heard, as if the voice were speaking at the minute, 'No promises, mark you.' He stumbled against a thick mat outside a door labelled 'Miss Stocks, IIA'. His footsteps were loud again banging against the walls and low ceiling. The corridor was presented to him in every detail, every stain and lick of paint.

But there was an important matter. He knew something now.

What he knew was that he ought to write a requiem for his father. Just that. Nothing about it. No details. There was no lavish outpouring of golden inspiration. In fact it was the opposite. It seemed as if his body was compressed inwards, like a spring, and that for the moment there was nothing happening. Soon the spring would be released and the energy generated in the proper direction.

It was odd that he hadn't known it when he'd shut Cooke's door. It could not be connected with the remembered phrase, or plimsolls, or Miss Stocks. The way to describe it would be that it was tremendous excitement about nothing. A Requiem.

There it was then. The steel springs were wound tight in.

He walked out at a brisk pace, but he looked round with affection at the impedimenta of school, the corner of a black-board seen through a glass door, a caretaker's mop and pail left about, a fire-bucket with two spent matches thrown on the sand.

## 12.

STAGE two of writing the Requiem was one that Harris did not like. It consisted largely in an examination of his qualifications to bring the work off. He was quite modest about his talent, but always worked on the assumption that he should aim higher than he first considered he could manage.

His knowledge of Requiem masses was not great; he had taken part in Brahms's, Verdi's, Mozart's and Faure's but had never thought of doing anything in that line himself. He wondered, for a start, what his father would have thought. The old man liked a sing, but didn't mind whether it was 'Messiah' or 'Comrades in Arms'. But that was beside the point. Harris wasn't convinced that the idea hadn't come on him too quickly to be any good. He'd never written a note commemorating his mother's death, and she was much closer, more like himself.

The actual idea of a mass stuck in his craw. Harris, not much of a church-goer, could not believe in hell, and the fine words of the Dies Irae, for instance, only struck skin deep. They were attractive on the surface; he felt he could make a splendid extrovert setting of them, but that was as far as he'd go; hell was bunk. If there was hell it was down here on earth. The tortures of the damned were real enough, but, in his view, we didn't have to wait for them. There was no great trumpet to call to blessedness or damnation; your ration was handed out here and now.

He tried to thrash over in his mind how deep his own beliefs were fixed. He recalled Attenborough talking one evening to the Bach Choir. They had the Christmas Oratorio nicely taped now and were mainly concerned with the Matthew Passion. At the end of a rehearsal he asked Attenborough if he'd like to give a word of advice to the singers. Attenborough, serious, with his cheeks puffed, had commended Harris's musical preparation, but had told the choir to go home and study the words, get them off by heart, and not only the choruses and chorales, but the recitative and solos. 'Because, my dear friends,' he said, 'Bach was not only a musical genius, he was a religious genius as well. When we think of Bach, we tend to concentrate on the massive talent, that overpowering intellect, but we should never forget the humble man on his knees before his God. It is as important as the other. The art of counterpoint was raised to a stupendous height to bring before the ears of the world the love of God and the sin of man. Bach understood all three equally well.'

Harris thought Attenborough was overdoing it a bit, but was impressed that old pomposity was moved to such overstatement. He himself had no such qualifications; that he was certain about. He wondered if he could put together a sort of libretto of his own, not exactly secular, but untied to beliefs he could not hold. Something parallel with Tippett's 'Child of Our Time' might do, but he felt that the high marks of Tippett's work were the Chorale-Spirituals, and that his own words could never match his music. Still, one could say that of Bach. The words were often trite. But again, Bach had the Bible to fall back on. It was all very trying, and, worst of all, it had so little to do with music at the present. He wanted to get down to the musical struggle, not to beat about the bushes of what he could or couldn't believe.

He was still deliberating when he went the next week to see Brand.

Brand, contacted by phone, had laughed and told Harris he knew why he was coming up, and that he ought to be ashamed of appearing such a Cookeified lickspittle, but, anyway, he was always ready for a chat with a pal, so come round Thursday and get a great big cheerful 'no' for an answer.

Harris, hearing that his step-mother was back, called on her first. His sister had come over for a half-day and with the neighbours had got the house shipshape. There was nobody there but Mrs. Harris, when her step-son arrived, and on the face of it she was cheerful. She looked young and alert, smiled, handed on news, spoke of Harris senior quite steadily and it wasn't until Harris said he had to go that he realised she was terrified. Not that she'd deliberately shoved up a facade of cheerfulness; the excitement of the return had done it for her. But now she came to see, for the first time, that she was to be left on her own, with nobody to be looked after. And it was to last for the rest of her life. Her zest dropped off. She glanced at the clock, the television set, the tea-caddy and knew they were her husbands now. Harris was surprised that he'd spotted this; he'd dreaded the meeting and was bucked that all had worked out so well. Now, and even he saw it, the woman had time on her hands, round her neck, and was frightened.

'You going to be all right?' he said.

'Oh, yes. Course I am. I've always had plenty to occupy myself with. Your dad didn't like to see me sittin' idle.' Then more slowly. 'I expect I shall be lonely, Tom. I s'll miss him.' She sighed. 'But time's a great healer.' It was plain she didn't believe that.

Her hands fluttered as if she were trying to explain some awkward point. 'Tom,' she said. 'Would you sit at the piano and play an 'ymn?'

'Yes,' he said. 'What would you like?'

'Any hymn. Something nice, like.'

He sat and played Vaughan Williams's 'Down Ampney'.

'Very nice,' she said. 'Play us "Abide with Me," now would you? Your dad used to like that.'

He did so, and he could hear her rocking in his father's chair. When he looked up, she smiled at him.

'Very nice,' she said. 'You've got a lovely touch, Tom. Your dad did like to hear you play.'

'I shall have to be off,' he said.

'I'll come to the front door with you.'

He looked back from well down the street. She was still at the door, making it last.

When he reached Brand's house, he knocked and was kept waiting. He knocked again. In the end, Brand came to the door, looked his caller over and invited him in. He was swaying slightly and pale.

'Come and sit down, Harris,' said Brand. He had a whisky bottle already out and had been going at it.

'What's this?' said Harris. 'Anything wrong?'

Brand leaned forward, with his hands on his knees. He was like a man after a race he'd lost, blown and disappointed.

'The missus,' he said.

'Ill?'

Brand nodded, then made an odd motion as if to ask for silence. He had not offered Harris a drink. It appeared he hardly knew where he was. From time to time he looked up at Harris as though he were going to say something in confidence, but his eyes would be lowered and his face drop back to a blank, unusual surliness.

'Is it serious?' said Harris.

'Eh?' Brand flinched and struggled to concentrate.

'Is it serious? Can I do anything?'

'I don't know,' said Brand. 'I don't know.' He took a noisy mouthful of whisky. 'There's been an accident. Young Chris got out into the street yesterday, and some learner practising turns ran over him.'

'Yes?' said Harris. It seemed he was forcing details out of Brand.

'The lad's all right. It broke his arm and they whipped him straight off to dock. He's back now; his arm's not even in plaster. But some fool woman came up here with a message that he'd been run over. You know how it is. Nance was all right then. Got off down to the hospital in a car, brought Chris back. In the night I thought she was going off her head. Punching and screaming and saying it was her fault and she wasn't fit for children to be entrusted to. You never heard such a performance. Scared the holy Jesus out of me.'

'I'm sorry,' said Harris.

'Would you go and see her?' said Brand.

'Would it do any good?'

'What would do any good?' said Brand. 'She's half doped now. She thinks a lot of you, Harris.'

'And how about you, mate?' said Harris.

'I'll get over it,' said Brand, trying to be himself. 'There's nothing I can do.'

'You could just put a touch of work in on *The Tempest* score.'

'Do you think of damn-all but your own concerns, Harris?' said Brand. He asked it in a natural way, without bitterness, quietly. 'Haven't I got enough on my plate for you?'

'Sorry,' said Harris. 'I shouldn't have brought it up.'

'I'll conduct it for you,' said Brand. 'You can tell Cooke, blast his eyes. What's it matter if Cookey conducts it himself. I'm a selfish cow, Harris, God's truth.' He put his teeth together and twisted his face into a grimace. 'Do you want a drink?' This was all said very fast, in a flat voice. It was mechanical, nothing alive. 'It shakes you, Harris and I've seen some service.' He blew his lips out. As he settled back into his chair, he tried an effect of nonchalance, 'Well,' he said, 'this won't buy the old woman her bloomers. How are you, Harris?'

'Can't grumble.'

'What about Cooke's wonderful commission? Did you get it?'

'As a matter of fact, I had thought of trying a Requiem,' said Harris steadily.

''Struth,' said Brand. 'For the old man?'

'Yes,' said Harris. 'Odd, isn't it?'

'Just sit here and talk a bit,' said Brand. 'It's what I want. Your father dies, you're half-way through a requiem mass and here you come, running Cookey's errands. You do me good, boy.'

'I suppose I should be at home in floods of tears and inspiration?'

'You should be right there,' said Brand, 'on your backside on that chair, doing good to your neighbour. Now just bash on a bit.'

'Well,' said Harris, 'I wouldn't mind asking you a question or two. Do you know anything about Requiems?'

'I feel like death now,' said Brand. 'No, I've fiddled through the viola part in most of 'em.'

'Could you see much sense, yourself, in setting a requiem mass?' said Harris.

'How do you mean? As I feel, brother, I couldn't set the table.'

'What relevance has a requiem mass for people these days?'

'Isn't that the wrong way?' said Brand. 'You write music for musicians. I'm not telling you that it doesn't matter whether you set the Tuba Mirum or the Telephone Directory, but choirs don't give a tinker's whether they believe what they're singing about. If your music's good enough, they'll believe while they're singing. That's enough.'

'Not for me.'

'I always thought you were a religious cove, Harris.'

'I don't believe in hell.'

'Eschatology,' said Brand. 'Nice word.'

'You don't know what I'm talking about,' said Harris. 'I want to write something that'll not only commemorate my father, but say something about every Tom, Dick and Hari Ram who's being pushed about by last judgements and deaths and earthquakes down here. I'm not selling the old, old story. I want to say something for myself.'

'Has it struck you,' said Brand, interested, 'that you're not consistent? What's the connection between your dad dying in bed, and some poor blackfeller with a flick-knife in his ribs, or somebody kicked to death by secret police, or even an old sheep killed by strontium fall-out? Where's the tie-up?'

'Perhaps I'm too big for my boots,' said Harris. 'When my dad died, it made me feel ready to say a word for these others.'

'You're a rum bloke, Harris,' said Brand. 'By God, you do me good.'

They sat together quietly in the room.

'I don't want to go to a literary type for a libretto,' said Harris. 'He wouldn't give me what I wanted.'

'What about old shag-bags, your pal, Winterburn?' said Brand. 'He's as near death as no matter.' Brand had met him one night with Harris. 'He's sorry all right. He'd knock you out a few stanzas to spare for your Arab refugees. No?' Harris shook his head. 'Would you go up and see my missus? I did ask you, didn't I? You won't get much sense out of me tonight.' He got up. 'Hang on a bit. Won't wake her if she's dropped off.'

Harris sat and listened to the clock ticking. He then walked across the room and started a metronome and tried to make the beats coincide. His chat with Brand had got him no further forward. The problem was still there. He wanted to communicate something definite to blokes like Brand on their beam-ends, who were too fagged and battered to understand the idea, but who'd get the music like comfort into their bones.

He plucked at the string of a viola lying in a case with the lid open. He grinned at a plaster, music-shop bust of Beethoven, lifted it and then blew into the hollow interior. It had done him some service to talk about his difficulties to Brand. That's what Cooke had meant when he'd said people should do some of your thinking for you. Once you'd put your idea into words it presented a simpler problem. Brand was a deuce of a time upstairs. Apart from the clock there was not a sound in the house. Harris lowered himself into a chair and took up Grove from the shelves. He'd look up Requiem. It was so still in the room that he let the book lie unopened on his knee, too idle to make the minute disturbance of the flick of a page. Brand had been gone a quarter of an hour.

Perhaps they were arguing upstairs as to whether he should visit. Perhaps Nance was unhinged again. Now Brand came in, harassed but smiling.

'Sorry I've been so long,' he said. 'I've been telling Nance about your Requiem.'

Harris stood up.

'Do you know,' said Brand, 'that's the first real conversation I've had with her this week. We don't seem to be able to spin anything out. It was a change.' He took Harris's arm. 'One should be able to talk... Why should you...? Come on up, Harris.' He made a wry, happy face.

The bedroom was unlike any Harris had known. The mirrors were bigger and clearer; the walls and coverlet matched and there were thick white rugs on the deep carpet. Money tells in a bedroom, Harris thought. Or waste of it.

Mrs. Brand lay back with a book in her hand. She did not look ill, and, in face, since her body was covered, she seemed more placid.

'Hello, there,' she said. 'Visiting the sick?'

'I don't think I should let these handsome men into your bedroom,' said Brand. 'Puts your temperature up.'

Harris began to move his lips politely into a smile, but saw that Mrs. Brand was staring unpleasantly across at her husband. When she noticed that Harris was observing her she relaxed with a kind of shrug.

'How are you feeling now?' asked Harris.

'John's been telling me about your Requiem,' she said, ignoring the question. 'It's going to be marvellous.'

'I thought Nance might help with the libretto,' said Brand. 'She's by way of being a poetess.'

'I'm not good enough,' she said. 'I'm like you, Mr. Harris,' she said. 'I'm not frightened of death; it's what comes before it. We are all dying, in a way.'

'Some quicker than others,' said Brand, laughing.

'Yes,' she said, 'quick and slow. You could have that, Mr. Harris; those who die in a minute and those who die all their lives. I should like them remembered.' She spoke to a far corner of the room.

'They ought to be well prepared, then,' said Brand. He was determined not to let the entertainment grow too grisly.

'Dying is not a preparation for death,' she said.

'Now there's a line for you to set, Harris,' said Brand. 'By God, I'll write that down. You could give that the four sorts, china.'

'I should like Mrs. Brand to help me,' said Harris. It seemed polite.

'I wish I could. Just tell me about it, will you? John, go downstairs, there's a dear. Mr. Harris is quite, quite safe with me.' There was a world of sanity in her last remark. It indicated that she could talk on Brand's own low, jovial level without trouble if she wanted. It spelt control. Brand went out.

'I shouldn't have sent him away,' she said, 'should I?'

'I suppose not.'

'But I want you to tell me what you've told him. We can talk about it afterwards. It'll be lovely when you've gone to talk to him and pretend I'm revealing secrets between us. I know I'm very silly, Mr. Harris. Now, hold my hand, and tell me.'

She stretched her fingers out like a child. Harris took them, and, embarrassed, explained dryly what he would like to do. She shut her eyes and listened. When he finished she still remained in the same position.

Now she was sitting upright in bed. The shawl, she seemed fond of the old-fashioned articles, was flicked away and her arms and shoulders were bare. She swayed a little and he could see far down into the cleft of her breasts. But there was no tremor of sexual excitement. There was an air of invalidism about her that did not exactly repel him, but held him away. He remembered kissing a girl, over twenty years ago, who had a cold and who smelt of menthol. She'd had a bit of silk rag tied round her neck. He had been uninterested; one does not make love to a disease. Once the idea of a body as a beautiful whole was lost, and the parts were visualized swarming with microbes, love became something unthinkable.

Suddenly Mrs. Brand opened her eyes.

'What gave you the idea?' she asked. 'In the first place. After all, a Requiem's for somebody who's dead, isn't it?'

'My father died a week last Sunday.'

'John never told me that. It's funny. Fancy not mentioning that. It's the important thing, isn't it? Come to think, Mr. Harris, you never mentioned it either.'

'I thought John would have told you.'

'And...?'

'Well, it might upset you, you know. No use harping on it.'

'That's exactly what you are going to do, isn't it?' she said. 'Why couldn't you mention that your father had died, and yet could talk about your Requiem? That's about death, isn't it? That's asking God to have mercy on somebody dead.'

'You brought the subject up.'

'I did,' said Mrs. Brand, 'yes. But it seems to me your Requiem must be a thin, vague, strangled affair if you can talk about it here, and yet skip the fact that your own father had died. Are you being honest?'

'You're ill, Mrs. Brand. You broached the subject and I went on.'

'Do you know what you're doing, Mr. Harris? You're saying, in effect, that the deaths of thousands of people all over the world won't upset me, but the death of one real old man, as unknown to me as any policeman shot in Cyprus,[13] is taboo because I know his son.'

'That's not quite…'

'Not quite, no. Not quite anything. You're either accusing me of having no imagination, or, and this is worse, you've none yourself and the thousand dyings you're celebrating mean absolutely damn-all to you. You've a streak of pity or something. You might as well set a requiem mass proper. You don't agree with it, but it sounds juicy and you've got your technique.'

She was excited, but Harris did not notice it.

'I'm a hypocrite, am I?'

'Well, aren't you?' She smiled, archly, playing a game.

'No. There's no man alive feels the death of unknown people more than that of his own kith and kin. It's not natural. I'd be a hypocrite if I claimed any other.'

'And yet you are prepared to set other people's emotions by the ears?'

'Do you mean,' he said, 'to tell me that Bach felt Christ's crucifixion more strongly than the death of his own youngsters?'

'They were perhaps the same. A son of God and a son of Bach. I don't know. I don't have any notion what it's like to write music. '

'My father's death,' he said, 'triggered this off.'

'Yes, yes,' she said, 'of course.' She was soothing him

'My father was alive,' he said, 'full of energy, seeing things, doing, wanting things and his heart just stopped.'

'Yes,' she said. 'His heart stopped. My boy only broke his arm.'

Harris stood up and gently wrapped the shawl round her shoulders. Then sat down again.

'I'm not very good at the bed-side manner,' he said. 'Every time we meet, we have words.'

'That's lovely, "have words". Why didn't you say "quarrel"?'

'Use,' he said. 'My mother always said that.'

'And you're a mother's boy? Did you write her a Requiem?'

'I wasn't ready,' he said gruffly.

She patted his head, rather sharply and absent-mindedly.

'We row,' she said, 'because we're in love a little.'

Harris felt his face flushing.

'Did you like me to say that?' she asked. 'Am I a forward hussy?' The cliché kept the air of banter, but he thought she was after information. Her wits might have been scattered, but they were scattered to collect intelligence from a wider field. She seemed hard, with her head screwed exactly on for her own purposes. He found it difficult to believe her own account of her neurosis, or her husband's of her behaviour. There was always something on, behind every twitch and start.

'Come on,' she said slowly. 'Let's hear from you.'

'No comment,' said Harris.

'That's not fair,' she said. 'I tell you I'm a little in love with you. You might confess the same back again, even out of politeness. Anyhow, it's true. You blushed like a boy.'

'Sorry,' Harris said.

'You're not very forthcoming. Do you think it's sin?'

'Do not adultery commit; Advantage rarely comes of it,' said Harris, lightly as he could.[14]

'Most men would be flattered when a nearly naked woman tells them she loves them. Are you a man at all?'

'Nothing doing,' said Harris.

'I hate you, Thomas Harris. You're a nasty inhuman puritan.'

'And that's that,' said Harris. 'Now let's talk about something else.'

'Yes, let's.' She sounded enthusiastic, like a schoolgirl invited to tennis.

'You can do something for me, if you like,' he said hesitantly. 'My step-mother is very lonely now my father's dead. You could visit her. It'll do her good. She'll think you're high society, and treat you like the Queen.'

'You'll turn me loose on her, with my tongue?' she asked mischievously.

'You'll behave yourself there. She'll see to that. But she'll be very sorry for you. That's what you want, isn't it?'

'I don't think I like you.'

'Will you go and see her? Take the kids, if you like, if you can manage them without a nanny.'

'Are you sending me to see a good woman?'

'I'm asking you to see my step-mother; that's all,' said Harris with a snap. 'If you don't want to go, don't make a song and dance of it.'

'I was really upset about Christopher,' she said. 'Any mother would be.'

'But most mothers wouldn't get the chance to lie on their backs acting the goat.'

'I know. Honestly, I know. I'm bad sometimes. I can feel...'

'Listen,' said Harris. 'I don't know whether you're ill or not. If I was certain I'd pull your nightie up and lace you.[15] I suppose that's what you want. Why don't you try to behave yourself?'

'I don't know what to do for the best.'

'Let your husband know that this visit's over.'

She sat in bed, quite still, pondering this and then rang a bell.

In a minute or two Brand came up.

'Well, doctor?' he said rubbing his hands. 'And how's the patient?'

'Cured,' said Harris stiffly. He was in no mood for badinage.

'He's done me good, John,' she said. 'And I'm going to do something for him in return. I'm going to write his libretto and visit his step-mother.'

'And when you've done,' said Brand in the manner of a lugubrious Lancashire comedian, 'tha can sweep t'snaw awaay.'

'Goodnight, Mr. Harris, and thank you very much,' she said. She held a hand straight out. It looked odd from a person sitting in bed, an out-of-doors gesture, something for the fully dressed. 'I'll try to get up tomorrow.'

'That's good,' said Harris. ''Bye.'

'I don't know about her,' said Brand, 'but you've put a bit of pep into me.'

They were walking down the wide staircase.

'Do you know, Harris,' said Brand, 'when you turn up here, it gives us a day or two's steady sailing. She talks to me as though I'm her husband. It's a bloody rest, mate, I can tell you.'

'This is only the third time I've been,' said Harris.

'Oh, well,' said Brand. 'Perhaps I'm as daft as she says she is. She often tells me she's in love with you, Harris. Did she tell you tonight? She's always threatening to. I tell her that I wish she was. Give her a decent hobby.'

'You want to get to bed,' said Harris.

'Oh, no,' said Brand. 'It'll be Harris's libretto and Harris's conversation until midnight, if I know anything about it.'

'I hope you won't mind this,' said Harris. 'Is she really ill?'

'Search me,' said Brand.

'But all these psychiatrists and so on you've had in, what do they think?'

'Yes. They say she's up the creek. I wish to God I knew. She can be a mischievous bitch if she wants. Makes a nice picture, doesn't it? "The lecher's wife".'

'You've just about had it for tonight, brother,' said Harris.

'You've done me good,' said Brand. 'I'm safe now from the gas-oven and my braces.'

They left it at that.

## 13.

TEN days later Harris received a libretto from Mrs. Brand.

With the half-dozen beautifully-typed copies was a letter which said that she and her husband had worked this out and had ideas about how it should be set. They wouldn't say what these were until Harris had worried through the script himself. The copies were to be tried out on his friends. There was also a message from Brand to say that he had reinforced *The Tempest* orchestra and that they were going to give a good account of themselves. Harris was to make alterations to the Requiem script, and send it back, when it would be revised.

The libretto was written in a sort of poetic prose; it was flowery, but rather more abstract than one would expect from such an account. It began with a prologue, which told the audience that they were involved in this, and the one certainty amongst them was that they would die. This was the lot of mankind. They were then invited to think what they were to do about it; to put it off, to make something of their time or bemoan humanity. Then a little episode followed in which Harris senior seemed to be speaking. He said that trees were green, that he enjoyed a pint, the light flashing on knitting needles, the love of women. He said he was old, that his heart was groggy and, despite appearance to the contrary, he deliberately took things steady. He did not, however, think about death, the consolations of religion and philosophy, and that death had surprised him when it came. 'I am one of the lucky ones,' he said, 'because I did not bend my mind or strain. Morbidity I hated.' Then came some comment on the provincialism of this view and this was answered by the widow who said her grief was the greater because her husband had not prepared her.

The script then went on to ask how this death had differed from the notable deaths of history; soldiers dying in victory, martyrs at the stake, statesmen for policy at the assassin's hand and then the thousand little deaths that were a concomitant of the death of a prince.

The world, it seemed, was full of death. This was not a statistical statement; it would be more precisely expressed if it said that the world seemed more packed with death than at any other time. An airman, it did not matter on which side, had been blown to bits in his plane; a Jew had been put out in a concentration camp; a Japanese by the atomic bombs; a child in

India had been starved; a Chinese drowned; a Russian had died by some abstract act of justice he did not understand; a Hungarian in the street; a Cypriot; a suicide in a rich community. The wild rush of news about the earth had made these the morning reading of Mr. Everyman in the civilised west.

In some ways, Mr. Everyman with his newspaper was responsible. Harris senior was responsible. Everyone who took things steady on his own account was responsible. A babel of argument broke out; everybody blamed everybody else and above all were the cries of the children who were too ignorant to accuse.

This uproar was stopped by Death himself who said that all must die; he would not say whether it was the end or a new translation, but advised them to come to terms with him and stoically bear what was inevitable. There was some comfort; they could see the next generation toddling about their feet. If men used their wits, and saw to it that the children were preserved from inhuman death, then men even took on a kind of immortality. Life added a plea, at this point, admitting the force of Death's argument but demanding a more cogent attitude of preparedness so that when the sun burnt up the earth, man's ingenuity would be ready to plan an escape in a new ark to a new place in the universe.

Harris senior reappeared and admitted that he had been wrong, but asked Death and Life about religion. Both refused to answer. If there was faith, an answer was not necessary; if certainty were admitted, faith became redundant and its complete value, the highest gift to humanity, lost.

The prologue then asked the audience where they stood, how they were prepared, what faith or God or gods they had, what fault they admitted in this death-wishing world. All the time the prologue was interrupted by voices of the dead, asking for vengeance, or reward, or renown, or pity, or hate and the work ended with a great chorus 'We are all mankind from the lowest ape-man to yourself, from the merest man-child to yourself, from the bloodiest victim to yourself, from the greatest victor to yourself, from the God-head crucified. Go out this night,' it said, 'and make your terms with the fire, the bullet, the fall-out, the unjust and the righteous judgement, the aching cancer. Lump of matter, make your choice, but do not deceive yourself or your brother. You are part of death's kingdom.'

The libretto shocked Harris. He didn't want a hymn in praise of brother death however trimmed with his own garnishings. On the other hand, there were dramatic possibilities. The very next post, he received another letter from Mrs. Brand telling him that this was only a sighting shot and that he was to collect opinions, have another talk with her and she'd start again.

He met Brand, by chance, or rather Brand saw him from his car and drew up.

'Lift?' said Brand. Harris got in. 'Well, how's the poem suit you?'

'Uh,' said Harris, 'well, er. A bit morbid, isn't it?'

'That's what I thought,' said Brand, 'when I read the typescript. But I tell you this, it was exciting while we were at it.'

'It might do,' said Harris, not enthusiastic.

'It's the way she thinks,' said Brand. 'And yet she got it down as cool as cucumber. Never seen her steadier. All that stuff about death just round the johnny-horner and she might have been writing that her heart was like a swinging brick or whatever it is.'

They went along in silence.

'There's a rum thing about it,' said Brand. He spoke seriously this time, almost nervously.

'Go on,' said Harris.

'Didn't you notice?' said Brand.

'No.'

'About your old man?' said Brand.

'What about him?'

'Well,' said Brand, 'she made him the villain of the piece, didn't she? It sounded as if it was his fault. She's not half got it in for him.'

'I didn't notice,' said Harris.

'You surprise me,' said Brand, very lightly. 'I told her you'd be round to wring her neck and that your father was a decent old stick, very like you in many ways. Do you know what she said?'

'No.'

'That's right, she said. He's just like Harris, ignorant.'

'And what do I do now?' said Harris. 'Jump through the sun-roof?'

'I thought you'd like to know,' said Brand.

'You sound as if you're fed up with her, and trying to get at her through me.'

Brand didn't answer that, but took Harris the rest of the way smiling.

Harris tried the script on the Friday Dining Club. Some of them were sitting at their table and Winterburn was with them.

'Would you literary gents do me a favour?' he asked.

They looked up and said nothing. They did not like interruptions. Then followed some little by-play, such as silent coughing fits and looking behind as if he were talking to somebody else.

'Try Hobson,' said the Scot, pointing to the raconteur.

'Ask Mortenson,' said Hobson, indicating the young man with the hair.

'He likes Kingsley Amis.'

'You want McManus for the all-round, reasoned, dialectical view,' said Mortenson. 'He'll analyse it.'

'Winterburn,' said McManus, with a rattle. 'He's just been saying there's no intellectual content in pedagogy.'

Winterburn looked away.

'One for each,' said Harris, pulling out the copies. He dropped four on the table. 'It's a libretto for a choral work. Or rather a first draft.'

'Do you want us to read all this?' said Hobson.

'It's about death,' said Mortenson. 'Here you are, Winterburn. Death. Read all abaht it.'

Winterburn did not pick his copy up.

'You can hang on to 'em,' said Harris. 'Read it tonight.'

'What's this word?' said McManus, lifting his copy and holding it to the light. 'Concernment? Do you mean "concern"?'

'Will you read it, Winterburn?' asked Harris.

No answer. Harris felt himself becoming angry.

'Are you deaf?' he said.

The others said nothing, but had put their typescripts down. There was a pause. Nobody did anything until Winterburn slowly slewed round and said,

'Why should I?'

'Harris would value your opinion,' said McManus in a friendly way.

'He can want,' said Winterburn; then suddenly he opened the papers. He read, breathing heavily. He went carefully through page one and flicked over the rest. Then he slowly pushed the script along the table away from him.

'Cock,' he said. 'Decadent cock. Delivered in the worst manner of a nonconformist extempore prayer.'

He rose and walked to the other side of the room.

On the following day, the Club were back with their criticisms. None thought very highly of the libretto. Mortenson conceded that it was an important subject, but felt the treatment was undistinguished. He had compiled a list of borrowings and literary echoes. Hobson, surprisingly, had written a long screed in his big slow handwriting. He said that death would do as a subject, but that what was said about it was trite and that the invitation to the audience to do something was mere question-begging. If the writer had any ideas, she would have dealt them out. If death was important, it was only important because it made you get on with life. Any interest the work might have was due only to contemporary events; fifty years would show what a rag-bag it was. A sort of Bulgarian Atrocities and Fashoda Incident, he said; and what if Elgar had been misguided enough to set that sort of old mush?

McManus had not written, but Harris thought he could guess his line, a stronger version of Hobson's. It was time that such mystical clap-trap was thrown out on to the garbage-heap. A backwash from Freud, etc., etc. Oddly enough, McManus did not talk like this at all. He tried to think himself into what was going on. Harris's father had died, this led to thoughts of death and the various fine or hopeless ends in the world. McManus said that such was a good subject, that it attempted to look round the world and relate it to an emotion strongly held. He hoped that Harris would set it powerfully.

However, McManus was a man with a conscience, and at every spare minute he withdrew with quirks and riders from his original position. It seemed to Harris that McManus was sorry he had no subject to suggest himself and felt that Harris was capable of making a success of this, but that everybody would have been happier had the subject been more forthright and healthy. His doubting, legalistic modesty intrigued.

After school, Harris saw McManus signalling with forefinger, and moved across to kiss the rod again.

McManus still wore his dusty gown; he was carefully sorting piles of exercise books.

'Your friend Winterburn is in there again,' said McManus, nodding towards the head's room.

'What's up now?' said Harris.

'Winterburn went into town this dinner-time. He should have been on duty. Leaman was waiting for him.'

'Why doesn't he leave the poor devil alone?' said Harris.

McManus sighed. He was everybody's friend. He shook his head.

'Now, that script of yours? There are certain passages in it that don't quite measure up either to the general philosophical trend of the whole work and in fact clash…'

The headmaster opened the door, looked round, closed the door. He did not seem pleased.

'Yes,' said Harris. 'You were saying?'

'Ah, now, where was I? Yes, if you look closely…'

'Mr. Harris.' It was Leaman's voice. Harris turned round. 'Could you come to my room for a minute?' He was usually politer than this.

Harris followed him.

Leaman pushed through his door and rushed for his chair. Winterburn was standing in front of the desk, his face a nasty red.

'Now, Winterburn,' said Leaman, 'would you be so good as to repeat what you have just said to me.' He spoke breathlessly, but in a harsh, staccato way;

a lieutenant-colonel's 28 days' voice.[16]

Winterburn did not answer; he moved his big shoes heavily about on the carpet.

'Well, Winterburn?'

No answer. Winterburn was now rubbing a thumb rapidly up and down the seam of his trousers. Leaman waited.

'Well, if you haven't the courage to repeat what you've said, I shall have to do it for you.' Leaman spoke as he addressed the boys from his rostrum, distantly. 'Harris, have I ever spoken to you about Winterburn?'

'Yes, sir,' said Harris. 'Once.'

'There you are then,' shouted Winterburn. He seemed to be dancing with excitement.

'Control yourself, Winterburn, for heaven's sake,' said Leaman, in a tired drawl.

'I'm not going to be ...'

'Shut up,' said Leaman. His voice was even quieter.

'I've got a right to say what I damn well like,' said Winterburn. 'And if I've got something to say, I say it straight out to a man's face. I don't go creeping round my toadies whispering.'

'Winterburn, will you please understand that while I am headmaster of this school...'

'I don't care who you are. I'll tell you one bloody thing. You're not in the army now.'

Leaman sat back and smiled, a handsome, arrogant, well-dressed man.

'All right, Winterburn, go on then. Have your say.'

For a minute Harris thought Winterburn was going to clamber over the desk to get at the head.

'Ph,' said Winterburn, 'you're not worth the breath.'

Leaman still leaned back, with his legs crossed, at ease. He began to bite the end of his thumb in a placid way. When he was sure Winterburn was not going to start again, he turned towards Harris.

'Winterburn believes,' he said, 'that you and other members of the staff have reported him to me for incompetence. As far as you are concerned, is that true?'

'No,' said Harris. He wished he could have said 'yes'.

'There you are, then, Winterburn,' said Leaman.

'What do you expect?' said Winterburn mildly.

'Are you saying that Harris is a liar?' said the head, determined not to let the point go.

'Yes,' said Winterburn.

The headmaster slapped his hands on to the desk, letting his breath out. Nobody spoke. Harris stood still, sorry for Winterburn, who also did not move.

'Harris interrupted one of my lessons,' said Winterburn at last.

'Chuck it,' said Harris.

'I know you don't want me to say anything about it. I don't blame you. But you've been blabbing, so what do you expect?' Winterburn was facing Harris now, his back to Leaman. He looked Harris straight in the eye. 'He came in,' said Winterburn, turning round, 'to quieten my class, and he beat up one of the boys. That's why he wants me gagged. He's only told you half the story.'

'Was your class noisy?' said Leaman.

'That's not the point,' said Winterburn. 'He set about one...'

'Was your class noisy?' said Leaman sharply.

'I suppose so.'

'Did Mr. Harris quieten them down for you?'

'He beat Blay,' said Winterburn, 'and then reported me to you.'

'Sometimes, Winterburn,' said Leaman, 'I begin to doubt if you're in your right mind. Don't you know who your friends are?'

'I know this,' said Winterburn, 'that you're not one of them. Why don't you say straight out that you're going to get me the sack?'

The headmaster looked down in embarrassment at his blotting pad.

'Why don't you?' said Winterburn loudly.

Leaman looked up. His eyes were bright blue.

'Winterburn,' he said, 'I am going to send in an adverse report on you to the director.'

Winterburn staggered.

'Well, that's something,' he said.

'I've covered up quite long enough,' said Leaman. 'You're not in a fit state to have charge of young boys...'

'Save it,' said Winterburn. 'Don't practise the report on me.'

'That's all then,' said Leaman. 'Thank you very much.'

It looked for a minute as if Winterburn were going to begin again, but he bundled himself out of the door, leaving it open. They could hear his footsteps on the corridor.

'That's about the limit,' said Leaman. Harris looked away from the door and at him. The headmaster was sweating and white. The handsome mountaineer, the clean-cut colonel had gone; there was a man tried to the extreme, who had been forced to do what he hated.

'Give him another chance,' said Harris. It took him all his time to get the words out. He'd never been able to talk to Leaman as man to man, to get past the official. 'He doesn't know what he's saying.'

'If ever you become a headmaster,' said Leaman, 'you'll realise that there comes a time when you have to take action.' He was recovering.

'I know...'

'You don't know, Harris. You're thinking of Winterburn. His wife's left him. Oh, yes, I know that. But I have to weigh one matter against another, and my first concern's for the school.' The head's blue eyes were raised. 'As a matter of fact, I'd thought he'd shown some improvement lately and I was going to let things slide, but I can't after this.'

'You can,' said Harris. 'Fetch him in tomorrow and tell him so. He's frightened to death.'

'He'd construe it as weakness on my part.'

'It doesn't matter. If you can get him to pull himself...'

'Harris,' said Leaman, 'listen. He should have been on duty today. He went into town. Knowing Winterburn, I expect he forgot if he ever knew. But it's my job to speak to him about it. He said it was persecution and that all my toadies were out to get him, that if it had been somebody else it would have been covered up and nothing said, but his face didn't fit and I was determined to get rid of him.'

'Let him say what the hell he likes,' said Harris. 'It's no matter.'

'If it were anybody else but Winterburn, I would,' said the head. 'But he won't keep his mouth shut. I can't afford trouble of that sort.'

'In other words, his face doesn't fit,' said Harris.

The headmaster jerked up, startled.

'I'm trying to be fair, Harris,' he said. 'I don't know why you stand up for him. I thought he wouldn't speak to you. Um, one does hear things.'

'Winterburn's right then.'

'Oh, grow up, Harris. You get fifty men around and some of them will talk.'

'And some listen.'

'Yes, Harris. I could be worse. I like to know what's happening to the staff.'

'Wouldn't it be a good idea,' said Harris, 'if you took it they were all doing their best?'

'It wouldn't. They aren't.'

'Couldn't you give that impression?'

'Harris, you don't find it easy to talk to me, do you? Oddly enough, neither does Winterburn. He says outrageous things but in a sort of shorthand of his usual self. I suppose it's my job; shall we call it an occupational risk?'

Harris couldn't answer the head's joke.

'I'd like to say something to you, if I may,' said Leaman.

'Yes, sir.'

'You're making quite a name for yourself, aren't you? Things are panning out nicely. You aren't thinking of leaving us yet?'

'No.'

'I shall be sorry if you do.' The headmaster frowned. 'Oh, yes. Everything's coming right for you and, well, you want to share your good fortune with the world. You're creating something, winning chips for yourself. I'm stuck here, to this desk.'

'Yes, sir. I don't...'

'It's not likely I shall leave, Harris. I'm here, keeping this place going. I can't afford to act as generously as you feel.'

'Don't you wish you could?' said Harris.

'That's impossible. I'm a realist. I expected you to tell me my job was creative, but it isn't. Too much paper-work, too many hole-and-corner jobs, too much staff-room politics to disregard. I cannot even deceive myself now when some boy or team does well. I'm not responsible. I'm not even the catalyst. The lab-boy's more like it.' The headmaster took out an elegant pipe and stuffed it with tawny, expensive tobacco. 'It embarrasses you to hear me say this, doesn't it? You want to side with Winterburn and the great unwashed? Against me and the jacks-in-office?'

'What are you going to do about Winterburn, sir?' said Harris.

'Oh,' said the head. 'That's different. Now we're off the generalisations.'

'Yes?' said Harris.

'Then,' said Leaman, 'I'm going to do what I said I'd do.'

It wasn't the expected answer. The periphrasis was slightly unpleasant.

'What would you do, Harris?' said the head. 'Honestly, now.'

'Leave him alone. At least for a bit.'

'Are you sure?' said Leaman. 'If you were in my place.'

'Yes.'

'When he said you hit that boy, I didn't mind. But do you know why the committee say you're not allowed to beat? It's because of the Winterburns. If you hit a boy, Harris, that's one thing; but if Winterburn started, I'd as soon see a tiger loosed in the classroom. Winterburn's quite right; one set of rules is permissible for one man, and not for another. That's cynical, isn't it? It turns a headmaster into a judge. And if he's the slightest inch out, and he always is in somebody's eyes, than he's accused of favouritism or not allowing a face to fit. That's how it is, Harris. You play with notes, a thing I couldn't do. I play with human beings, a thing nobody can do.' The head stopped. 'Winterburn upsets me, I see. Or perhaps garrulity's setting in.'

Harris didn't reply again. He was stuck for words.

'Right you are, then, Harris. Thanks very much.'

'Will you think again about Winterburn, sir?' Harris forced himself to say it.

'No. I'm sorry. No.'

'Goodnight, sir.'

'I've made up my mind now.'

Harris went out into the corridor. In the cloakroom, Winterburn's gown hung untidily on a hanger. A. E. Winterburn, M.A. Harris straightened it. It was all he could do.

# 14.

MRS. BRAND kept her promise to visit Mrs. Harris senior.

The arrangement worked better than Harris had hoped. Mrs. Harris saw in her young visitor something of the high-life to which her incursion into the bottom-end of the middle class, in Elias Jones's shop, had attracted her. But here it was more than a sketch. As Mrs. Jones she had spoken, in the way of business, with the well-dressed ladies who arrived in cars and had walked on Sunday afternoons past their houses with conservatories and plate-glass windows. She had, however, not come to grips with them. Now Mrs. Brand had children and she knew them by name. That was no great improvement; but she knew that one was hard on shoes, another delicate and had to be kept out of draughts. She learnt what Mr. Brand liked for his tea, and what his father did at weekends. By proxy, she became one of the privileged.

She prepared for Mrs. Brand's visits. Her speech acquired a gentility that William Harris would have laughed out of the house. Mrs. Freer, who had been in and out, kindness itself, was not allowed to share the new prize. She was introduced, once and curtly, and though Mrs. Brand was staple diet for backdoor conversation, Mrs. Freer was not permitted the real thing.

With Mrs. Brand, the situation was equally delightful. She admired admiration, and met it too little at home or with her husband's friends. Further, it was as if she had been introduced into an alien society. She enjoyed the reminiscences of shop and pit; they were as exciting to her as revelations of life in Samoa or Sumeria. And, both women, of course, had a common interest in Thomas Harris.

Harris now called regularly at his step-mother's, and sometimes found Mrs. Brand there. If her car was not outside, he observed, to his surprise, that he was disappointed. They'd discuss the libretto, while Mrs. Harris knitted, and Mrs. Brand would take Harris back.

All this was fine. Preliminary head-work was still going into the script. He had reported his colleagues' comment, and Mrs. Brand had looked anxious.

'The trouble is,' she said, 'that they won't look at your subject. We've either got to deal with it or not. They prefer to talk about life, and that's sensible in the main, but we're not being particularly sensible and this is not our whole life. So, let's be serious. Or give the idea up.'

She spoke in her usual retreating manner, but was clearly not to be easily moved. She was so certain that she could allow notions of common-sense; indeed she put them forward herself. She did so, however, with the air of one who knew that these ideas carried no weight. 'I know,' she said, 'that when I've finished this you'll spend all the best time of several months working on it. And if you're doubtful at the start, you'll soon be convinced once the grind's on that you're wasting your time. So make your mind up here and now. It doesn't matter to me. I've enjoyed myself and that's that.'

Harris had no idea how to answer. In a way, he felt like setting the work; in fact, he already had musical ideas down in his notebook 'Work for Chorus and Orchestra.' But the strictures of his friends carried weight. They represented the sort of people who'd hear the requiem, and he feared that their opinion, the opinion of unbiased, healthy men, would kill it stone-dead, however brilliant his part. On the other hand, Mrs. Brand's certainty was a challenge. After he'd talked ten minutes with her, he'd be sure he must get on with it.

The dilemma was not pressing.

His preoccupation with the new work had sparked off other interests. The string trio was finished; he'd written an organ suite for Attenborough's young man, Dr. Morley. He knocked off another batch of songs, which were snatched up by Forde, and he was now certain that a cello sonata wasn't far off.

Mrs. Brand didn't force the libretto on him, but he noticed that she always carried a copy of the script, brought up-to-date with her. If he mentioned it, she'd make him sit at the table and carefully go over what she'd done.

'Don't you think,' said Harris once, 'that you could leave me a bit of thinking?'

'You're not serious, yet.'

'How do you know?' he asked.

She was standing over him, like a schoolma'am. Mrs. Harris was upstairs, pottering round.

'This means something to me,' she said. 'To you, well, you've not even decided to start.'

'If you only knew how much...'

'You've had long enough,' she said. 'Either you start, or I throw this in the fire.'

She walked across and held it by one corner over the flames.

'You'll scorch it,' said Harris mildly. He was unprepared for this.

'What's your answer?' she said.

'You're not getting a thing about this as well, are you?' said Harris.

She lifted the pages back.

'What if I am?' she said. Her voice was innocent and violent.

'It won't do you any good,' said Harris, roughly.

'Nor you.' She put the papers on the table. 'You go away and make your mind up,' she said, 'one way or the other.'

'Hold your horses,' said Harris.

She put her hands on his shoulders. He could feel her fingers gripping hard.

'You'll spoil the padding,' he said.

She did not speak; dug in with her finger ends. They could hear Mrs. Harris coming down. When the stairs-door was opened, the old lady stood watching them from the bottom step.

'You make a pretty pair,' she said. 'It's like something from the films.'

It cleared the air, with Mrs. Harris smiling. 'Pretty' was her superlative.

When they got outside into the car, Mrs. Brand resumed the argument.

'I haven't pressed you so far,' she said. 'I'm going to start now.'

'Look here,' said Harris. 'If I'm to do this, I'll do it in my own way and in my own time.'

'You'll never do it, then. You haven't the wit.'

'Right,' said Harris. 'Let's leave it.'

'You don't care for me,' she said. Caution was thrown on one side. 'When you aren't here there's a great lump of lead inside me. When I turn into this street, I tremble like a leaf. You know why, don't you? I love you.'

'Is that why you come here?' he asked. The question, he felt, gave him away.

'I like to visit your step-mother. I like her. I don't like you. I love you.'

'Well, well.'

'Is that all you can say?' She had her hands round the steering-wheel now as if she were touching ninety.

'I don't want to be unkind,' he said.

'Go on.' She flung the words at him, poisoned darts.

'Home, James,' he said. He was tired.

It worked this time. She let the clutch in and drove off. Her handling of the car was good but unpleasant. Her technique did not allow her to make the mistakes she wanted to perpetrate. When they stopped at Harris's place, he fetched out one of his ending-phrases.

'Fine it down a bit,' he said. 'It's too fancy yet.'

He enjoyed these. 'Cut the adjectives in half.' 'Work more drama into the situations.' 'Simplify the language.' He thought them up without real relevance to the text, and she obeyed. Next time they met she would show him how instructions had been followed. It put off the day when the libretto would be complete, and, worse, Harris thought, it made a date, arranged an excuse for the next meeting.

*The Tempest* was over now. It had created ill-feeling. The local paper had given its usual column of praise; Beauchamp's ideas were noted and a series of useless encomiums in journalese flowed beneath. There had followed, however, a long article, over the initials W. E. M., about Harris's music, which praised this at the expense of 'cheap tricks and savage hacking at the text'. W. E. M., was Dr. Morley, Attenborough's protegé, and it was thought, by Beauchamp at least, that Harris had put Morley up to this attack. Correspondence was still going on, and in the Shakespeare Society Harris's introduction was regarded as a fatal mistake.

Not that this bothered Harris. The business was over and done in his eyes. If people wanted a private war about it, let 'em get on. He seemed, however, to have noticed a change in Cooke's attitude. He'd met him several times during the week of the performance, and he'd been affable, if oblique.

'And how's our other little business, eh, Master Harris?'

'I'm working.'

'And so am I, boy. If you only knew the half. Blood out of stones. Phoo!' He blew his lips out and laughed.

But since the article, he'd lost his playfulness. He turned up at a Bach rehearsal, expressed himself satisfied, and then turned on Attenborough and Harris.

'I hope you two behave yourselves,' he said. They didn't reply.

'Who's W. E. M.?' he asked. 'No, don't bother, Attenborough. I know. You keep that monkey chained to his organ, mister.'

'The article was very fair, I thought,' said Attenborough. 'He's young yet, you know. Perhaps he was rather too forthright, but that's a juvenile fault. He'll learn.'

'He'd better,' said Cooke.

'I had no hand in the matter,' said Attenborough. 'Of that I can readily assure you.'

'I'm not accusing anybody,' said Cooke. 'Don't rock your boat. That's all.'

'And if we do?' said Harris.

'It'll sink,' said Cooke.

'I didn't know you were temperamental,' said Harris. Attenborough tried to look disengaged.

'You hardly know you're born yet, Harris,' said Cooke.

He went away.

'You oughtn't to rile him,' said Attenborough. 'He's, er, well, he's not well.'

'What's up with him?' said Harris.

'The common failing. Overwork,' said Attenborough. 'His job's as exacting as yours. Don't forget that, Harris. Try to put yourself in the position of the other man.'

'What good is this doing you?' asked Harris. 'Cooke's not here to hear it.'

'Sometimes, Harris, I dislike your manner.' Attenborough heaved himself into his musicianly top-coat.

'I'm sorry,' said Harris.

'Ah, my boy. Your heart's right. I know that. But we must be careful.'

Harris looked round for the Gestapo.

At school, Winterburn was more cheerful. It was as if his period of waiting was done, and the new reality bearable. He said as much to the Club.

'Our friend won't be quite so pleased with himself. When the inspector comes, I imagine I'll be able to knock off a decent period or two. It's very hard to sack a man for inefficiency.'

'Don't harangue the inspector,' said McManus diffidently.

'I shan't be such a fool,' said Winterburn. 'I like the head; I enjoy teaching; I have some difficulty but time will iron the wrinkles from the cloth.' He laughed at his expression. 'I prepare my lessons carefully. You never know. When's our visitor coming?' He asked Harris the question.

'I don't know,' said Harris, surprised. 'Should I?'

'He hasn't told *you?'* said Winterburn.

'No.'

'Polish your boots every day now,' said Winterburn. 'We want a good show when he sends you to open the inspectorial car-door.'

Harris was sorry, not angry, and wished to prolong the conversation.

'Give us a match, Winterburn,' he said.

Winterburn jerked angrily upright, thought better and handed over the box.

'Thanks, mate,' said Harris.

Winterburn watched him put the light to his cigarette.

'Take one or two,' he said. 'You're sure to need a drag.'

'Thanks,' said Harris. 'I've got to fumigate the stockroom.'

He passed the matches back.

'Coming for a bit of a stroll, Winterburn?' he asked.

Winterburn looked at the clock.

'Quarter to two,' he said. 'It's hardly worth getting up.'

That conversation left Harris pleased. He was cheerful through his first period, an unusual thing now. The burst of creative energy left little time for teaching properly. He knew how to handle his classes with the minimal wear-and-tear to himself, but he became anxious towards the end of the day to be off to do some real work. However, he made a virtue of necessity and told himself that time passed in school was valuable; it gave the subconscious room to expand and prevented him from clearing himself out too violently. He didn't know if either of these were true, but he was keen on these small attempts at the psychology of aesthetics. They were the full stops which gave your hand a rest.

Brand came round to see him one evening.

'I'm not stopping,' said Brand. 'I know you're busy.' Harris, in fact, was eating his tea. 'I'm just on my way home.'

'You made a marvellous job of that *Tempest,*' said Harris.

'Didn't like it much,' said Brand.

'What? My score? Your performance?'

'Score.'

'What's up with it?' asked Harris.

'Dunno,' said Brand. 'Didn't click. That's all. Perhaps it was hearing yon keg-handed crowd scrape at it put me off.'

'Spoken like a Cooke,' said Harris.

'I'm learning,' said Brand.

They sat still. Brand seemed ashamed to have committed himself.

'Your wife's made a hit with my step-mother,' said Harris, friendly.

'Yes.'

'I see her quite often up there. She's grooming me for the Requiem.'

'So I hear.'

'Does she seem any better?' asked Harris.

'You should know. You see as much of her as I do.'

'Me?' said Harris.

'She's always tearing off up to your mother's. I wish she'd put in a bit of time on her own family.'

'Hey,' said Harris, 'what's this?'

Once more there was a pause. It was hard work keeping the conversation going. Brand hadn't said what he'd come for.

'I'm not allowed in on the Requiem now,' said Brand. 'We started together. She's taken over.'

'Does your wife ever do anything steadily?' asked Harris.

'What's that to you?' said Brand sharply.

'Oh, nothing, nothing. I just wondered. She seems as obsessed with this as she was with atom bombs a month or two ago.'

'Same thing,' said Brand. 'You're doing no good encouraging her.'

'What am I ...?'

'Stop worrying her with it. She might drop the whole shoot.'

'Would she? She's more likely to get another thing about that.'

'Well, let her. And I'll deal with it myself, without your help.'

Harris watched Brand with exaggerated ease.

'Look here, Brand,' he said. 'Now, just what's wrong?'

'Nothing.'

'You're not picking a quarrel, are you?'

'And why should I?'

'You might think I've alienated your wife's affections. Is that the phrase?'

'I don't think that,' said Brand. He spoke in a lumpy, leaden voice. 'All I think is that you're doing no good driving her on as she is being driven. What she wants is a bit of peace and quiet, a sit-down, a breather... She doesn't want the local genius kicking her up the wall. She's there already.'

'What do I do?'

'Drop the Requiem. If it's no better than *The Tempest*, you won't lose much. You're first-class on chamber-works, but, well, you've got your limits.'

'Suppose,' said Harris, 'I went on with it myself. With the libretto as it is, or altered to suit me, would that do?'

'Use your head,' said Brand. 'Once you're at it; she's at it. No, it's "drop it", for good and all.'

'And keep away from her?' asked Harris.

'Why should you? Just tell her you've scrapped the idea.'

'You tell her,' said Harris. The schoolboy expression comforted him.

'Right, I will.'

'And what do you think she'll say? At one time you were all for getting me to find some interest for her; now, you're dead against it.'

'I've got to do my best. It may be rotten.'

'You'll tell her that I've dropped it?'

'Yes, I will. Thanks, Harris.'

Harris gloomily looked at the floor. He didn't particularly want to get on with the Requiem, but it seemed the most stupid folly to throw out any chance of trying it just on a mere word in a chance conversation.

'Suppose,' said Harris, 'I can't chuck it.'

'You said you would.'

'Did you, Mr. Brand,' said Harris heavily, 'never hear of temptation?'

'Come off it,' said Brand. 'Your head's several sizes too large as it is.'

'And then there's Cooke.'

'You can set something else. I'm not stopping you writing music. If you want my honest opinion you won't get anywhere with choral works, but that's neither here nor there. Do something else. Just don't get my wife involved.'

Harris thought again.

'I ought to think about this,' he said.

'Yes,' said Brand. 'You ought to have done some thinking about it long enough ago.'

'Is that all you came to see me about?' said Harris.

They looked at each other.

'Harris,' said Brand. 'I realise, old man, what I've asked you to do.'

'Uh.'

'You don't want a speech, do you? I'll make it right with you, don't you fret yourself.'

'Brand,' said Harris, 'had you any idea of asking me to do this when you first came in?'

A smirk of embarrassment crossed Brand's face.

'To tell you the honest truth,' he said.

'Oh, ah,' said Harris.

Brand's mouth opened, and he forced a smile.

'I had thought of it,' he said, 'before. Often enough, really. But I didn't realise when I walked in that door tonight that I was going to ask you.'

'I thought as much,' said Harris.

'I want to be straight,' said Brand.

'You want your brains testing,' said Harris. 'I've spent hours of serious work on this thing and you expect me to throw it over for some idea that's this minute flitted across your bat-brain. Where's your sense of proportion, man?'

'Which do you consider more important,' said Brand steadily, 'to write a masterpiece or drive my wife mad?'

'Don't act the goat,' said Harris.

Brand blew out his cheeks.

'And I tell you something else,' said Harris. 'Your wife hit the nail on the head when she told me that you thought she was ill worrying about your chasing other women. Have you settled that bit of bother?'

'As a matter of interest,' said Brand, 'I'm now as pure as the driven snow.'

'For how long?'

'Until death or Harris's Requiem do us part. Amen,' said Brand.

Harris's anger had drilled into his cheekbones. He felt the red fire of his face. As they sat, saying nothing, he found himself steady again, subnormal, tired, aware that the pair of them had changed positions. First Brand had been seriously angry, and then like a comic turn, they'd exchanged masks. Harris thinking back realised how like Winterburn's his conversation had been over the last few minutes.

Brand was buttoning his overcoat, pulling on his driving gauntlets.

'Well,' he said, 'that's over.'

'You don't think I can bring this off?' said Harris.

'No, I don't.'

'I shan't know until I've tried. Surely you can see that.'

'My eyes are opened,' said Brand with unction. 'Cheerio.'

'I've got to try,' said Harris.

'Yes,' said Brand. 'Good old No. I. You're like everybody else.'

'Do you really think,' said Harris quietly, 'we could do any good?'

'Dunno.'

'Do you care for your wife?'

'Dunno.' Brand's expression was ironically cheerful. 'You tell me.'

'I've never seen you before as you were when you first came in,' said Harris. He wanted to check Brand.

'And what does that make me?'

'It shook me. I thought something like this: "young gold pants has woken up to himself." And I didn't like it. I didn't want to see it.'

Brand bit his lips. He was chalk-white and drew his glove back and forward across his face. He was like a man recovering from a jolt in the solar plexus. It seemed that Harris's words had reduced him, shrunken him. The biting on his lips was so violent that Harris, scared to see the bloodless flesh under the teeth, flailed round for something to say. But it was Brand who spoke first.

'You know those gob-stopper pills,' he said, 'that vets blow down cows' throats; you take a couple.' His voice was shaky.

'I don't know what to do,' Harris said.

'Do as you like.'

'I don't know what I like,' said Harris.

'Well, do the other thing, then,' said Brand. He laughed and walked dizzily for the door.

'Will you come and talk to me again?' Harris said.

'Like a father,' said Brand, and went out.

Harris crawled into his chair, licked. He wanted to groan out loud, to translate his state into some communicable sound. The butter on his toast soaked or congealed; the tea in the pot stewed and cooled. He lounged for an hour with his arms dangling to the floor.

It took him ten minutes to get down the MS of 'Work for Orchestra and Chorus'. He looked over it without seeing it, all the time giving Brand the answers that he hadn't thought of. It was hopeless. He took his pen out, scribbled a maltese cross with dots in the margin, made it a flag, then the top of a sky-scraper, filled in the windows, drew oblongs of cars in the street. He crossed the lot out.

He had been working on the wife's lament, with the shrill voices of a women's choir, and sharp thoughtless shouts of children, while in the background men were bawling 'Gaudeamus Igitur' in a drunk jazz over a nasty, buzzing fugue. He'd hardly started; it was enormous.

He looked, still scribbling across the sky-scraper street. This idea was interesting. It got him going.

Exactly seventy minutes later he remembered Brand, thought about him coldly, pushed him without trouble out of his head and went on with his work.

## 15.

A WEEK or two later, Harris received a letter from Mrs. Cooke, demanding an interview.

She arrived in a very large car, was inspected by Sanderson and humbly shown upstairs. Sanderson was disappointed that he had no doors to fling open for the 'magnificent lady', Harris had tidied his room and when Mrs. Cooke was shown in was surprised again by her beauty. The terms of her letter had been stiff, but the handwriting large and untidy. This had in some way helped him to forget what she looked like, so that when he sat facing her he felt at a disadvantage.

'I don't expect to keep you long, Mr. Harris,' she said. Harris told her he would be delighted to help. She stared at him as if he'd proposed to jump out of the window.

'I see, then, that you've no idea why I've called to see you.'

She delivered this in a manner that appeared to Harris significant, as if by the right word he could dispose of preliminaries. He did not know the word.

'No. I'm afraid not.'

She took in breath.

'You are not going to be awkward,' she said, and paused.

'I'm sorry,' said Harris.

'You know perfectly well why I ...' again the stop, the invitation to do something.

'This could go on for a long time,' said Harris cheerfully. He enjoyed looking at a beautiful woman, running his eye over cheekbone, breast, shoulder, thigh. Bending forward he picked up the poker and fiddled with the fire.

Mrs. Cooke looked round the room as Harris squatted. There was no arrogance in her scrutiny, mere interest.

'You are not very perceptive,' she said.

'No?' said Harris. He felt like putting on a fake foreign accent.

'I have come about my friend, Nancy Brand,' said Mrs. Cooke. 'You are making unwarrantable, that is, you are attempting...' She stopped. 'I am not putting this clearly. Let's begin again. You are either committing adultery with her or trying to do so.'

'That's plain,' said Harris.

'You admit it?'

'No.'

'Then I shall have to point out to you, Mr. Harris, that your attentions to Mrs. Brand are being talked about.'

Harris shrugged.

'You may wonder how I'm concerned.'

'I may well,' he said.

'I am a close friend of both Brands. I think I know her as well as anybody. Don't imagine, Mr. Harris, that I'm not broadminded. Or that I'm doing this to get a front seat at any scandal that's going. But since her husband spoke to me last week about this, and you'll admit that John's not the sort of person to go scattering needless confidences about, I decided to come and say what I'm going to say to you.' She stopped, nodded at the fire, held a hand towards it momentarily and went on, 'I am trying to be as fair as I can. You've forced me into plain speaking. I hardly know you, Mr. Harris, and I don't in any way propose to judge you. I hope you understand that. I am trying to use words as clearly as I can.'

'You sound to me,' said Harris, 'as if you're translating them from some foreign language.'

She had begun to assume an air of quiet acquiescence to the sensible remark she had expected Harris to make. When she heard what he said she was taken aback. It was obvious that she was no hand at argument. For a moment she thought, and appeared to do so. It was delightful to watch. There was none of the grimacing and hair-raking of a schoolboy at a hard sum. She sat quite still, except that she made slight movements of her right forefinger as if ticking off what she had said and considering how Harris could have arrived at this conclusion. It was all very elegant; it was a poem; it was stupid.

'That's as may be.' She made it schoolma'amish to cover her unease. 'You see, Mr. Harris, Nancy Brand is not normal. She needs to be very carefully watched because even under the most favourable circumstances she's likely to make herself seriously ill. And it's not as though there is the woman herself. There are the children. Though, Mr. Harris, if you'd have known her, as I did, a young high-spirited girl, you would want to save her for her own sake.'

'Has Brand complained?' said Harris.

'Confided rather.' She smiled as if she had made the most exact correction. 'And I had to come to see you. I am throwing myself on your generosity. We've only met once, and I had the impression you did not like me. That's so, isn't it? Though perhaps it wasn't so much myself you disliked as your idea of what I represented. '

She stopped again. Harris himself thought her last sentence rather good. He did not say so.

'So I came along to ask you to be careful. Or,' she fairly wriggled with excitement, 'to make the situation crystal clear to you. You may not understand. You are immersed in your work. You may not have heard what people have said.'

'What people?' said Harris.

'Several sources. Most you wouldn't know. But I think you can believe me. I ask you to.' She leaned earnestly, gracefully forward. 'And scandal's a heady draught. For poor Nancy. She needs quietness, soothing.'

'What do these sources say?' said Harris. He was hot under the collar.

'Nothing much, as yet. The two of you are often together. Nancy looks excited. You're a dark horse. You know how these things go. There's no chapter and verse, exactly. Neat little touches.'

'And who takes notice of this tittle-tattle?'

'Plenty of people. You're a somebody now, Mr. Harris. You've made a mark. I know that to yourself you're the same fellow, carpet-slippers and pipe, but for good or bad you're a target for scandal. They like to pass on hints about you; it shows they're in the know. And I don't mean "your enemies" by "they". This town and this world are full of busybodies who like to be one up on the Jones about men like yourself. It's a score for them. They don't mean any harm.'

'All very fine and handsome,' said Harris, 'but...'

'One minute, Mr. Harris, before you tell me to mind my own business. This climate of scandal is growing. You can be as gruff and bluff as you like about it, but Nancy Brand can't. It might even bolster your ego, but she's a broken bit of a child.'

'A what?' said Harris.

'She has no defences against this. And, ironically enough, the fact that you claim you are both innocent makes matters worse. Suppose you were in love, she could turn and lean on you. She'd give up much, but she'd win much in return. As it is, she is likely to lose the sympathy of her husband, and you, quite innocently, of course, and be forced back upon her own resources, which aren't there. She depends, you see. She does not exist in her own right.'

They looked hard at each other.

'Mr. Harris,' she said, 'do you get what I'm driving at?'

'Yes,' said Harris, 'unfortunately I do.'

'Well, then,' and she smiled and put her hands together, caressing herself.

'You sit there,' said Harris as amicably as he could, 'for one reason. To enjoy yourself. If I said to you, "Describe a mousetrap in detail for me," you'd soon find yourself in difficulties, I can tell you. And in my view, nobody but Almighty God can speak of a person as you've done tonight. You don't know what makes Mrs. Brand tick any more than I do. And your claim that you can is as bogus as the language you've couched it in.' She half stood. 'No, Mrs. Cooke. Don't interrupt me. You've had your bang at the big analysis. I'll have mine. You're here to poke and pry because you like it. In other words, you're here as I told you to enjoy yourself. And I'll get this in, while I'm at it; you won't enjoy yourself at my expense.'

Mrs. Cooke had sat down. Harris's outburst did not appear to affect her. She seemed to concentrate on assuming the most beautiful pose she could in the chair. Harris might have been some Victorian poetaster spilling his musical syllables of half-baked passion at some lady of rank, who, herself, only half-enchanted, was intent on forming some even more idealised image to evoke a further flight of literature.

'Yes,' she said. 'I can see your attraction for Mrs. Brand.'

'Good for you,' said Harris.

'That's not nice of you, Mr. Harris,' she said. 'Besides you are my husband's protegé. He's chosen you, from a great crowd. You mustn't let him down. You're not secure enough yet to risk any scandal, and especially of this kind, when a young mother is dragged in with you. That's the point. You might even flourish; but she would not.'

Harris saw that he had made no impression on her.

I don't think we're getting anywhere,' he said. 'You'd do better to start on the threats.'

'What threats are these?' she asked.

'Oh, wrap up. What'll you tell your husband if I kick you out.'

'Yes,' she said. 'It's a point. It must be clear to you that you'll lose a certain amount of goodwill if you go on as you are doing.'

'A certain amount,' said Harris.

'Sneering's no use. Your music has been pushed by two people, John Brand and my husband. Brand's already against you. You didn't know that, did you? He's just an amusing type to you, nothing else. A comedian. You must forgive me it I tell you he's a temperamental young man, on edge the whole time, and this is the final straw. You can laugh; you can disbelieve me. Just watch, that's all.'

'I will,' said Harris.

'And as to my husband, I must tell you straight out that I have some influence there. Any man as busy as he is wants quiet at home. He may not get it. You know he's great things in store for you. You wouldn't want them thrown away.'

'Shall I tell you,' said Harris, 'what Mrs. Brand and I have been up to?'
'You're going to be sensible, then?' she said, satisfied.
'Oh, yes,' said Harris. 'I'm always sensible, especially when I know which side my bread is buttered. Mrs. Brand has been working on the libretto of a choral work for me. That's all. We meet to discuss it. We meet too often in my view, but that's nothing.'
'Ah,' said Mrs. Cooke, letting breath out.
'There's no more to it than that. They can talk as they like.'
'You are not in love with Mrs. Brand?'
'No.'
'But, Mr. Harris,' she said, 'you've surely noticed that there are more ways than one to be in love.' She paused as if to let Harris master this idea. 'When I was a girl in school we had a man come in to teach us chemistry. I fell in love, but I didn't write poems. I swotted formulae and got a distinction.'
'You were a youngster.'
'So's she. So's she. And the slavery she puts in on your libretto is as sure a sign of sexual attraction as if she ran into your bedroom stark naked. You see that, surely?'
'Let's suppose it is,' said Harris. 'What can I do?'
'Keep away from her. It's as easy as that. It might be possible that this was doing Nancy a power of good, if only it were private. But it isn't now. It's common talk.'
'It's common talk,' said Harris, 'that you've been Brand's mistress.' Now he'd shake her.
'I have heard it said. It's not true. But I wouldn't like it mentioned in Nancy's hearing.'
'You wouldn't mind for yourself?'
'No,' she said, 'of course I wouldn't. I'm in a position to,' she moved her hands, 'push it aside.'
They sat still, thinking over what they had said.
'Now, Mr. Harris, what are you going to do?'
'Nothing. There's nothing I can.'
'That's not true.'
'I've noticed,' Harris said, 'that once people start talking, they don't stop. If they think without any evidence that we're lovers, and it's noticed that we're never seen together, they'll say that we've gone underground.'
'That's your opinion?'
'Yes. I told you I was sensible. In my view, what Nancy Brand's doing for me is for good. And no amount of tittle-tattle among your friends will convince me otherwise.'

'You sound cocksure, Mr. Harris. Aren't you falling into my fault?'

'Maybe. What are you going to do, Mrs. Cooke?'

She faltered. 'I just don't know. I really don't. I feel inclined to believe you. I think it remarkably silly of myself to do so; it cuts against all my experience but there you are.'

'You've heard,' said Harris, 'that your husband's supposed to be arranging for this choral work to be commissioned. You do know that, don't you?'

'Yes.'

'You could put the screws on him and stop it. It wouldn't be hard. He doesn't love me much now.'

'Why are you telling me this?' Mrs. Cooke asked.

'If he said it was no-go, it would be stupid for me to continue, wouldn't it? You have the remedy there. Scotch the whole programme, and bob's your uncle.'

'Would you stop, Mr. Harris? Once you've begun, I mean?'

'Probably. I keep telling you I'm sensible. I want a hearing just as much as the next client.'

'You're laughing at me again. You couldn't give in. Not even if my husband went the whole hog and put a wholesale ban on you with all his people.'

'You don't know me,' said Harris. He felt more cheerful. 'You're a bit of a romantic, aren't you? You've lived too long with that old man of yours. I should in all probability knock off writing. A sad come-down, isn't it? But that's life.'

'So you're willing to accept my terms, if I press my husband for your commission.'

'Are you willing to do that?' he asked.

'I suppose so. Yes. You're not asking too much.'

Harris screwed his eyebrows together.

'Well,' he said, 'there, now.' He reminded himself of his stepmother. She put little phrases together, to keep herself comforted and going, even when she was on her own. 'But I don't think I'm willing, Mrs. Cooke. Now I've come out with it, I'm sure I'm not. I'm not going to be pushed around by drawing-room gossip, even yours.'

'You realise what you're saying?' she said. She was not without intelligence. 'You're willing to commit suicide as a composer, on your showing, because you dislike scandal. It isn't right.' She sounded very young.

'Well, it's wrong, then,' said Harris.

'And you're not in love with her?'

'No.'

'You're mad.'

'Am I?' said Harris. 'All right, I'm mad. Isn't that lovely? How did you divine my secret, dear Mrs. Cooke?' He was making a hash of this.

She rose.

'I don't know what to do,' she said.

'If you believe what you've been telling me,' said Harris, 'you'll take action.'

'Yes,' she said. 'I suppose I shall. Thank you for talking to me, Mr. Harris. I really do like you.'

'Thanks,' said Harris.

He showed her out. On the step outside it was cold. She turned round.

'Mr. Harris,' she said. 'When you talk, as you've just been doing, in that trivial, frothy way, you frighten me. It's not sane.'

Harris held out his hand. They shook and she drove off.

When she had gone Harris sat down. He had to. This had hit him, and hard. He was thoroughly unconvinced by Mrs. Cooke's performance. He put his reactions into words. She had been dramatising, hamming, was as shallow as a bird-bath, but... That is what amazed him. If only he could have believed sense, he'd have shrugged her vapourisings off. He couldn't...

He lounged in his chair.

His legs were heavy and his feet bursting. The beginnings of a headache began to poke. Perhaps there was something in her story about Brand. He had been a bit off. It seemed unlike Brand to say that *The Tempest* was rotten because he was jealous, but it was possible. Now Harris was up against it all round. It wasn't a hap'orth of good posturing, claiming that he wasn't going to be shoved around by scandal-mongers. He was. Or then may be he wasn't. It would be more honest to say that he didn't want to give up his meetings with Mrs. Brand. All right; he certainly didn't want that to develop into an affair, but he liked the little jaunts in the car. Boo-hoo.

This ought to be right up a musician's street; one man against the world. Beethoven in his cellar with the cannons knocking houses over. That wouldn't wash. Why couldn't they leave him alone? They were doing. He'd only Mrs. Cooke's word for it that folks were talking. But she meant business. If they weren't talking now, she'd soon see to it that they were. No, that was wrong. Why should she queer the pitch for Nance Brand when she was supposed to be protecting the girl? She wasn't. That was the answer. She was making trouble. She picked out the sore spot and rubbed the germs in. Why couldn't they leave him alone? Oh, oh, Antonio.[17]

He was frightened, as he was not often frightened now he was grown up. It was strange now this empty, hollow hardness of his body, as if he'd been multiplied into steel, brought back another memory of school which he'd completely forgotten. He remembered how he'd felt on the rare occasions he'd not done his homework and was waiting for the lesson to come round to collect his detention ticket. And that reminded him of the times he'd been let off, and the sort of fizzy lightness of the head had made him cheeky and brilliant in the next period. That side-track offered no relief. His body, with its metallic core, was there, warning him.

Harris made no attempt to get on with his work.

He was abjectly sorry for himself.

Why had this not happened when Brand had seen him? Brand had shown him... what? Something unexpected and shocking. It had upset Harris for half-an-hour. But Mrs. Bogus-breeches, with her blathering, had put him out cold. What was it Leaman had said? That he wanted to share his good fortune with the world? Some fortune. He'd share this little lot with all the takers.

He was like Winterburn. No, not quite. He was at the beginning of the series while Winterburn was well on. Often he'd told himself that what Winterburn lacked was a sense of proportion.

Now he did, himself. Any fool could have told him that Mrs. Cooke's visit was about as serious as a football comic. It did not shift his fright. That was right inside him. And if a few other Mrs. Cookes perked up, and he was as defenceless, what happened next?

The right thing he told himself was six fingers of whisky. He took out his dental plate and held it in the palm of his hand. It looked a forlorn, pink, helpless thing, like a baby. Now he was going off his rocker, shedding a furtive tear over his false teeth.

He got up, staggered into his raincoat, and walked about the room. Harris, the great Harris, versus the wide, whirling world. Harris scratched. He found himself tramping about the place, putting his hand on pieces of furniture, actually groaning.

There is nothing for it.

Lighting his pipe, he went down, and out, to the pictures.

## 16.

FROM November until Easter Harris spent his time writing mainly at the Requiem. It amazed him that he could do so, for the world had gone sour on him.

At the Christmas Oratorio performance, he'd had a superb evening. He'd begun to grudge the time he'd spent on his choir, but their performance was outstanding. Cooke's wisdom in forcing the young principals into consultation lessons with Harris paid dividends. The church was crammed; every notability for miles had turned up, paid up and liked it, every one of any musical consequence, and Cooke had even deigned to squeeze in a couple of hundred concert-goers, who'd queued for hours.

The choir had excelled itself; it was agreed that there wasn't its equal in England. Cooke was beside himself. He'd invited Harris and Brand to his home; rushed them away in a car of ducal splendour.

Once the drinks were out, and flowing, Cooke edged the man-of-the-moment, Sir Archbold Staleybridge with Harris and Brand into a spare room.

'This is the bloke, Archie,' he said. Staleybridge congratulated Harris on the oratorio. He was a tall man, in a light, hairy suit. He spoke very quietly and hardly seemed to move.

'You don't drink alcohol, Mr. Harris?' he said.

'No,' said Harris, surprised.

'The usual egoism?' Staleybridge said to Cooke. 'I've noticed it before.' He turned to Harris. 'Not a bad thing in a musician, eh?'

'Being a teetotaller?' said Harris, out of his depth.

'Egomania,' said Sir Archbold. 'Heard your *Tempest*. Too good for the job. That's so, eh, Brand?'

'Yes,' said Brand smiling.

'You don't think so,' said Sir Archbold. This big, whispering man didn't waste anything. 'Why not?'

'Not a touch on the Passacaglia,' said Brand.

'Didn't hear the broadcasts,' said Sir Archbold. 'The critics set about it.'

'The critics always set about what they don't understand.' Brand glared.

'Is that your experience, Cooke?'

'Mountain says it's the best string work since the war,' said Cooke.

'He'd back his own judgement,' said Staleybridge. 'What do you expect?

What do you think?'

'Exceptionally good,' said Cooke, rubbing his hands. 'Big stuff.'

'You didn't like it, either,' said Staleybridge. 'You know why I'm asking these questions, Harris? Expect you do. I don't want to appear a fool. I'm willing to encourage local talent. All the same to me who writes it. But it's going to be good.'

'I can't promise that,' said Harris. He didn't know why he'd said it.

Staleybridge looked at him suspiciously.

'You can't? Where's your confidence? If you think it's n.b.g. what will the others say? And we've got to get moving. This business is in three years. If you don't write it, somebody else will, and they've got to be given time.'

'I'm not promising anything,' said Harris.

'Not to get it finished?'

'I'll do that,' said Harris.

'You can see this pair,' whispered Staleybridge, 'hanging about in the background, can't you? What are they saying? Nothing, you'll notice. Three months ago they were mad to have you. Now they're not. Why not?'

'Perhaps they don't think I'm capable,' said Harris lamely.

'Do you?' Staleybridge asked Brand.

'How do I know?' said Brand. 'I'm an amateur fiddler.'

'Charles?'

'I think he can do it; said Cooke, not enthusiastically.

'You see,' said Staleybridge, 'my predicament. Why've they changed their minds?'

'You ask them,' said Harris, annoyed.

'I'm asking you.'

'Perhaps their wives have been getting at them,' said Harris, trying to laugh.

'This is no time for jokes, Harris,' said Staleybridge. 'You compose *The Tempest* score, and it nearly stopped the performance. Cooke pulled you out of that. When it's over, some other fool steps in, and stirs mud up. He won't last long. But the mud's sticking. I thought the stuff was good, but it upset all of three counties. Now we've had the experts on the Passacaglia.' He took out a bunch of cuttings, held together with a small, bronze paper-clip. 'Look at these, Mr. Harris. Of ten notable critics who heard your work, eight are unfavourable. Eight.'

Harris knew very well. The caning had cut deep.

'What do they say?' He flicked through the papers. '"Grandiose, but failed to achieve coherence." "Immodest in conception." Rather good that, eh, Charles? "Would be advised to restrict himself to the more limited fields where he has achieved some success." "Musically disappointing when compared with even what is obviously popular in manner, the Blidworth March." "Not without moments of vivid excitement, but lacking an overall unity." They don't like you, Harris, do they?'

'No,' said Harris.

'And what's your reply?'

'Nothing.'

Sir Archbold all but turned away. He swung back as if to strike Harris.

'I suppose so. I suppose so. Now then. Let's look at our little situation.' Staleybridge pulled his lips in. 'You've irritated the locals. Not that that's hard, but you've done it double-quick. Your friends are apathetic and the critics of the national papers think you're a washout. That's how we stand. Why should I give you this commission?'

'You can please your dead aunt,' said Harris.

'What do I get out of it?' said Staleybridge. 'I put money down. And what for? A work that the people here will refuse to sing, and which, if they do, will get slated all over England. Why should I put myself out?'

'You shouldn't,' said Harris.

'Why do you say that?'

'Why do I say anything?' said Harris. 'What sort of man are you? You make your mind up with the help of a few snippets from the paper, written by hacks who couldn't harmonise a simple hymn-tune between them, let alone judge what I was getting at. What am I supposed to do? Drop on my knees and swear blind I'll write another Missa Solemnis, especially dedicated to Sir Archbold Staleybridge. I'm a professional musician. I write as best I can. If it doesn't please you, you can tell me what to do with it. But don't expect me to thank you. I shan't.'

'Let's be reasonable, Harris.'

'Oh, let's. I would if I knew how, but I don't.'

'Come, come, Harris,' said Cooke. 'This won't do. You can't expect Sir Archbold to give you the commission without some sort of preliminary enquiries.'

'Can't I?' said Harris. 'That shows all you know. What I do is so much ink on paper to him. Nothing else. If his newspaper says it's nice, it is. If not, it's nasty.'

'Sir Archbold doesn't claim to be anything but an amateur,' said Cooke. 'In the best sense of the word. But he's a business man. And he likes to form his judgement of a man before he sets him on with a long assignment.'

'I know enough,' said Staleybridge, 'to know that a stable character's required. How do you fare there, Harris?'

'I don't suffer fools...'

'Yes,' said Staleybridge, 'oh yes. We all realise that.' He looked across at Harris, dropped his eyes and shuffled a foot or two further away. He spoke over his shoulder, in a more matter-of-fact way. 'There is one other thing. I've looked over the libretto, or whatever you call it. Mr. Brand was kind enough to show it me. And with all respect to Mrs. Brand, and to you, it's hardly what I should have chosen to mark a celebration of this sort. Don't you agree?'

'How much does it concern you,' said Harris, 'whether this city's four hundred or four thousand years old?'

'I've as much civic pride as the next man.'

'Ay,' said Harris. 'Damn-all.'

'Mr. Harris, you are not...'

'No, I'm not. That's right. You tell me to creep back in my hole; I'll go.'

'Come, come, Harris,' said Staleybridge. 'You won't put me off. I don't let go as easily as all that. If...'

'If,' said Harris. 'If you want a six part setting of Nellie Dean to celebrate the grand and glorious heritage of this noble pile of factories and public conveniences, I'll sit down and write it here and now.'

'You're pressing me, are you, to put you off?'

'I'm telling you to make your mind up one way or the other.'

'Those critics hurt you, Harris. Cooke said they would. I thought you fellows were impervious to slush of that sort. Have you done any of that Requiem yet?'

'Yes.'

'Much?'

'No. One scena. And the prologue.'

'What's it like?'

'Marvellous,' said Harris. 'Stupendous. Thrilling to the marrow of the bone.'

'I don't take much notice of these two either,' said Sir Archbold. 'I expect you haven't licked Cooke's boots hard enough, and I suppose young Brand's jealous. His father's always a cry-baby. Now I'll suggest a compromise.'

'I'll buy it.'

'Shall we go out,' said Brand to Cooke, 'and let 'em get together?'

'We've got to get these local worthies behind us,' said Sir Archbold. 'I can be as rude as I like, but you can't. Cooke pulled your chestnuts out of the fire last time, and will probably have to do the same again. Now what I'm suggesting is this. That we add your scena to the April concert; how long will it take?'

'Ten minutes or so.'

'Just the ticket. And we'll make a final decision then. What do you think?'

'I don't mind,' said Harris.

'There you are, Harris. Score to me by tomorrow. I'll arrange for parts to be got out, and pay for them. Right, Charles?'

'Like the idea,' said Cooke.

'It's not long,' said Harris. 'My stuff's difficult.'

'Can't help it. I'm not chucking money away. What do you say?'

'Right,' said Harris. 'In April.'

'You'll do the fixing, Charles?'

'I will,' said Cooke. 'I'll move 'em. You won't see their lower regions for dust.'

'What do you think, Brand?' said Sir Archbold. 'You're disinterested.'

'Great, great,' said Brand. 'It doesn't give Harris a dog in hell's chance, and you'll have no idea of the completed work when you've done. It's wonderful.'

'You don't approve,' said Sir Archbold. 'I'll let you into a secret. This is Cooke's idea.'

'You're telling me,' said Brand. 'I could see old clever-cuts behind this. If I were Harris, I'd be insulted. As I'm not, I'll go quietly in a corner and ponder deep on you two great big panjamdrums. Nasty, unpleasant cut-throat thoughts.'

'What do you make of that, Harris?' said Sir Archbold, rumbling.

'I'm sorry,' said Harris slowly, trying to be honest, 'that Brand doesn't think I'm up to it.'

'And I'm frightened,' said Brand, 'that you are, and then what a mug I shall look.'

Cooke, with his way earned, shepherded them back.

Harris did not know what to think. This idea of Cooke's for a try-out of the scena at Easter, didn't seem too bad. It would be under-rehearsed, but the Philharmonic were quite a virtuoso choir, in the football-crowd style, and the soloists for the Easter concert were all youngsters not yet in the big-time, who would at least try to learn the stuff.

It might come off.

Some things did. He'd dreaded the break with Nancy Brand, for instance, but it had been easy. Too easy, in fact, for his peace of mind for a week or two, but there'd been no repercussions.

He'd detained her one night in the car.

'Did your husband say anything about this Requiem to you?' he said, casually.

'Not really. He's been humming and haing for a few days now. He thinks I should give it up. Is that what you mean?'

'Yes, it is.'

'Why should I?'

'Now,' Harris said, 'I want an honest answer out of you. Has your work on it in the last fortnight improved it? Honest, now.'

'I think so.' She opened her eyes wide, and brushed her forehead.

'And how long's the improving process to go on?'

'I don't know. Might be months, or even years.' She giggled as if this was ridiculous but inevitable.

'That's what I think. And it's not worth any more time. I like it now, as much as I ever shall. And it's time I got down to it, without being scared that the next time I see you, you've altered the very bit I'm working up to.'

'You can't stop me,' she said.

'I didn't say I could. All I shall do is to take it as it stands. Any brainwaves you have from this day forward are wasted. See?'

'Yes. I see. Shan't we meet?'

'In the ordinary course of things. I'll keep you posted how I'm going.'

'Have you,' she spoke slowly, as though she were pulling words out of the air which would drop together to make a sensible question, 'have you only just made your mind up?'

'In a way.'

'It's not very fair to me, is it?'

'No. But that's the librettist's life. Nobody knows or cares who wrote the words.'

'I don't mind about that,' she said. 'I'd like to get it right.'

'No, Nance. Sorry. No.'

She leaned back and rubbed a hand down the window. She stuck out a finger, tracing a complicated pattern on the misty glass. When she had finished, she turned and spoke in a low, breathless voice.

'I wonder,' she said, 'if there's not something behind all this.'

'Such as what?' He was not beyond wondering himself whether Mrs. Cooke or Brand had let the cat out of the bag. He didn't put that past them.

'Oh, I don't know. Perhaps you've had enough of me.' She looked tired, sulky. 'Are you one of these people who drop women when they've got all they want out of them?'

'I'm not proposing to drop you.'

'You are,' she said. She was more engaged now.

'Oh, rubbish. I'm proposing that we look on the libretto as complete. No more, no less.'

'And what about between me and you?'

'What about it?' he said.

'I don't do this for nothing. I do it because of you. It's an excuse to meet you.'

'I wondered,' he said. Then more cheerfully, 'Never mind. Once the libretto's out of the way, you might find the desire to see me gone too.'

'Do you think so?'

'I shouldn't be surprised. Perhaps your interest in me is really something else. You want to make sure I'm going to do it. You can set your mind at rest. I am, come hell and high weather.'

'That's cruel,' she said.

'By no means. It's only a suggestion. Not even a good one.'

'You won't take me seriously, will you?' she asked. 'Nobody takes me seriously. I'm a comic turn.'

'I'm going to set your words.'

'That's different. Why won't you love me, Tom? That's what I want. I won't have your compliments; they mean nothing. But if you loved me, I'd know you were taking me seriously. I'd know I was an adult.'

He shrugged.

'It needn't come to anything, you know. You needn't make physical love to me if you don't want. If you'd only tell me, out straight, that you thought something of me.'

'I like you, Nance,' said Harris, and stopped.

'That's no use,' she said.

'But I'll tell you this. I'm going no further. Once I said I loved you, you'd be content to hold hands tonight, but tomorrow you'd be on with some other demand. I know you. You won't be satisfied.'

'You're frightened of me?'

'Perhaps.'

'You do love me, then?'

'Because I'm frightened? No. Why have you got to make it so hard? I don't want to say out loud, Jack Blunt, that I don't love you.'

'Why not?' she leaned forward.

'I don't want to hurt you.' He put a hand on her arm steadying her.

'And don't you think,' she said, 'you're hurting me now? You like it. You know I'm mad for you, and you hold yourself back for the pleasure of killing me, slowly, in your own time.' She pushed his arm away. 'I'd like to hate you.'

'You mustn't do that.'

'Oh, no,' she said. 'I won't do that. I shall love you.'

They sat still, two people in the car, both enjoying themselves. Harris realised at once that she was right. He did not love her. But, by God, it was good to have her on a leash. He knew, too, that she enjoyed playing this emotional game. They both were hypocrites. But he told himself, as far as his knowledge went, he was normal and she wasn't. There was no telling where she'd stop. He'd better put the screw on now. It suited his mood.

'In which case,' he said steadily, 'it would be better if we didn't see each other. At least for a bit.'

She gave a sort of howl and fell on to him. He could feel her heavy breasts on his arms.

'Get up,' he said. 'It's no good acting the goat.' It would have been very easy to kiss her. He heaved her upright. She sagged in her seat with her head thrown back, catching the lamplight from the street on her profile, like a film actress playing a drowned girl. Everything she did was a still, a battered cliché from some good old film.

She began to cry. This was the biggest foolery of all. Tears rolled down her cheeks. Harris was bored by the posturing, but asked himself how he knew that her emotion was not genuine. The answer was that he didn't. For all he knew, she was quite overwhelmed. He hoped she wasn't, but hope wasn't knowledge. He tucked his arm through hers.

After a moment, she dried her eyes and took out her compact. This was more like it. He didn't feel ashamed of smiling at the apparently workmanlike dabs at her nose. This, drawing-room comedy manner, and the pleasant smell of the powder set him at his ease so that he stretched his legs and put his hands in his pockets.

When she'd finished she turned and said,

'The critics didn't like your Passacaglia, did they?' Her voice was still tremulous, and she snuffed at the end of the sentence.

'They did not.' Harris considered whether she was trying to get her own back.

'Do you mind?'

He did. The condemnation had been in general terms. They did not suggest this or that was bad, merely that he'd overshot his limits. Perhaps these taciturn abstractions were due to the shortness of the notices, but even that was an added insult. Harris was raving angry when he thought consciously about it, and miserable when he didn't. It did no good to say that he knew the work was good, he'd had it performed only by the back door of influence. If it were as fine as he thought it, the B.B.C. wouldn't have kicked it out. He wished to God he'd stuck to two-part songs for schools.

Now, three days since the last notice, he was beginning to recover. He didn't think about it all the time. For an hour on end, he could forget that the highest-paid critics in England thought his best work inflated rubbish.

'It doesn't make much difference what I think, does it?' he said, limply.

'You don't want to talk about it?'

'I don't care.' He wished it were true.

'I wish I were like that.' She believed him. What twaddle people talked about womanly intuition. A blind and deaf-mute imbecile could see he was kicked into the gutter. 'Poor stupid girl,' he thought. A pang of compassion for her passed through him.

'We can't all be the same.' Why had he come out with that masterpiece of truth?

'It won't stop you writing the Requiem, will it?' she asked.

'No. When I showed you my pal's criticism, you didn't stop your work, did you? It seemed to do you good.'

'Good?' she said. 'It nearly drove me mad. I cried. I couldn't sleep. I was angry with no provocation. I was a nasty, little animal, all bite scratch and scream.'

'I didn't notice it,' he said.

'You're a man,' she said. 'And not a very sensitive man at that. I don't know how you come to write music. I suppose you make up on technique what you lack in feeling.'

'Your old man doesn't think I'm much good in the larger forms.'

'You ought to have heard him. "That greasy set of venal lechers" he called them. He was savage.'

'He thinks *The Tempest* rotten.'

'He can't stand Beauchamp. That's what put him off there.'

'Is that so? Well, I've done one thing on his advice. I was going to use a big orchestra, but now I'm using a few strings, string-quartet, solo wood-wind and brass. That's all. And bags of percussion. If the Philharmonic do it, they'll swamp the orchestra with their Baal Chorus larks.'

'Never mind,' she said.

They sat quiet.

'I must be off now,' he said. 'Goodbye, Nance.'

'You're not going to see me?'

'No, Nance.'

'I expect you're wise. Goodbye, Tom.'

They shook hands, and he got out. He waved as she drove off. She raised a hand like the Queen.

For some weeks Harris was frightened to death that Mrs. Brand would do something silly for which he could be blamed or, worse, blame himself. He looked through the evening papers dreading the accident or the suicide he might find there. Walking along the road, he'd find himself stopped, locked into a sort of trembling fit of doubt. Perhaps he should have been less brusque; there was something in Mrs. Cooke's plea. Before he went to sleep he'd be held awake in a dream from which he had no escape and in which he had to watch Mrs. Brand fling herself into an unnecessary tragedy. And while the moment was on, he was held. He could no more throw off the fear than he could wriggle out of a nightmare.

Gradually he began to learn sense. Nothing happened. As far as he could tell, for he never saw them, the Brands were right enough. But it wasn't until the new excitement of Sir Archbold Staleybridge's proposal that he felt himself over the worst.

In his spare minutes during the next few weeks Harris tried to decide why he was so strong about the Requiem. It was not merely his father's death he was dealing with; the second theme, the defenceless harried by authority was of paramount importance now. Nance Brand and Winterburn were his exemplars. He'd chosen them as typical of mankind, rather than Brand, for instance, or Leaman or Cooke with whom he'd had as much to do. He would not have liked to defend his thesis in words, but it roused him emotionally, rang some fighting echo. When he looked over the libretto or began to set it, excitement flooded his cheeks. For some reason, perhaps his own experience, certainly his own experience, it was imperative that he should get this music down.

He was not pleased with this amateur philosophising; if anything it tended to weaken his regard for the work, but his emotional impulses finally determined what he should write. That was his sort of thinking.

He got on with it.

## 17.

HARRIS now went at it in a frenzy.

It wasn't that his new-found convictions about the Requiem gave him the urgency; rather the other way about. The pressure of ideas threw up the convictions; his whole mind was ablaze with energy. He felt as if he could not only write music but throw off without a by-your-leave suggestions for preventing draughts or unblocking drains. This was marvellous; he ran creative to the finger tips. Nothing could stop him. He was staying with his step-mother at the seaside. At the beginning of December an old friend of Mrs. Harris's had written from Wellsthorpe on the east coast to say that the bungalow next door was for sale. Mrs. Harris went to the solicitor's office at once, got out some of Gentleman Jones's cash and was installed within a week.

Harris spent Christmas there. His step-mother made no demands on him; served him four square meals, kept the house hot and let him play and write or walk by the sea as he wished. Mrs. Next-door didn't think highly of Harris as a son; he was too brusque, too fast on his way, but Mrs. Harris spent dizzy hours of conversation explaining why he couldn't stop long enough to pass the time of day. The two old ladies sat and gossipped at each other with years to make up. Harris provided a decent point of entry; he was the starting blocks for the natter-sprint.

Soon after Christmas, and Harris hadn't stopped for that, he realised that he wasn't likely to get his stint finished before the school opened again in the second week in January. For the first time in his life, he decided he'd have time off. It gave him an air of importance in his own eyes. He was independent. He could afford to miss a couple of week's pay. He didn't consider his colleagues who'd have to take his periods. It didn't matter a hoot that he'd miss a fortnight with the Bach choir. He only grudged the time it took to write a letter asking Attenborough or Morley to take over.

He rang up Leaman. The Headmaster was noncommital. He didn't sound pleased, but when he saw that Harris meant business, he advised him to write a formal application to the Director. Harris did so at once. Some subordinate granted permission and told him how much of his salary would be docked, but the Director scribbled in his own writing a p.s. wishing Harris success.

Mrs. Harris was perturbed. She'd never seen her step-son at close quarters for so long, and certainly never in this excited frame of mind. When they met, he kissed her, or picked her up and chaffed her for a minute, then grew silent as he ate and thought. She watched him carefully, crumbling his bread or drumming his spoon.

'Eh, Tom,' she said, 'you're just like your dad.'

'Uh?'

'Nothing would stop him once he'd set his mind on.'

'No.'

'I often wonder what he'd have been if he'd been educated like you.'

Harris never took up these conversations. He was too busy elsewhere, but he saw the force of the comparison and was not displeased.

The change of scene was good. Walking along by the gunmetal, wrinkling sea, his nostrils dilated, he burst with life. He'd belt along on the coldest days without an overcoat so that when he came in to compose, his frozen hands could barely keep up with his racing mind. He gave up work with a pen and wrote in pencil, page after page; ideas swelled and jumped, bustled, fought to get themselves down. He'd never felt so lively before nor so dog-tired at night. He could barely drag himself into bed before he was asleep.

By the third week in January the pace had abated; he'd had a month's non-stop work and he decided he'd go back and write out a neat score. He disliked this, but knew it was imperative now that the flush of creation was on the way out. The rewriting, he realised, often brought the best ideas.

Once he was back at school, the tempo relaxed. Truancy has its uses, but so has steady grind. He rehearsed songs, transposed hymns, 'appreciated' A Night on a Bare Mountain or Till Eulenspiegel and crossed out consecutive perfect fifths in ordinary-level exercises. He worked late at night, but more easily. He was a human being, not a machine to be threshed.

Returning humanity posed its problems. He wondered, for the first time, how the Philharmonic were progressing with the Prologue and Scena. At Wellsthorpe, he'd not given them a fraction of a thought. Now it seemed fairly important that they should serve him out a fair deal.

The best thing, he thought, was to get hold of Brand, who'd know how matters were shaping. Harris wasn't sure how he'd be received, but that didn't matter. That month's worth of oversized energy wasn't to be wasted.

He rang Brand at work, and was invited, cordially, to go round that night.

Brand showed him into the music room, the place where they'd met the first time they'd gone round to see Cooke. Harris carefully looked Brand over, but could see no difference. He didn't know why he should have expected a change in Brand, but supposed that the image of the man at their last interview had stuck, had coloured his imagination. Nance was not to be seen;

his stepmother had received a Christmas card, and that was all he'd heard of her.

'Well, cocker,' said Brand, putting himself into a chair, 'and what can I do you for?'

'A friendly visit,' said Harris. 'I wanted to know how the Prologue and Scena were going?'

'They've started rehearsing. Sir George Gilbert who's conducting has got his score. So have the soloists.'

'And all's well?'

'Um. They've started. They look as if they're playing fair.'

'Good,' said Harris. 'Good.'

'Is it?' said Brand. 'I suppose so. I don't want to put ideas into your head.'

'Come on,' said Harris. 'Out with it.'

'Look here, Harris, I don't want to start any trouble, but has Sturton asked you to mark his score, or attend rehearsals?'

'No. But it's early. And I've been away.'

'Right, then, if you're satisfied, that's it.'

Harris leaned back.

'What are you trying to say?' he asked.

'Nothing,' said Brand. 'In slow time.'

'You sound as if things weren't too happy.'

'I sound like nothing on earth,' said Brand. 'I'm the proverbial clam.'

'That won't do,' Harris said. 'Are you suggesting that the Philharmonic aren't...?'

'Me? I'm suggesting nothing. I've said so.'

'Fair enough,' said Harris. 'If you won't, you won't.'

Brand frowned, ran fingers through pale hair and shifted in his seat.

'Friend Cooke doesn't love you so much,' he said, in the end, slowly.

'Oh.'

'That's how it is, brother. Take it or leave it.'

'Why?'

'I'm no mind reader. Perhaps he's like me and thinks you'll make a hash of it. Or more likely, he sees you as a trouble-maker. He had a job with your *Tempest,* and this is likely to be worse. He's probably decided it's not worth the bother. He'll let the Philo muddle through the try-out, and that'll be that. Not that I know. I'm just guessing.'

'You've no proof?'

'I've said so. Put it down to my suspicious mind, brother, and leave it there.' He sighed and wriggled like a man who has done his duty. 'You know, Harris, you've bitten off more than you can chew. Why so keen on the perishing thing?'

Harris sat up.

'If I told you, you'd laugh.'

'I could do with that,' said Brand. 'Open up.'

'My Requiem,' said Harris, 'makes some sort of claim for all the clods who are pushed about by this life we're trying to lead. Somebody's got to say something.'

'Refugees and Hungarians and what not?' said Brand, off-hand and embarrassed.

'Yes,' said Harris. 'And your wife and Edwin Winterburn. They don't know what they're at. Your wife thinks all the governments of the world are conspiring in lunacy to do your youngsters in. Winterburn's driven up the pole by the kids he teaches and thinks there's a caucus of inspectors and headmasters out to fix him. They may be wrong. But there are thousands like them. Pushed around by authorities they don't understand and who don't explain.'

'And what's your bit of singing and fiddling going to do?' said Brand languidly. 'I suppose Harris's mighty Requiem will have such a therapeutic effect that the kingdom of God will be established on earth there and then. Why, you want locking up. Let's imagine it gets performed. What thanks will you get from Nance and old Rot-guts let alone anybody else? She'll be interested in the batty words you've misunderstood, and he'll be as jealous as hell because Tom Harris is getting on in the world.'

'Never mind,' said Harris. 'I've done what I could.'

Brand sat back impressed.

'Say, Harris, old jockey,' he said, 'do you really think there is an upper ten kicking the beans out of the rest of us?'

Harris pulled on his pipe, a plain man's guide to school mastery, and laughed.

'If you pinned me down to it, I don't suppose I do. But I've seen people I care for believing it, far too many for safety, and it's got me emotionally. And when that happens I'm like my dad, I've got to get up and shout.'

'Does Nance's mystical palaver about death make this point?' said Brand.

'We've slashed it down. All the historical stuff's gone. There's a lament for my father and then we get smack into a world full of death and everybody, men of goodwill and all, responsible. Oh, it's there all right, believe you me.'

'Harris,' said Brand. 'Don't you think some of your lads at school might look on you as a sort of malicious authority?'

'Yes,' said Harris. He thought of Mrs. Brand. 'That's what I mean. We'd all throw our weight about if we'd half a chance.'

'Thanks, china,' said Brand, almost whispering.

'I might be wrong,' said Harris. 'But it's the way I see the world. Through the eyes of people I like best and respect. Through my own. I don't like licking boots.' He smiled. 'Perhaps I've got it round my neck. It's hard to talk about music. Words won't do.'

Once more they sat there, two fellows exhausted.

'Oh,' said Brand, 'Cooke said he wanted to see you. Shall I ring him to see if you can go round now?'

'Fair enough.'

Brand got up and very slowly went out to the phone. Harris knocked his pipe out and closed his eyes. He wondered if he'd done right to try to explain to Brand. The effort had sucked virtue out of him. His hands were lead weights pulling his arms to the floor. Tears prickled at the back of his eyelids. A faint pain, like indigestion, scraped the length of his chest. His face felt like melted rubber, slopped quite out of shape, into the inhuman imbecility of a child's Guy Fawkes.

He dropped asleep.

Brand shook him by the shoulder with gentle fingers.

'You all right, boyo? You put the wind up my tail. I thought you'd gone and joined our great and glorious dead yourself.' He was laughing but white and serious.

'What's Cooke say?' said Harris, heaving himself up.

'You can go straight round.'

'Good,' said Harris, and straightened his tie. His pockets bulged with pipes, tobacco, handkerchiefs and keys. 'Look here, Brand, can I tell him that you think he's out to sink my Requiem?'

'That's a puzzler,' said Brand. 'Don't see why not. He won't hold it against me. Mark you, chum, it won't do you three ha'porth of good.'

'Thanks,' said Harris. 'I took your advice, you know. I've cut my orchestra down to chamberish size.'

Brand looked up, his face alight.

'You did?' he said. 'That's good. Well, I'm in on it now, aren't I? I tell you what, Harris, my old bird, I'll come round with you and let him have it myself.'

'Yes,' said Harris, pleased. 'No, I don't know.'

Brand laughed out loud.

'Don't worry. I shan't change my mind and help Cookey to sling you out. I'll say this, Harris lad, and then I'll put my coat on. I don't believe a single word of what you've told me this evening's right, but I like the way you said it. By God, it's a change to hear somebody who believes something even if it's that old... No. Let me get my coat on, before I start howling.'

They went out.

* * *

When Cooke received his guests he appeared displeased to see Brand, but said nothing. After the two were seated, he opened the business with a proposition for Harris and walked across to play four notes on the piano, A, E, B flat, C. These, he said were his wife's initials; he'd often wished he could use them as a musical theme. Now he wanted Harris to take them, work them into a big piano piece, which he would get one of the leading concert pianists to record and then he'd present the finished article to his wife as a birthday-present. Harris said he was busy with the Requiem. It was pointed out this wouldn't detain him long. More tit-for-tat, Harris thought, and grudgingly consented. He hated himself.

Mention of the Requiem gave Brand his chance. He asked how rehearsals were going.

Cooke acted exactly as he had done with the Shakespearians. Very temperately he put into plain words the worse case against himself. He knew, he said, what Brand was hinting at. He, Cooke, was out to ruin the Requiem just to show whipper-snappers like Harris where they really stood. He smiled and waved his soft palms. There was no truth in it; Sturton was working hard; Gilbert had praised the work. Moreover, they were going to ask Brand to lead the viola section. That didn't look like conspiracy, did it? He was promising nothing, of course, about the acceptance of the whole; that was out of his hands. Even there he wasn't sitting back, they could believe him.

Brand blew into his fingers like a schoolboy who had been caned and Cooke went on.

There were snags, he said; the difficulties inherent in the Prologue and Scena for one. That was to be accepted. But he knew exactly what Brand thought. And he'd kindly point out that there had to be somebody in authority, to take the decisions. But he could see no reason at all why Brand should look on that authority as anything but benevolent.

Brand, he said, was always the same. You didn't hear Harris talking in this wild way. Because Brand had been pushed about by some ignorant schoolmaster or sergeant-major at one time, that was no reason to think like an adolescent for the rest of his life. The next thing he'd go on to do would be to argue himself into the frame of mind where all authority was malevolent, merely out to scotch talent and banish individuality. A moment's thought would convince any sane man that such a suggestion was monstrous.

He seriously advised Harris not to listen to rubbish of that sort, but to get on with his job, writing music. However, if he'd any sense, Harris would be pleasant to Staleybridge, because it cost nothing.

Brand then lost his temper.

That, he said, was what he was talking about. Why should Harris lick Staleybridge's boots? Harris was worth three million peasants like Staleybridge.

Cooke was easy. Staleybridge liked flattery. He also provided money for concerts. It did no harm to Bach or Mozart to be civil to their patrons. It wouldn't hurt Harris. If he couldn't stomach it, then he should keep out of Staleybridge's way and he, Cooke, would provide the soft-soap. That was all, gentlemen; he hoped the piano piece could be done inside the month. They were to go home and stop worrying; the Requiem was all it should be. He wished them a very good night, with thanks.

When they stood outside, Brand was livid.

'And what do you think of that?' he said.

Harris, who'd said nothing inside, shrugged his shoulders. Brand walked on.

'Put me down,' he shouted, 'with the great afflicted. A modern Requiem dedicated to Nance Brand, Edwin Winterburn and John Brand's battered body.'

'Eh?' said Harris.

'The bottom, dirtiest dog of all,' said Brand, and kicked a lamp-post.

## 18.

WINTERBURN surprised everybody, himself included, by applying for and obtaining a senior post in a grammar school in Belsthorpe, a new town. Not only did the job carry a fat responsibility payment but a council house was also provided.

The effect on Winterburn was immediate. He affected a charming modesty, consulted colleagues on choice of books and examining-bodies, took a tome or two on education out of the library. His attitude to the headmaster was cunningly ambivalent. It was clear now that Leaman had not made his adverse report, and had supported Winterburn strongly in his application.

'You know how it is,' Winterburn said. 'It's easier to kick a man upstairs than down. And that's what our dear colonel's done.'

'He wouldn't support you without reason,' said McManus. 'He's more about him than that.'

'I'm not cribbing,' said Winterburn. 'It suits us both.'

Next he sold his house, stored the furniture and moved into digs. His teaching improved a little. He got through the day now without killing himself, because he'd had a smell of success. His temper was easier; his indigestion less frequent. Emboldened, he wrote to his wife and asked her to try again with him in Belsthorpe. She, without any show of reluctance, because it was not easy to live on her parents, agreed. Winterburn now went occasionally to see his family at the week-end.

Harris was pleased with Winterburn's success, not so much for the future as for the present. You could now talk to him with enjoyment. You could employ his intelligence, and Harris was grateful. If Harris had been asked how he thought Winterburn would shape, he would have said 'well' and thought 'badly'. Winterburn had no sense of humour and thus no staying-power. If things didn't turn his way at the new place, he'd sulk. He'd probably never make such a mess of teaching again as he had, but he'd never be capable of doing what Harris could, that is, shutting his mind off from his classes for as long as a whole week, and still give the impression of teaching adequately. With Winterburn, there'd always be wear and tear. Still, that wasn't so bad. How the marriage would make shift, Harris did not know. He guessed that when the first flush of family-reunion had gone, Winterburn would be intelligent enough to spot that his wife was glad to get away from the old people, and he would play loud and long on that, if it suited his book.

Still, Winterburn the successful man was a change for the better. Harris even ragged him.

'What's it like to be nearly a responsibility-man?' he asked.

'Like a composer, whose last inspired notes of a heaven-spanning requiem are splashing off the end of his pen.'

'What about the underlings?' said Harris. 'Those whose timetable you fix with the rubbish while you sit all day in the library with three boys in the schol. sixth?'

'Just like you, Harris,' said Winterburn. 'Got it round your neck. We haven't got any sixth. They're all little cherubs. You know, shining hair and chubby cheeks. The sort that unmarried choirmasters go to prison for.'

It was a change. Harris liked it, and wrote Mrs. Cooke's birthday piece. He made it contemporary sugar-sweet, too hard for himself to play, all over the keyboard and then some. He enjoyed this; you've always some spare ideas when a really big job's in progress, and he gave it a private title 'Queens hereafter' from Drayton's sonnet.

'And Queens hereafter shall be pleased to live
Upon the alms of thy superfluous praise.'

This tickled him, and he worked a flowing cantilena to this couplet into the piece. It won a little of his own back, somehow, and he shared the dig with Brand, who didn't care for it. Cooke, however, was delighted and promised that this 'Intermezzo' would soon be in the concert repertoire. Once it was over, Harris didn't mind if it was soon in the dustbin and went back to the Requiem.

He had wondered, while he was away from it, if Winterburn's up-grading had made any difference. It had not. The same flurry of temper displayed itself on behalf of the downtrodden, and if Winterburn had suddenly appeared as Minister of Education, it wouldn't matter. The thesis was in under Harris's skin, and had to be worked out. If the millennium had established itself, and every man found himself every other's equal in gifts, abilities, wealth, opportunities, Harris's Requiem would have to be got on to paper, be it even for the slugs and snails, or other vermin enlightened humanity would need to exterminate in this saner, brighter regime. Then it would be Requiem for the Tubercle Bacillus, or the Spirochaeta pallida or the Oidium Albicans, but it would be the same big shout after authority. Curiously enough, Harris did not feel cynical about this.

Now that Winterburn had broken into success, it occurred to Harris that he might inquire again into Mrs. Brand's circumstances. This was not easy, since they did not meet and he did not wish to get himself involved again with her. The only method left was that of casual inquiry from Brand, whom he saw often and who made a point of reporting regularly on the Prologue and Scena. It was difficult to edge him away from the politics of this production and his answers were the usual concoction of slang and hot air, showing that he didn't consider the matter worth inquiry.

'Nance?' he'd say. 'All right. What d'you want to know for? Thought you'd got no axe in there? She's fine. Joined some sort of anti-H-bomb campaign. Knocks about half the day with Quakers and nonconformist parsons. Don't know if it's doing them much good, but she's thriving on it. She has more letters on House of Commons notepaper than I get football-pools.'

'And in herself?' said Harris.

'In herself? How do I know? She's cheerful and nice to the kids. She talks to me. But it'll blow over. She'll be back where she started, when the craze's gone.'

'Can't you do anything?'

'Such as what?' said Brand. 'It's the white man's burden. I'll get by, boy. Now everything's smooth as treacle. I'm thankful, but I don't think it'll last. I've had some before. Don't see why you should fret yourself, though. You've enough on your plate.'

Harris left it at that.

He got quietly on with his teaching and his writing. His thesis, if it merited that name, gradually grew to have less importance. He was concerned with the minutiae of the job; getting this piece of scoring straight, seeing that he preserved an exact balance through the work, making it eloquent from moment to precise moment.

This was full-time business, and occupied him steadily. As the spring came on, however, and the day of the concert approached, he found he was giving less time to creative work and more to introspection, to consideration of what would happen if Staleybridge said 'no'. He didn't meet Staleybridge; Cooke and Attenborough were uniformly sanguine as to prospects, but within three weeks of the concert Harris found himself at a standstill, unable to work because of his anxiety. The wheel had come full circle. He was thrust back to his thesis. He was now the representative of his beat generation,[18] waiting, unable to fend for himself, his bowels watery, waiting for authority to speak one way or the other. According to his friends, authority, Staleybridge and Co., was certain to come down exactly where it should, firmly in favour. Harris could not believe it. He found himself suddenly shivering in the classroom, when talking to his colleagues, pulling Sanderson's leg.

At no time was he happy. Only when he became interested in a lesson, or a snippet of common-room scandal, could he forget his fear. His Requiem was laid by permanently now; he did not want to do anything at it.

Malevolent authority had done its stuff.

He discussed this with nobody. He felt morally bound to carry his fear on his own. This was perhaps a confession of weakness, an acknowledgement that what trouble there was lay not with authority but with himself. Dredging this to the surface brought no relief. Grin and abide was the word. At least, he could abide.

Only once did his defence nearly cave in. He'd been talking to Brand, who'd been full of a marvellous performance by the orchestra of the Prologue, and in the course of the rehearsal, it appeared, the leader of the seconds,[19] a rubicund man, had asked some stupid question. Sturton had given him his usual courteous, slow-witted attention, but Brand who wanted to get on had shouted, 'Ah, soap your bow, you café-fiddler.' Some were shocked.

Harris tried to smile; thought he had succeeded. All his mind registered icily was that here was one extra enemy, one more to the big band-wagon.

Suddenly he saw Brand looking at him.

'I know,' said Brand, 'how you feel. And there's nothing you can do about it, boy.'

He crossed the room, put his arm through Harris's, and gently, as if he were coaxing a child, massaged the cloth of his coat.

'Put the fourth name down,' he said. 'Tom Harris.'

Harris was unable to speak and stood enduring the embarrassing strokes at his sleeve, until Brand, utterly sensitive, began to describe in a rough jargon the fiddler's colour-changes.

## 19.

AS time pushed on, Harris grew glad that the Requiem had dried up on him, since he had time now to devote to the Matthew Passion. He spent hours with the score; coached the principals, by letter and occasional lesson, and delighted in the virtuosity of his choir which could give his ideas quick, beautiful shape.

He saw much of Brand. They were on the old footing. The Bach orchestra was always on call now if Harris wanted it, and Brand himself led his own violas. There was between the two men a kind of intimacy that could not be revealed for fear of loss. Brand talked, joked, encouraged, criticised but never tackled personal relationships or dilated again upon the theme of the Requiem.

Harris preferred it like this. Brand on top of the world was stimulating; Brand out-at-the-emotional-elbow was too much, too unexpected. If Winterburn exploded or gave himself away it was exactly as it should be, in character; when Brand did so, some existing, permanent order seemed jerked upside down. Brand was like a balloon, bright, smooth, gay, to be played with; when the toy burst and poison gas spread, absolute malevolence was revealed beyond Harris's credulity. Now his friend was what he should be; bright and beautiful.

Brand brought snippets of news about the Requiem preparations. He was himself won over by the Prologue and Scena and confessed himself 'disturbed' by it. Beyond this he wouldn't go, and Harris didn't probe. Both the Philharmonic Orchestra and Choir were now on top of the notes, and were therefore generally in favour. Attenborough had borrowed the score and had given a semi-official lecture on it to undergraduates at the university; Morley had followed this up with private sessions and was reported to be whipping a sizeable group of students into enthusiastic frenzy. Though the concert was to take place in the Easter vac., two bunches had already booked seats and were determined to get the work encored.

'These lads shout for anything with a discord or two,' Brand said. 'But they can shout. There'll be no lack of support, whatever sort of job we make of it.'

Harris was delighted with this, and with a letter from Button, who was bringing a bus-load or two of his band and supporters. 'We're going to clap the heads off us,' Button wrote.

As well as the canvassing that Brand, Attenborough, Morley and Button were doing, Cooke was also reported to be coming down strong in Harris's favour in the right places. 'You tell Harris,' he said to Brand, 'that we're creating the climate of opinion to get his Requiem accepted.'

Harris went to London to see Sir George Gilbert. He was what Harris expected, off-hand, holier than any other half dozen and very quick on the uptake. It was clear he had Harris's Scena practically complete in his head, though he couldn't have spent much time on it, and his questions were of the sort that Harris wanted. After half-an-hour of Gilbert's grilling, Harris felt wrung out, but certain that justice would be done to him. While the cross-examination was on Gilbert treated him as an equal, but, once that was done, he was superbly on his high horse again.

'I'm doing you a great favour, my boy. Finish a concert in London Thursday night, fly up to Welstead, motor the rest and spend the week-end with Cooke. That means you get two rehearsals out of me, Friday night and Saturday afternoon. You can come Friday, but I don't want you there, wet-ragging, on Saturday. Keep away. Leave me to myself.'

'Will the soloists be there twice?' asked Harris.

'Why not? Of course they will. Youngsters on the way up. Told to keep Friday clear. They've got to consider my dictates, and Cooke's, if they want to get anywhere. Good material.' He bit on his false teeth. 'You wait till you've heard Eleanor Marlowe. Sings Galatea like a bird, and yet she'll be marv'llous in this thing of yours. Does the wife, y'know. Contralto part. But she'll be peerless. Best voice in England. Twenty-five. Good-looking piece and sharp. Barrow-boy's daughter. Come on Friday. Watch me excoriate the lot then. They'll not get any sleep any of 'em that night. They'll all have bags like bunkers under their eyes on Saturday, but by God they'll sing. Well, that's it. Afternoon, Harris. You're more sensible than most composers. I wasn't born yesterday. Trick or two up my sleeve. You trust experience, my boy. See you through. Right. Let yourself out.'

He stepped away, without shaking hands, leaving Harris standing there as he sat at his desk studying a score. He did not look up as Harris left the place. A character.

Of Sir Archbold Staleybridge Harris saw nothing until the second performance at the Cathedral of the Saint Matthew Passion. The Cathedral was eighteen miles out in the country and thus there was no junketing after the performance as there had been in the city. Both occasions had been wonderfully successful, but found Harris deadly tired. There was no elation for him, merely routine movements with baton and fingers, though rehearsal had done the trick. The choir and orchestra were indefatigable and as the closing, thoughtful movements of the Passion sang on, they seemed to gain a clarity, a clear, unhampered texture that was quite out of Harris's hands. It was a rare chance for him; he seemed to be conducting some unearthly machine, some heavenly diapason, which awed him, was quite beyond any effort of his own. As the oboes swept for the last time from leading-note to tonic, he put away his baton, downed his head for the voice hollowly pronouncing the benediction and stumbled away.

The buzz of noise, magnified in the roof, of socialites shaking hands, of musicians comparing notes, of the packing of instruments, the unscrewing of stands seemed, though perfectly audible, in some way removed from him, cut off by a wall of glass or water. He stood with his hand on a chair watching the movements of the crowd and not understanding them, like a man in an aquarium watching the goggle-eyed darting of fishes, taking pleasure in the artfully-lit flick of fin or tails, but wondering what the rush was about. People spoke to him and he answered, pleasantly; modestly smiling he thanked them for their congratulations. Both he and they were speaking gold-fish language.

Staleybridge and his wife came up. Harris saw them, recognised Staleybridge, but had no idea what to do. In his state there were no problems; if Staleybridge asked a question, it could be answered. But if he had to work his way into Staleybridge's favour, that was impossible. Perhaps he would try, as one runs a finger nail down the glass case, to make the fishes dive, but no more than that. One had no idea whether that was the correct approach.

'Wonderful performance,' said Staleybridge. The lady with him smiled, and spoke at length of her thanks. She was beautifully dressed, had once been herself beautiful; she was exactly the sort of woman Harris disliked, a lady of some artificial creation, but he could see she was trying to be kind. The thought sidled in dispassionately. One of the upper ten was being pleasant to him. Did she mean it? Was it that he had made for the moment an impression and she was therefore willing to condescend to speak to him? There was no apparent condescension about her. Her clothes, accent, perfume, jewellery, stance, air got him on the raw, but that said nothing about her as a woman, a naked, thinking heart. The thought slid away. He was too tired to bear malice even on principle.

'It's a great work,' he said.

'I have never been so moved before,' said Lady Staleybridge. Harris looked at her in surprise, a smarting pimple of emotion, on the dead skin of weariness. 'You must be a firm believer, Mr. Harris.'

He did not answer, and she did not seem to expect one. Sir Archbold nodded as if the evangelical statement were the one to be made. Perhaps it was. Harris decided he did not understand people. He wished he had a biscuit to eat; a thick one, with whorled, crumbly edges that he could hold in his hand and bite. He'd feel the crumbs crackle and burst on his lips and tongue; he would know how to handle it. He looked down the long line of arches, and the darkness of the roof over the slight swing of the chandeliers. Pathetic thought. For Bach, read biscuit. Lady Staleybridge was talking again.

'We're hoping to hear your work next Saturday, Mr. Harris. Sir George Gilbert says how fine it is. We are really looking forward to it. It's an honour to have a man like you, Mr. Harris, with us. It is indeed.'

Harris peeled the accent from the words, and there they stood. She meant it. He could not believe she meant it; such things should be said by the woman behind the mop or the linen-draper's counter.

'Yes,' said Harris. 'It will be interesting.'

'It must be very exciting for you, all this. I'd give anything to be able to stand up and conduct as you did...'

Harris thought of himself in the last chorus, dog-tired, going through the motions, wishing it were over. That counterpoint which had touched him to tears time and again as he worked over it in his room, at rehearsal, was so much noise. He knew the choir was achieving it to perfection, but not for or to him.

'... and to write music, to create for others to create again must be an experience that...'

Staleybridge touched his wife's arm.

'Come 'long, m'dear,' he said. 'Long drive in front of us.'

Lady Staleybridge subsided and smiled. Staleybridge had moved away. She took Harris's hand, pressing it between both of hers. Staleybridge noticed this, nodded again with curt approval and stepped back to shake hands himself, briskly. As the pair walked down the aisle, Harris noticed that, in spite of a straight spine, Staleybridge had a limp and his wife's ankles were swollen. The retreating backs joined Harris and humanity.

Harris's contacts with Winterburn and Mrs. Brand were neither here nor there. The flush of success had disappeared from Winterburn and he was only moderately cheerful. He grumbled, but spoke to Leaman; he would walk to the bus with Harris, but said little about his wife's return. He seemed interested in Harris's reactions to the forthcoming Prologue, but he never made a frontal attack for information. Harris would have been glad for a chance to spill what he felt. He himself would have been reticent, diffident, but the offering of scraps of confidence might have eased the period of waiting.

The days stumbled past. They had nearly finished at school and most nights were taken up with study, administration or rehearsal of the Matthew. But there were gaps when his fear for the Requiem stabbed him. That the dread was there was clear; it became worse when the first Passion was so outstandingly successful. To Harris, a success meant one thing; you were placed higher, more carelessly, for the next disaster to slug you down. Each time you won something, and got it hard, you held out another trophy for catastrophe to steal away. In Harris's world there was no such thing as a series of successes; his boyhood had engineered that. One up; one down was the scheme. You stuck, of course; you didn't give in; in fact, you counted yourself lucky that it wasn't one up, two, three, four down. When Brand told him that the full Requiem was as good as accepted, Harris had to fight, not an elation of delight but a shudder. Sometimes he thought he had been happier when he was up against it. Down, he'd need fear no fall. Up, he expected nothing else.

One night, as he was going to a rehearsal of the Passion, he met Mrs. Brand in the street. It was raining very slightly and she wore a raincoat and little waterproof hat, the shape of those they'd called in the army 'caps, ridiculous'. She saw him first.

'Hello, Mr. Harris,' she said, shyly. He stopped. Under the light of the street-lamp she looked waxy, with the rain faintly on her nose, as if she were in a fever.

'Hello,' he said. 'What's wrong? Car bust?'

'Oh, no. I like to walk. Too much driving makes you fat, doesn't it?' He eyed her diminutive, curving shape.

'Suppose so.'

She looked at him and smiled. He saw a pale shadow of a line at the side of her mouth. Apparently she wasn't using lipstick.

'I'm off to a meeting,' she said. She rubbed the side of her nose with a forefinger like a child and then examined the upturned finger-end. 'Will you come with me?'

'What sort of meeting?' he asked.

'To protest against H-bomb tests. We're trying to get the government to take unilateral action. Will you come?'

'I'm sorry,' he said. 'I can't. Got a rehearsal.'

'What of?'

'The Matthew Passion.'

'Then don't go. Come with me.' She spoke in her sharp, sergeant-major voice.

'I can't. I've something like a hundred people waiting for me.'

'Well, I'll tell you what. I'll go along to the rehearsal-room and then you can tell them where you're going. Perhaps they'll come with us. And if they don't, they'll still think it's important. And it is. It's the most important thing on earth.'

'Is it?' he said, annoyed at her simplicity.

'You know it is,' she said. 'It's no good singing the Matthew Passion when they drop a cobalt-bomb. We've got to make the world fit for Bach, and when it is, then we can sing, because we shall be happy.'

'Well, I'll just continue rehearsing,' he said. 'And when you've set the world to rights I'll be ready to do my bit.'

She looked at him abashed, and slapped her hand in a pet against her coat. There were tears in her eyes.

'You're a fool,' she said.

'Many people would consider you equally foolish,' he said.

'I wish I hadn't done that libretto for you now. John tells me it's certain to get a performance. I see now that I was only playing with words round about a serious thing. I'm taking some action now. Foolish action, you say, but action. I think I'd have done better to write letters to the Prime Minister.'

'They wouldn't have reached him,' he said.

'Somebody would have read them. Some seed of doubt and sanity might have been planted.'

'You've got the real platform manner,' he said.

'What I'm saying is a cliché,' she said. 'But it's right. A cliché's only a cliché to those who bother about words, and art, and such. What I was doing in that libretto was wrapping truth up in nice words so that nobody would understand them. That's what you're doing in your music. You're putting a barrier between people and understanding.'

'What a little puritan,' he said laughing.

'Call me what you like,' she said, 'as long as you come.'

'I'm sorry,' he said. 'I can't.'

'You won't.'

'All right. I won't.'

She shook her head, flinging off a few drops of rain. A warm, damp wind was blowing. Suddenly she put her hand out. He was reminded again of the films. She could not help posturing, even when she was utterly sincere. This was the Big Goodbye. This Thing is Bigger than the Both of Us. So They Walked Out into the Night. He felt small, cheated, deflated.

He took her hand after an interval.

'Goodbye, Nance,' he said.

'Goodbye,' she said. 'Don't forget what I've told you.'

'No,' he said. 'Doubtless some seed of doubt is sown.'

She dropped his hand, and left, almost running.

He stood, ashamed. He could not help treating her badly. For a minute, he saw himself as she saw him, malevolent authority; blind, stupid nastiness going to any length to gall her. Cooke, Leaman, Staleybridge, all powers-that-were were no worse than he was. We were all tarred with the brush of violent malice. Some had more elbow-room; that was all.

There was the pavement, where she'd stood with her hand out. He was reminded of his father at the conclusion of the Button business offering to shake hands. A gesture? A snippet of human foolishness? Tinpot foolery towards a tin-god? He shook his head miserably.

Curiously enough, when he was at rehearsal he was no longer troubled. Now his search for an outlet to power was properly employed.

The week before the concert shot away, although each minute considered in its own right was interminable. The weather was good; a wash of blue sky, bunched clouds, sun on wet pavements, poet's weather. Harris, on holiday, had nothing to do. He noted, without rancour, that nobody seemed concerned with his ordeal; he could talk to friends and nothing would be said about the Prologue and Scena. No word came from Cooke or Brand. Sitting in the Central Library, he'd watch the showers pelt over the stained, gothic windows and read Shakespeare sometimes, at others a large score of Berlioz' Messe Des Morts. Both were dull dogs, flat boys. Now and again he'd be attracted by some phrase or touch or conception, but forcing his eye back he'd discover the ephemeral delight was done. Then he'd get up, smile at the assistant-librarians sitting at a desk cutting up and endlessly pasting newspapers, go down to the coffee-bar across the way, sit at a chromium table in bamboo-hung windows and watch the variety turns from the music-hall over the road sinking their serious cups of tea, massaging dry-skinned jowls. Or he'd take his umbrella and walk in the frowsty park, past the Victorian busts and the Chinese pagoda and watch the ducks on the pond behind the low, lurching railing. Not much of a life; but then he was barely alive. An habitual act, such as lighting a pipe, came as a surprise. He'd wonder why he was doing it, and exactly how he should hold his match. The taste of smoke was new, but dull.

On some such moments, he'd feel a surge of success. He was Thomas Harris. His Requiem was about to be commissioned. Then he'd drag his feet like a boy showing off, and flick his spent match whirling into a bin and nod to some loiterer on a bench. But the elation did not last. He did not want it to; he was too cautious, but, either way, he'd no choice. The impetuous instant lost momentum, sagged; he was left wondering if it was time to start back for lunch, or if the last shower had damped his trouser-bottoms sufficiently for him to go home and change and thus put back the meal and hurry the day through.

No word came about the Friday rehearsal. He knew the time, but expected an invitation. He watched the postman twice. Nothing. What about the cinema then? He'd go to the pictures and would show 'em. He was already in the queue under the red-rose bands of neon light when he gave in to himself and walked to the Albert Hall.

The rehearsal had started. Gilbert was imposing himself on the choir, catching people out, driving them, stampeding flat faces into headlong music. They did Zadok the Priest and then, Harris had never heard this bit of fancy work before, the Academic Festival Overture with the Philharmonic Society hammering in at the end singing Gaudeamus Igitur. Under a new arrangement, this was to precede Harris's work which brought the first half to a conclusion and left the second to the gentler gales of Acis and Galatea. Harris wondered, distantly, if this unison bawling of Gaudeamus, and Gilbert made it flash sparks, was a bit of programme-planning by Cooke, an ironical preparation for the use of the song in the alto-wife's solo. Good for Cooke.

'Prologue and Scena,' said Gilbert, wiping his hands. He took his coat off and nodded to the tenor of the Prologue who sat huddled in a topcoat. 'I want this eloquent. Speaking. Talking. This is the language of our time, the language everyone of us understands. Brahms and Handel are the pure Latin and Greek. This is the contemporary, racy, unsmug vernacular.'

With this oracle he got on with it, and spent forty-five minutes of agony, cursing and gibing, until Harris thought the whole choir, three hundred or so, would rush on him in mutiny and fling his mangled bits into the street. Heads bowed, feet shifted as he concerned himself with notes, dynamics, power-points, as he called them, but then, suddenly, he thanked them in an offhand, courtly fashion which charmed the usual row of well-to-do be-bosomed grandmas and briefly looked at Acis.

'Good strong-arm stuff,' said Cooke to Harris after the rehearsal. 'My eye, he's a shaker.'

He told Harris where to sit on the next night so that he could be fetched up, gave him a ticket, posh as a workhouse master, waved a hand and said,

'Now get into kip for twenty-four hours.'

'Have you heard anything from Staleybridge?' asked Harris. He hated the question.

Cooke smiled and spread his arms wide, palms outwards and walked away towards Gilbert.

* * *

It was pleasant to find yourself arriving at the concert after waiting all day. Every action, the polishing of shoes, choosing a shirt or handkerchief had seemed an obstacle; Harris would have liked to have done none, to have gone dirty but his mother had knocked him too firmly into line in these affairs.

Now he was walking to the Albert Hall, worried because his polished toecap had two spots of mud on it, wondering if he dare stop and wipe it off on the back of his trousers.

A quarter of an hour to go. He'd walk round the Circus and finish his pipe. The doors were wide open, and the usual people were there. The tall young fellow with blond hair, holding his umbrella, Oxford-fashion, with the handle pointing away from him. The fur-coat brigade. The family party, all of a rush from their car, with mother's white silk, the Philharmonic's badge, showing eighteen inches under her coat. Sugar-bag or was it flour-bag? The students with their scarves. The honest man with scores. The worried man raking his raincoat pocket for the tickets. The man with glasses and cloth-cap, wondering about the babysitter and the television-set. The young ladies in threes, all licentiates or associates of somewhere-or-other, who'd put their pupils off for the night. The gushers, the screamers, the nodders, the grunters, the hand-shakers, clerks in holy orders, the mothball stinkers, the tweed-coat and pocketful of fountain-pen men, they were all there. This was the audience. Harris had appealed to them. They judged. Death and the man-in-the street? A vestal virgin hit into him with an elbow like a breaking wing-forward. 'Beg pardon,' she said. He had a momentary glance of a parrot's powdered nose, with flared nostrils, and she rushed inside, side-stepping and hacking. Why her hurry? He smelt her scent again.

From a little way up the hill, at the other side of the Circus, he stood and watched them again. Three oblongs of light on the pavement and black figures flitting. The moon shifted amongst clouds like railway-smoke. Full house tonight.

Harris knocked his pipe out on his heel and finally wiped his toe-caps on his trousers. He examined the result under the next street-lamp. He went into the Hall.

As he walked down the steps, the warmth of the building wrapped round him and the whole structure seemed to tingle in the buzz of intense noise. There were fiddlers in the foyer who tucked handkerchiefs into their collars. A man swinging a bassoon was deep in serious talk. Harris showed his ticket. The steward pointed briefly with a finger and turned away to peer at a large incoming group. Harris had not been recognised as a holder of a seat-of-the-mighty. Bad luck. A girl sold him a programme casually. Sixpence to see his own name, large as Brahms's or Handel's, but smaller than Gilbert's; Thomas

Harris (b 1916).

He tipped his seat down and folded his coat on his knee. The seat on his right was empty; that on the left occupied by a young lady from the university who was going through her handbag at breakneck speed. He looked round quickly. It was certainly full. Everywhere there was the hot rush of noise. The gallery writhed like an ant-hill. It was as if some order had been given to clamber over the seat-backs and start twenty press-ups. Harris recognised nobody. A figure stood out here and there strangely; a fat man, waving; a pale boy polishing his glasses.

The choir were up and at ease. Ladies wore white silk; ghosts, cobwebs, night-gowns, cement-bags. The men expanded chests under evening wear and talked to the bloke three places away. The oboe wailed to the organ; fiddles flashed to the chandeliers; the harpist wittled up and down her strings unheard.

At 7.15 the leader appeared and was perfunctorily clapped. Gilbert ranged on, bowed once straight ahead, into the cheers, turned about, stuck both arms in the air like a muezzin, wagged his hair at the timps and they were having the National Anthem. Once that was over, Gilbert relaxed, put his back to the orchestra and swinging his baton in his finger-tips like a newly-commissioned orderly-officer watched the late-comers paddle in. Having derived satisfaction from that, he flicked up the baton, scrutinized it in surprise, stared at the choir, bit his lip, rubbed his disengaged hand over his face and tapped the stand.

He bent towards the firsts,[20] and the strings were away. Zadok the Priest and Nathan the Prophet anointed Solomon King. The Philharmonic roared. Gilbert ended with a great shuddering passion of energy. Item No. 1 was done. Gilbert spent little time at the rostrum, went down. Sturton appeared, white-tie, tails, the whole hog, head-surrag[21] for once, and was greeted with a friendly outburst. He took his choir through the Four Sacred Pieces with power, Harris thought. He'd none of Gilbert's platform manner; he conducted like a man suffering from rheumatism, but the performance was excellent. If there were broadcasts going, Sturton pulled them in. Local boy made good. The Philharmonic were a virtuoso choir; too extrovert perhaps for Harris, too many with brass lungs, but magnificently trained. At the end of the Sacred Pieces, Gilbert brought Sturton back, leading him by the hand.

The orchestra were now tuning again and Gilbert, hands in pockets, was talking to the cellos, amongst them, one of the boys. A steward opened the swing door to let Sturton in; he took the vacant seat next to Harris. His face was quite covered with beads of sweat, which staggered together and ran off in high trickles like rain down a window. Eyes switched in his direction. He breathed heavily like a sick man, and mopped his face; his hairy hands were trembling.

'Jolly good,' said Harris. 'First rate. Marvellous.'

Sturton nodded, rubbing the handkerchief, big as a blanket, round the back of his thick neck. Gilbert looked out, smiled at Sturton, remounted the rostrum, crouched, waggled shoulders, flashed his baton and was stuck across the Academic Festival Overture. Though his movements were minute, the driving power was plainly seen; an eye up, a flat wave of the left hand, and somebody else was pushed beyond his limits. He radiated confidence, and when finally he fetched the men in to sing Gaudeamus Igitur he stood tall, whipping his baton, as if he was calling a yapping dog to heel. Harris noticed some of his own choir there, rollicking with the rest, giving all they had to the big, broad, chummy Brahmsy tone. Sir George, meanwhile, scratched at his ribs through his white waistcoat with the left hand as though the climax were already accounted for, played off to perfection.

The audience went for this in a big way. They stood to clap. True, the young woman from the university whispered that it was a 'gimmick' and her friend agreed it was 'vulgar', but they were a minority. The clapping was furious. Harris noted that Gilbert had not yet used a score, and wondered if the Scena would force him to open the book. Certainly there wasn't one on the desk.

The orchestra diminished itself rapidly. Strings, woodwind and brass soloists, harp, additional percussion re-arranged themselves. Gilbert watched the changes easily. When it seemed they were about to start, he recrossed his rostrum and left the platform. People began to talk. It was impossible to discover, Harris thought, whether or not there was tension. The crowd round him were mainly happy, caught up still in the Brahmsian heartiness. A few considered the programme note. Harris did likewise. He had not been consulted, but the thing was sensible. 'These excerpts from a Requiem in the modern idiom and on which the composer is currently engaged consist of (i) a prologue, (tenor, orchestra, chorus), which reminds all humanity that it is mortal and (ii) a scena in which a widow (mezzo-soprano) laments for her dead husband while the chorus broods on the universality of violence and death in the world.'

'This is it,' said Sturton. He was cooler now.

Harris nodded. He was cold, attacked by trembling ice cracking the spine. He could not keep his legs still and goose pimples pricked on his arms. His bowels were loose; his face locked in a mask of cool steel. With an effort he jerked his head round. Behind him a man was taking a caramel from a paper, a woman fanning herself with a programme; up in the gallery Staleybridge, in full evening regalia, was talking to the Duchess. Cooke was there, smiling. They didn't care.

Gilbert came up the steps on to the platform, leading his soloists, a tall, attractive girl with big arms and a fair young man with glasses. Nobody had thought to put out chairs for the singers. An omen. Gilbert imperiously did his stick-drill at the violas and they brought two vacated chairs forward. Harris saw Brand get up to let the chairs pass. He held his instrument and bow in one hand and continued a laughing conversation with the girl next to him who was adjusting their stand. The soloists finally sat down. Gilbert seemed in no hurry; he said something to the mezzo and listened, nodding his head to her reply. It seemed minutes before he tapped his desk.

No, he was not using a score.

He hunched again, shoulders right down. His baton bounced and bows leapt with white fire across the strings. Sound galloped down the hall. Elbows crooked and straightened, heads jumped and the biting noise of strings driving themselves into ears blotted out each others consideration. With an uneven, unstoppable, flinging motion the fiddles smashed themselves along, like a bulldozer in twigs, chased by the violent hammer of the timps and interrupted, though not stopped, hurried rather, by the thin chafing of the solo woodwind. This was elemental music; no soft-soap, no syrup; the rough edge of the composer's tongue. We're not in here to muck about; dewy-eyed, starry-eyed, bat-eyed, boss-eyed, out. This is not comfort, we aren't here to lick your chops and wounds in A minor. This gets you on your toes; army-fashion; outside for P.T.[22] You don't drag, you're dragged, up high; you come out fighting or you stop where you are.

The strings belted at it, scurry and beat, until a great golden clash of percussion, bass-drum, kettles, timps, cymbals, triangle, gong, iron-bars wiped the strings' sound clean and clear out and the tenor, unaccompanied, opened fortissimo.

'You who are listening, easy in your pew and your mind,
This concerns you.'

The strings bit again, dived and died to a muttering.

'I am speaking about death. That concerns You.'

The word death was flung round the choir, in eight parts; it seemed an echo of the race and beat of the strings' beginning, but the question 'Death?' was put. Now here, now there; now in a close harmony, now spaced soaring and quiet with soprano, growling with the men. 'Death?' The soloist interrupted. He said death was the concern of all; they all shared it alike; they might as well think about it. The choir, pianissimo, fierce, moved, trained to a hair, questioned every statement, flung his plain words about, twisted them until the word 'death' flew like a cloud of stinging insects spat about by a backing wind. The world was full of death, the soloist declaimed and the three men on the timpani let loose a maddened tom-tom of pain; a clarinet exactly mimicked his line over fighting strings; the ladies, fainting and high began to mimic but let the phrase drool away into an uncontrolled wail into which the other parts sagged, gibbering and anguished. 'This is your concern'. 'It's ours.' 'Is it ours?' 'It cannot be'. 'It is and can'. These the choir took up in a marvellous canon like forked lightning at a quaver's remove, prestissimo while the soloist shouted 'your concern' over and over again with a wooden idiocy that bespoke the perfection of practice until the strings from a remote key broke in with the initial hammering, the wildly hitting surge. Again the golden clangour of the percussion, but the strings were this time unchecked; recklessly they bundled on, dragging the eyes out of you, sloshing the blood to your temples, drilling in, killing, racking. Again the burst of iron. Nothing stopped. A murderous crescendo was on, which rattled up in intensity until it seemed as if every man-jack and woman on the platform would fling himself, herself off the stage, smashing the polished wood, trampling the delicate bows, splitting the flattened bridges and splintered bellies. Again the great hammer of percussion, fighting to hold the gallop into chaos, and with a shattering second of discord the whole dissolved, thrashed itself into a chord of C major with trumpets up high and a thunder of two great organ pedals.

There was dead silence in the hall, the frightened silence of consternation. Gilbert stood locked leaning towards the violas, baton up, to start the Scena. Harris sat dumbfounded. Gilbert had done it, first shot. The trembling had left his legs. He was holding on to the seat in front, knuckles white as leprosy, but the man there didn't seem to notice. Sturton was rubbing his hand over his face. The young lady from the university was gnawing at a lace-edged handkerchief, a shilling-sized ring of colour burning on her cheek bones. Harris knew he'd won. They'd listened; they were going to listen. Now you big bugs, you weight-chuckers, where were you? Tom Harris was shouting at you from Sinai and Horeb.[23]

Gilbert's baton curled through a lovely circle and the violas began to sing. The tenor sat down and wiped his head; the young woman with big arms was standing. Harris could see Brand's partner; her left hand was in a frenzy of vibrato as the broken, gleaming tune spoke across the hall. There was sorrow; a modern man speaking sorrow; a full man and his grief. The girl began, 'He, whom I loved, is dead.' The violas paraded gently round her, easy and supple, stroking her voice with hands like athletic lovers.

The woman sang with balance; her voice was rich but she was not content with mere beautiful noise. She was into her part, determined to carry her audience. The tune Harris had written her was simple enough, at least, to hear, and round it the other instruments moved with short, eloquent phrases, which underlined the poignancy of her part. It was all easy; only those who knew the score knew how delicately the accompanying counterpoint was bandied from instrument to instrument and how difficult each change, each gradation of tone, was to make. Gilbert didn't put a foot wrong. The whole of the intricate writing was in his head, and slight movements here and there, spoke his control. The girl's lament poured out, filling the hall and the orchestra supported her to the very limit.

The middle section of the song asked a question. 'Who am I to complain? I might almost be called lucky.' Harris had broken up the flow for this. The wife was to ask her questions like some teacher of morals. The girl had it perfectly. She asked, but both as one with a conscience and as one with real grief; she wound the two together so that her sorrow threw up the doubts, and the doubts doubled the grief. The women of the choir howled about her; mothers and wives. The men sang snatches of Gaudeamus over a rough fugetto in the orchestra and that was all suddenly bound into a high, unaccompanied chorus, a kind of cappella shout, 'The world is full of death; the world is full of death' and then the violas were back, on the first, broken, heart-breaking obbligato and the full voice briefly, soothed by the shifting instruments, sang her personal grief. 'The world is riddled with death' said the choir. 'He whom I loved is dead' and the cellos turned the melting theme into a molten, high, angry buzz, a gesture, thin, angry, narked, dyspeptic. 'The world is full of death', pianissimo, fading, insistent from the choir, and it was over.

There was quiet again for some seconds. It seemed longer. Then the case-hardened types spattered into clapping and the whole concourse applauded. The clapping was strong, Harris noted. Gilbert motioned his soloists to stand, and stood holding their finger-tips. Now from here and there came a drumming, banging of feet on the floor, and some shouts. ''Core, 'core.' That must be the students. The audience elsewhere took the shouts up. There was tremendous applause; it was not the ear-splitting chaos of Blidworth, but then the hall was too big for that. There was more and more shouting. The young lady from the university next to Harris was flailing her arms together like a maniac windmill. Gilbert let go the tenor's hand and beckoned Harris. Sturton tugged at his coat, pulled him up, pushed him. He was walking out now, through the swing doors, in another entrance, up the steps, and on the platform. The fiddles moved their chairs for him; a huge roar of approval burst from the choir.

Harris bowed, dazzled. He ran his hand through his hair, ruffling it. The students were giving it four sorts now.

'Thanks,' said Harris to Gilbert; 'marvellous.' He shook hands with the soloists and the leader.

Gilbert stepped forward and held a hand up. Clapping died.

'You seem determined to have a long concert,' he said, smiling. 'But it's great stuff, great stuff. I've done it once for you. How about doing it again now for,' he paused, 'Thomas Harris?' He put an arm over Harris's shoulder. The audience let rip.

'O.K.' said Gilbert to the leader. 'Again.'

Harris scuttled off the platform. When he got back into the hall, Gilbert was waiting up there for him, clapping. People craned to see him; there was more applause. The young lady from the university looked as if she'd have a fit. Gilbert waved, a sort of salute, turned round, tapped, hunched and the strings banged into it again.

Harris was excited.

After the first rush for the doors in the interval he sat still until he had filled his pipe and had his hand shaken off by Sturton before moving himself. People looked at him now. He was somebody. He'd done something.

As he moved towards the door he was battered by excitement. He wanted to jump and kick, but compelled himself to appear modest, a middle-aged man going quietly out for a smoke. People looked at him, stopped their conversations to look. One or two of the orchestra nodded as if they were in a secret with him; a choir woman, yards of white silk and a fur-stole, stopped in a rush to thank him for the experience. It was good to be recognised. That fact was unpalatable enough, but it was there. What price Harris the mouthpiece of the underdog now? He was delighted with himself, a big noise. Perhaps that was all his Prologue and Scena was about, a place in the sun for Tom Harris. He was up aloft with Cooke and Staleybridge now; they coined money, he minted music. 'Strewth.

The thought of Staleybridge was no discomfort. He could look him in the eye. The thing was a success. Staleybridge could hardly refuse the completed Requiem a hearing. But couldn't he? Wasn't that what big bugs were for? To get a climate of opinion, a great will-to-power from the thousands, and then scatter it, shred it. Staleybridge might refuse; it was like him.

Not that it mattered. Harris was bursting at the seams with joy. He had power. He'd proved it.

Somebody shook him hard by both hands. It was Button.

'Ah, Mest'r 'Arris, ma duck, ma duck.' That was all. Marby stood alongside, a cigarette dangling. He shook his head, beyond words. A marvellous compliment.

'Got t'be gooin',' said Button. They rushed off.

Harris saw some of his colleagues. Through an open door he caught a glimpse of Hobson and his wife. Hobson, his face quite straight, his jacket of the people's cut, like Stalin's, was conveying information to his wife in his slow, deliberate way. There was McManus now, coming down the stairs, still in his overcoat in spite of the heat, shy, with his scholar's stoop, head down watching for bawbees. Harris wondered if he'd come on his bike and peered to see his clips. He couldn't; then suddenly it became important to know. Probably the excitement. Harris pushed through the crowd.

'McManus,' he shouted. McManus pulled his head up. 'Have you come on your bike?'

McManus was baffled.

'Your bike?' said Harris. 'Socialist realism?'

'Yes.'

McManus shook his hand, nodded several times, eyed the crowd, said, 'A lot here,' and moved off.

'Absolutely wonderful, Mr. Harris,' said a woman's voice. Leaman and his wife.

'First-rate,' said Leaman, colonel-wise.

'The rest'll be just anti-climax,' said Mrs. Leaman. 'We should all go home.'

'Not Handel,' said Harris.

'You admire Handel?' she said in her party voice. She was glad to be seen talking to Harris. McManus crept back by them. Mrs. Leaman looked him up and down. She knew him quite well, but wasn't stopping to speak now with more important matters to hand.

'Now for the real music, eh, Mac?' said Harris.

McManus stopped, and stuttered, gathering his wits.

'Good evening, Mr. McManus,' said Mrs. Leaman.

'Mr. Harris, Mr. Harris,' somebody was calling in the crush a yard or two away. People stopped talking.

'Excuse me,' said Harris and stepped back. It was a steward with a note from Cooke. Harris ripped it open, watched by a hundred eyes. An invitation to come round to the artists' room immediately the concert was done. This was it. Harris rammed it into his pocket. The Leamans had gone back in. The choir were shuffling up to their places.

'Well, if it's not the old Archduke himself.' Brand's voice. 'We did you a little bit of good there, eh, boy, eh?'

Brand, carrying his viola, stood at his back with Nance. She looked small, and smiling. Her eyes were large, wet.

'Jolly good,' said Harris. 'Hello, Mrs. Brand.'

'Yes, comrade,' said Brand. 'You're honoured. The missus's here. Took time off from camping on atom-bomb sites for an earful of the great forthcoming attraction.'

'Marvellous,' said Mrs. Brand, in a distant way.

'Glad you liked it,' said Harris, hearty.

'Oh, yes,' she said. 'I did.'

'Got to scapa,' said Brand. 'Have to play in tune in Handel. Doesn't matter in his nib's. Fact is, the real edge was given by me playing a bit off all the time.' He stuck his instrument under his chin and struck the open strings.

'Goodbye, Mr. Harris,' Nance said. 'And thank you.'

She touched her husband's arm, playfully almost, and walked away. Harris watched her. A small, beautifully-dressed woman, walking under the flickering red-sign, Exit.

'Made an impression, son,' said Brand. 'You've got what it takes, and then some.'

Harris wasn't listening. He watched, over the far side, Winterburn and his wife, hurrying back to take their seats. Winterburn was red in the face and at least two yards in the lead of his wife. He was holding a programme in his hand and looked like an important person, an Emperor-figure, without whose presence the Games could not start. They did not see Harris.

'Hob-nobbing afterwards?' said Brand. 'Bad luck.'

Harris went in. Sturton stood up, over-ceremoniously, to let him find his seat. The young lady from the university blushed, looked away, played with her handkerchief. The leader came on; the soloists; Gilbert. Harris stopped himself from applauding too violently. For a moment, he'd thought he'd be sick, but the stately presto opening of Acis and Galatea steadied him.

He sat back, winded, to hear Handel, the King of Pros, knock off, easy as kiss my hand, winner after winner. It was then he first noticed that he was still holding the plugged, unlighted pipe.

Once the concert was over, Harris found himself reluctant to go in to meet Staleybridge. There were plenty of people to detain him; people he did not know insisted on shaking hands and making congratulatory conversation. By the time he got through the swing doors the hall was practically empty. The young lady from the university came up and asked him to autograph her programme.

'Weren't you sitting next to me?' asked Harris, signing.

'Yes.' She blushed; she had not expected him to have noticed her. This man, who had thought out those marvels of sound, had taken in what she,

Miss Nobody, was like.

'The Handel was good,' said Harris, waving the programme to dry the ink. He noticed the duke and duchess, with a parcel of notables, entering the artists' room.

'Marvellous,' the girl said. 'Oh, your Prologue and Scena.'

'You liked it?' said Harris, smiling.

'Oh, yes.'

He returned the programme. She left him walking backwards. It was then that Harris saw the Winterburns. They were hanging about, obviously to have a word with him, but Winterburn, unwilling to admit this, was going through some sort of performance of his own, looking about, consulting his watch, frowning as if they were waiting for some unpunctual friend. Mrs. Winterburn stood quite still, obedient to her husband's foolishness.

'Hello, Winterburn,' Harris called out. It would waste time before the interview.

Winterburn who had seen him, it was clear, from the time he came into the foyer, went through another face-saving game. He bent towards his wife, took her arm, murmured something about going and then broke this off to see Harris, smiled at him, strode over with his hand out, leaving his wife where she was.

'Why, Harris.' A heavy shake. 'My goodness. Congratulations. We thoroughly enjoyed it.' He looked back for his wife, and nodded for her to come up and share the moment.

'You know my wife, don't you, Harris?'

They shook hands. She made the right faces for a moment or two, then let her eyes fall.

'Powerful writing,' said Winterburn. 'Forthright.'

He spoke as one who knew. Harris guessed it was all for the wife.

'Very nice,' said Mrs. Winterburn, in a small, flat voice. The secondary-modern type. Her husband frowned.

'Intensely realised,' he said. 'Spoken straight out.' He nodded. Harris noticed how curiously like Leaman Winterburn was in this mood. 'A wonderful evening, Tom, wonderful.' He took a big breath and manhandled the lapel of his overcoat. 'Well, we shall have to be off. Goodnight, and thank you.'

His hand came out, large, firmly-gripping.

'Goodnight, Mrs. Winterburn,' said Harris. 'Nice to have seen you again.' He would have liked to clap her shoulder or give her a kiss. He did neither, but watched them go, Winterburn engaged in a Fuchsian struggle with his top-coat, his wife a yard behind, tripping.

Harris treated his face to a grimace; slightly shifted his dentures. He was still excited, but scared now. He was glad he'd seen Winterburn. That little scene had made it explicit that he'd had a success.

He walked across the foyer and confronted the polished door. There was a legend on it 'Minister's Vestry.' He tapped and waited.

Nobody answered. He knocked again. No sign. Unwillingly he turned the handle and went in.

As he pushed open the door, he was startled by the immense jazz of noise, of which there had been no inkling outside through the thick walls. The room was long, and full. Everybody was talking. He collided gently with a tall, wooden hat-and-umbrella stand. Quietly he closed the door.

Round three of the walls were enormous photographs, a yard square, of parsons. The hall was in the first place a Mission and these were previous incumbents, if non-conformists ever used such a word. He looked at the one by his elbow; the Rev. T. Mainwaring Harvey (1921-23) and studied the pose of twinkling benevolence.

'Ah, the man of the moment.' A big voice interrupted, and a big paw advanced. A balding young fellow with a beard swept him forward. Some glanced up from their talk. Cooke waved the big hello from the far side. 'Great stuff, sir, great stuff.'

With that Beaver felt he had done his bit, and retired. Harris moved up the room towards Cooke, who managed to lean outwards from his conversational group.

'Seen Staleybridge?' Cooke asked.

'No. Has he said anything to you yet?'

Cooke shook his head, puzzled, pointed to where Staleybridge was standing, and swayed back to his companions.

Harris looked about him. Five or six groups becking hard. Beaver talking to the big-armed soprano; Gilbert with the duchess and Sir Archbold and Lady Staleybridge; no Brand. The racket crackled on.

Gilbert was going nineteen to the dozen to the ladies and Staleybridge stood by, quite impassive, tapping his teeth with a Dunhill briar. Harris caught his eye. Staleybridge stared, frowned minutely, nodded and went back to his pipe play.

That was all.

Gilbert suddenly looked up.

'Harris. The man,' he said. He waved him across. 'Here he is, the local genius. You know the Duchess of Annesley, do you?'

The duchess put out her hand, and smiled.

'It must be wonderful to be you, Mr. Harris, at this moment,' she said. She spoke like anybody else, very pleasantly.

'Magnificent,' said Lady Staleybridge.

'You know Lady…' began Gilbert.

'We have met,' she said. 'I saw Mr. Harris conducting Bach.'

'Is he as good as I am?' said Gilbert, ignorant as the R.S.M.

'No fishing now,' said the duchess. 'Wonderful, Mr. Harris.' She drifted quickly back into her interrupted conversation.

Harris, high and dry, noticed that the ladies had converged on Gilbert, and had left Staleybridge a yard or so away. His moment.

'Enjoyed the concert, sir?' said Harris.

Staleybridge brought his face slowly upward. He seemed affronted.

'Very much,' he said in his soft voice. 'Very good. Liked that thing of yours.' He began to drag his pipe-stem up and down his waistcoat.

'I'm glad.'

'Oh, yes, very good.' Staleybridge went back to his statuesque pose.

'Have you come to any decision…?' Harris said.

Staleybridge suddenly twisted his pipe in his fingers. The knuckles cracked.

'Begy'r pardon.'

A stab of temper tightened Harris's throat.

'Have you come to any decision,' he said, 'about commissioning my Requiem for the city's celebrations?' He seemed to himself to be speaking through gritted teeth. His face was thrust forward and his jaw out and locked. Bulldog Drummond.

'Oh,' said Staleybridge easily, 'didn't Cooke tell you?'

'Tell me what?' said Harris.

Staleybridge commenced the pipe-and-waistcoat drill. He watched himself, fascinated, draw intricate, wheeling designs.

'We met last week,' said Staleybridge. 'A few of us. We've decided on Beethoven's Choral Symphony. We're approaching Klemperer to see if he'll conduct. Should be a good show. Ode to Joy, what.'

This was it.

Ode to up-and-down Joy. No Requiem.

Now he'd got the answer he'd expected. Or was it the answer he wanted? Staleybridge had run true to type. Anger and lassitude struggled up to Harris's shoulder. Finally he achieved equilibrium, a sort of total anaesthesia. His fingers stuck straight downwards and he looked Staleybridge in the face.

'You're not doing my Requiem,' he said stupidly.

'No,' said Staleybridge surprised. 'The Ninth Symphony.'

If Harris had been his father, this would have been the time. Composer clouts knight. Or perhaps a deluge of abuse; good, short, vulgar, pig-sticking insult. He wondered what Staleybridge would do. The man was no fool, and couldn't have lived so long and so rich without getting into tight corners.

Harris stared rudely at Staleybridge, whose unconcern was disconcerting. With a start it came to Harris that Staleybridge did not realise there was anything wrong. The great, self-centred dolt hadn't allowed it to cross the ivory between his ears that Harris might be annoyed.

'That's that done then,' said Harris.

'Yes,' said Staleybridge, pleasantly. 'I've nothing against your work, Harris. You can be sure of that. But we had a look through the words again. They were just not suitable. Death and so forth.' He rubbed the corner of his jacket between thumb and forefinger.

'You might have told me,' said Harris.

'Yes. I took it that Cooke would do so. Very fly, that gentleman.' He smiled. 'Very good, your work tonight, very good indeed.'

'Not good enough to get a performance,' said Harris, vaguely trying to keep up hostility.

'No connection at all. It's over a week ago.'

'Why didn't you tell me last Saturday?' said Harris. 'You knew.'

'Never entered my head.'

'This evening was supposed to be the try-out, wasn't it?' What use was that?

'Well, yes, there was something said, something of the sort, now you remind me. Still, it's done now. Pity.'

'And I lump it,' said Harris.

'Yes,' said Staleybridge, 'you do. I shouldn't be disappointed if I were you. Cooke said it was certain you'd get a performance.'

'When?'

'I don't arrange these things,' said Staleybridge. 'I don't know. You see Cooke.'

'Uh,' said Harris. He scratched his chin, trying to work himself into a philosophical state of mind. This was the sort of setback that hurried him on.

'Well, thank you for speaking to me, Mr. Harris, about this matter. Glad you reminded me. I was very impressed with your Scena tonight. Don't usually like modern stuff. But you had me with you there.'

He patted Harris's arm and retired back to himself and teeth-tapping. Dismissal with blessing.

Harris backed away, uncertainly, made up his mind and went towards Cooke, who was still talking. Harris grabbed his elbow, hard and rude, and jerked him away from his companions.

'No Requiem,' said Harris. 'You knew all the time.'

Cooke raised his eyes to heaven.

'Cool off,' he said. 'They'd decided on Klemperer and that was that. Might be a good thing for you. You probably won't have to wait three years now.' He smiled. 'Ill wind, you know, boy. Leave it to Cooke.' No apology.

'Too many Cookes have spoilt this particular broth,' said Harris.

'Be nice to me,' said Cooke. He was jovial. 'I spit gold guineas. You've worked the trick tonight, done yourself a real bit of good. You go home and remember that in your prayers.'

He shook himself free of Harris's grip, turned his back and was laughing with his friends within seconds.

Harris looked round. They'd sorted themselves into cliques. The singers were left out on their own; they weren't important enough yet to be included in the real royalty of conversation. He went across and thanked them briefly. They seemed pleased.

He moved towards the door.

No Requiem. No fear.

The door opened and Harris, swerving, nudged the hat-stand again. Mrs. Cooke flashed in. She scrutinised Harris.

'Mr. Harris, isn't it? Lovely performance of your work tonight. And, oh, by the way, thanks for the other thing.'

'What other thing?'

'Not so loud. The birthday present. Very nice. Charles got Dargomizhsky to record it. I've heard it. Charming. But I'm not supposed to know. Don't say anything. Charles can't keep a secret, can he?'

'Can't he?' said Harris, thinking of his Requiem.

She looked at him curiously.

'Have you seen Nancy Brand lately?' she asked.

'Tonight.'

'Do you see much of her?'

'No,' he said, annoyed. 'Hardly at all.'

'She's going off the rails properly, I'm sorry to say. Got in with some pacifist crowd. Tries to convert me. She's a silly little thing. I told her that she'll end up in the papers being carted along like a sack of coal by two policemen, if not prison.' She laughed.

'Nothing wrong with that,' said Harris.

'Nothing wrong?' she said. 'Well, no, I suppose not if you do it on some sort of principle. But she doesn't. She does it because she's cracked. I imagine they all are. I shall leave her to it.'

'I bet she'll be sorry,' said Harris.

'She will,' Mrs. Cooke said blindly, 'she will. I really have tried hard for that girl.'

She pushed away. Harris got out, furious.

The night nipped after the crowded room. It had rained. As he began to walk home, the road shone like black glass and the trolley wires darted in the street-lights. He buttoned his coat and walked in the shadows of tall shops. People passed him, honest people, with a pint or two inside, talking rather loud. A courting couple swayed in a doorway. A cat slithered along the gutter before crossing the road fast and flat on its belly. Not much traffic. No Requiem. Neon-signs with dancing yellow boundaries marked the 'Lord Nelson.' It was still open and he could see a hatless youth lolling on the wall of the corridor swinging a jar on his forefinger.

Blessed is he that expecteth nothing; he won't be disappointed. The winner of tonight's booby prize is ... You don't have to tell me; I know.

'Yo' tak' 'er hom, an' Ah'll manage yo'r missus, I ses to him.' A raucous voice from a bus-queue and the shrill laughter of those who knew that alarm clocks rattled at half-past five. 'Yo' don't want much, surrey, 'e ses.'

As Harris walked he felt better. When he reached Forest Road the pubs had turned out. There was companionship and rough shouting; a woman swore for no reason. A spatter of rain blew down and was gone. Clouds raced above the shaking trees and Thomas Harris was thinking. The problems he'd lost a few weeks ago were back in his head exactly as they had been, unsolved but with the glimmer of a solution there. He knew now he could take the Requiem up again.

There was no sense of a marvellous epiphany about this. It was a sort of uncertain certainty that if he bothered to get down to it, there'd be results. It had no connection, apparently, with the evening's events; it co-existed with his disappointment, anger, frustration and excitement, but stood apart from them. At present the feeling was small. He would have to concentrate on it to the exclusion of others, but it was there and was real. It did not even remind him of the time in the school corridor when he knew he had to write a Requiem. That was a kind of pointer; this was the real thing. There was a musical job to be faced and with it the lick-and-promise of success. He walked along, humming, then stood stock still.

For a minute, he deliberately recalled the evening's performance, the strapping strings, the burst of the drums, the full voice of the young woman at the lament. Magnificent, but it meant nothing now compared with these obstacles he'd hack at tomorrow morning.

He was off again.

Sanderson let him in. He'd been waiting.

'All go well, Mr. Harris?'

'Yes, thanks.'

'Good performance of your work?'

'Very.'

'I should have liked to have gone myself,' said Sanderson, 'but you know how it is here. Like a cup of anything?' Decent man.

'No, thanks, Mr. Sanderson.'

'Right you are, Mr. Harris. Goodnight.'

Harris walked up the stairs, let himself into his room. Sanderson's voice was held perfectly in his head. 'Right you are, Mr. Harris.'

Right he was, perhaps. Perhaps not.

Grinning, he began to unlace his shoes.

STANLEY MIDDLETON

# The Golden Evening

A brother and sister – Bernard is at college, Mary is still at school – are struggling with their own young lives and loves, near the end of one beautiful summer. At the same time, their mother Ivy is dying from cancer whilst their father, a simple and dignified man, is barely coping. A family faces fundamental changes, together and apart.

*'This humane book digs patiently beneath the surface of ordinary lives to the rock of universal truths.'*

SUNDAY TIMES

*'Stanley Middleton, once dubbed "The Chekhov of suburbia", is to the Midlands suburb what* Anne Tyler *is to the Midwest picket fence. His careful writing creates an always precise and often unnerving picture of reality.'*

THE TIMES

STANLEY MIDDLETON

# Holiday

The Booker Prize-winning Novel

On holiday at an English seaside resort, Edwin Fisher is trying to come to terms with the breakdown of his marriage to Meg after the death of their baby son. But Meg's parents are also staying in the same town and are keen to help them patch up their relationship. As Edwin seeks to understand what went wrong, he must confront the past and decide upon his future.

*'We need Stanley Middleton to remind us what the novel is about.* Holiday *is vintage Middleton . . . One has to look at nineteenth-century writing for comparable storytelling.'*

SUNDAY TIMES

*'At first glance, or even at second, Stanley Middleton's world is easily recognisable . . . The excellence of art, for Middleton, is an exact vision of real things as they are. And because he is himself so exact an observer, his world at third glance can seem strange and disturbing or newly and brilliantly lit with colour.'*

A.S. BYATT

STANLEY MIDDLETON

# *An After-Dinner's Sleep*

One winter evening Alistair Murray opens his door to Eleanor Franks, a woman he has not seen for decades. A man apparently content with his life, he accepts even his retirement and bereavement as part of the natural order of things. But just when he thinks he must get used to the slow, lonely decline into old age, Eleanor arrives to make him call into question everything he has taken for granted.

*'He shows us the way we age and die now, with real and graceful distinction.'*
SUNDAY TIMES

*'Middleton wrote books you remember decades on . . . He wrote a calm, whispering prose, full of unspoken suggestion between ordinary acts of daily living . . . I think of Middleton, and a few others, who keep still and write and then write more, because they are writers and that's what they have to do, as the real ones, the sort to aspire to.'*
JENNY DISKI

STANLEY MIDDLETON

# Married Past Redemption

David and Alison are a successful young couple planning their wedding, but they are surrounded by family and friends whose marriages have ended in failure. As each member of this close community struggles to make or re-make a life, Stanley Middleton tests the reality of present and past marriage, its possibilities and dangers, its hopes and fears.

*'Every page is taut with inner strength and truth.'*
MAIL ON SUNDAY

*'His reputation, built book by book, as an astute observer of middle-England bourgeois life and as a writer whose reach extends far beyond his immediate milieu, is probably now invulnerable.'*
GUARDIAN